FIRST MONTHS AFTER

Book Three in the Cataclysm Series

Jay Vielle

Amazon

ACKNOWLEDGMENTS

I want to thank the many, many people who have helped me make this series possible. My family (including my wife, Lauren, and her family)--all of whom have been extremely supportive. To the real people who have lent their names (and perhaps even a little of their personalities) to the characters: Maureen, Wendy, The Colonel, Josh, Boo, Matt (a.k.a Mark), Casey (a.k.a. Eddie) Gail & Kristen, Eric, Greg, and Morgan-- thanks so much for listening, reading, commenting, and sharing. To my sister-in-law Renee--who embraced the daunting task of being my editor with a firm but caring hand--and who, I think--may know my characters better than I do. To my eldest son, Hunter, for his artwork and his creative ear. To my newest marketing advisor and former athlete, Taylor, whose guidance I look forward to hearing. And finally to my biggest fan and sister, Barb, in whose eyes I can do no wrong. Thanks so much to all of your.

--JVL

FIRST MONTHS AFTER

Book 3 in the Cataclysm Series

PROLOGUE

Where do I begin? Well, how about for starters that in a million years I would not have predicted I would be doing what I'm doing. I might have guessed I'd be doing it here, where I grew up, in rural Frederick County, Maryland. Yeah. Maybe the "where," but definitely not the "what" and absolutely not the "with whom." My name is Eduardo Reyes —Eddie to my friends, and Señor Reyes to my high school social studies students…that is, if I had any students. At the moment, I do not. At the moment, like the rest of the country, I am in the process of trying to figure out how to survive, live through, and even thrive during The Cataclysm. That's the name the news people gave it the first day or so after the bombings began. Now we just pretty much call it what it is— World War III.

Of course, everyone likes to invoke World War III in hyperbole. It's used all the time to describe arguments, fights, rows of any kind that people want to exaggerate about. "Wow, that hockey game was World War III out there." That kind of thing. And people do that because everyone expected World War III to be the complete destruction of the planet by nuclear bombs—but that's not exactly how it all went down. I say "went"—but I actually mean "going"—because we are just getting warmed up. We're only in the first weeks and months following the earliest round of bombings. After movies like *War Games* and *Red Dawn* came out in the Cold War 1980's, everyone began to imagine World War III as something distant, disastrous, and beyond imagination. The obliteration of life on this planet. Only the last one of those descriptions turned out to be accurate.

First, I should tell you that this one started like many altercations do—with a pissing contest. Our president--who had spent the bulk of his first years in office annoying, challenging, and verbally engaging nearly every powerful dictator in the world—continued the trend until someone became desperate and angry enough to do something about it. The battle lines were drawn pretty much as you might have predicted. Russia, North Korea, China, Iran, Pakistan, Venezuela and Cuba all joined forces against us. Those have been the countries that have caused us the most consternation over the years for one reason or another. But also predictable was the coalition of U.S. allies—England, France, Spain, Canada, Israel, Japan, Australia, India, and South Korea. There were a number of key neutral parties—places like Mexico, Germany, pretty much all of Africa and most of South America. Oddly, though, those alliances we were situational and tenuous. Many of those places were happy to befriend us. Not all of them were willing to fight alongside us. And alliances in World Wars are fluid and subject to change. Remember, I teach history. That kind of thing has happened before.

The short version is this—thanks to intelligence picked up by folks that Fate was oddly kind enough to place along our path over the last few weeks—we know that the Russians developed new weapons that allowed for maximum casualties with minimum destruction. That would allow them to conquer the actual real estate known as the United States of America, and they wouldn't have to rebuild. By not physically destroying buildings, roads, bridges, and infrastructure, the Russians would have the benefit of a "turnkey takeover." All they would have to do is dispose of the dead and subdue the few who managed to dodge their horrific new weapon: a combination of explosive, quickly-dissipating radiation and its aerially-distributed and synthetically-engineered Ebola virus.

Our most advanced experts in defending that weapon, Colonel Raymond Cannaveral and NIH research scientist Wendy Yubashiri, were among the people we rescued and restored after the first bombings. They returned the favor by helping us begin to get our lives back together. For me, that meant rescuing my parents from a bomb shelter in Washington D.C. For my colleague, Jake Fisher, it involved a lot more.

Jake Fisher had been my friend and colleague at Hunter's Run High School in Emmitsburg, Maryland. He was my teacher when I attended Hunter's Run seven years ago. We formed an unlikely comradeship there as fellow professionals being in the same Social Studies Department. But Jake was actually nothing like me. Jake was much older—pushing fifty—and had traveled some rough roads in his time. A career pugilist, in addition to teaching history, Jake had competed and coached wrestling for the past twenty years, including a stint competing for the All-Marine Corps Team. He had done a tour in Iraq during project Iraqi Freedom and had participated in a very bloody and controversial skirmish that had made him both a hero and a figure of blame. Jake would say he was probably neither, but I think he's more the former than the latter if I had to pick one. After a brief and brutal competitive career— followed by hip surgeries, Jake was left with scars, a limp, and a past he didn't like talking about.

Jake is central to this story, because regardless of how he feels about himself, he's the hero of it. The first days after the bombing began, most people left the school and tried to hunker down at home. Jake stayed at the school and helped about thirty of us set up camp and prepare for extended survival. He defended us from attack from a gang of looters twice before ending up at odds with a faction of teachers who were members of a hard-core right-wing church in town. See, even though Jake is a pretty middle-of-the road kind of guy, he isn't picky about his friends. Take me, for example. I'm a gay Hispanic teacher in my early twenties in a very red county in a pretty blue state. Jake always likes to say, "I don't care where you piss or who you kiss, just don't be an asshole." The members of the right-wing Church of Many Blessings are a bit more discerning in their taste, so they asked Jake and me to leave—something Jake was planning on doing anyway, as he had to go find his sons who were stranded at college. We had a few others join us on that journey, and we picked up a few strays along the way.

Those strays included a couple of ultra-liberal friends of mine, Maureen Kelly and Al DeFillipo. Maureen and Al came with us to Virginia's Shenandoah Valley as Jake went to collect his sons at Virginia Military Academy and Virginia Tech, where they had been attending on wrestling scholarships. We also picked up an assistant manager of the local Wal-Mart, Estela Fuentes, as well as Morgan Branson—a friend of Jake's son Vinny, who later ended up becoming Estela's girlfriend. We also rescued the aforementioned Wendy Yubashiri and Colonel Ray Cannaveral at Fort Detrick, where they were being attacked by orange, mutated, carnivorous humanoids bent on making them a meal. After some pretty hairy run-ins with a town run by convicts and another visit by the orange mutates, we eventually returned The Colonel to Washington D.C. and made it back to Emmitsburg safe and sound. Then things really got interesting.

After returning home, we came to find out that Jake's wife, Laura—whom he presumed dead from the Washington D.C. bombings—was actually alive, but she herself had turned into one of the mutates as a result of exposure to the Russian weapons. We made our way past military blockades of the capital city--which was under Martial Law—by horseback and by boat, and into the Pentagon where Colonel Cannaveral was waiting to help us locate and capture Laura Fisher, with the pleasant and surprising side effect of finding my parents hunkered down in a bomb shelter below a government building. After several attempts we were finally successful at capturing Laura, but as Wendy and the Colonel had much research and experimentation to do before trying to reverse the effects of the bomb, it was decided to put Laura into a coma until the treatments had gone through a testing phase on other captured mutates.

Meanwhile, while we were off trying to find and save both Laura Fisher and my parents, the Church of Many Blessings, led by Father Joseph Clarque, was in the process of taking over the town of Emmitsburg and remaking it into New Plymouth—a place where Puritan values could take hold more readily in a post-Apocalyptic small town scenario. Unbeknownst to many of his followers, however, Father Joe was able to preserve the town by going into business early with the Russians. In exchange for providing them a town where they could get a foothold for their new conquest, Father Joe demanded the townspeople alive, so that he could create his New Plymouth with the help of his congregation and their newly converted fellow citizens. The Russians were all too happy to oblige, and provided chemical water treatments to prevent the residents of Emmitsburg—now New Plymouth— from succumbing to radiation and Ebola, meanwhile planting one of their own agents at the church.

But that plot was discovered by Morgan and Estela, with the help of another member of our Social Studies Department, Mark Longaberger. Mark at first had bristled at Jake Fisher's leadership of the school and had readily joined the bandwagon of those against him. He found out later, however, that the people with whom he had allied himself were Puritanical white supremacists. To make matters worse, those supremacists were being led by a secret Russian collaborator in Father Joe Clarque. Once Father Joe had discovered that his secret was out, he set out to eliminate Estela and Morgan by turning them over to Oleg Stravinsky, his allied Russian assassin, who took them to the woods behind a Catholic shrine to murder them. But Mark intervened and saved the girls, later learning of the Russian plot that they had unwittingly uncovered.

Now Father Joe finds himself in a race to eliminate the people who know his secret before it gets out. In an ironic turn, it is Maureen Kelly and Al DeFillipo who come to Mark's rescue, and the entire bunch elude the pursuit of members of the Church of Many Blessings--who have been told that Mark, Morgan, and Estela were stealing secret passwords and account information from a church whose ideologies they disagreed with. They are also blamed for attacking Oleg, who sought only to bring them to justice for breaking and entering. While church members swarm to try and find them, the five fugitives manage to find a place to hide on the farm of Maureen's best friend, Kristen Faust—our librarian at Hunter's Run.

Oleg, however, has since reached out to his Russian superiors, and they responded by sending a dangerous cell of spy warriors to locate and eliminate the threat. But Maureen has called the cavalry--Jake Fisher, his sons Tommy and Vinny, and I are on our way to intervene. Colonel Cannaveral has provided us with another asset as well—the mysterious and bizarre mercenary Josh Rimone, who specializes in this kind of business.

Sound crazy enough for you? Well, you should try telling it. I am charged with that duty—as it is the tradition of my people to be the story tellers, the rememberers, the *camayocs.* I am Peruvian, and my Inca ancestors prided themselves on keeping accounts of things in their minds and passing them on in stories to other generations. I have had the boon of knowing how this story ends, so I can tell it to you now with as much vivid color and detail as possible, so that you can then, in turn, become the next *camayoc*--the next rememberer—and pass it along yourself.

CHAPTER 1—
JOSH RIMONE

Josh Rimone just got done telling us—"This shit's probably gonna take months."

"Months?" I said. "We don't have months. Our friends are in trouble now. Jake, let's forget this guy."

"Fuck you, Edmundo," said Josh Rimone. "I don't need this job."

"Eddie, give him a chance," Jake said. "The Colonel swears by this guy."

'This guy' in Jake's reference, was a weird-looking mercenary consultant named Josh Rimone, and he did, in fact, come highly recommended by our friend and colleague, Col. Raymond Cannaveral, who had saved our asses in Washington, helped rescue Jake's wife, Laura, and was currently working to find a way to reverse the horrible effects of the Russian radiation-virus-bomb that had turned her into an orange-skinned, white-haired, Neanderthal-like mutate. The Colonel had heard of our plight—our need to find and rescue our friends, who were being pursued by a Russian cell on its way to Emmitsburg—now called "New Plymouth"—to murder them.

But by my early impressions, Josh Rimone was at best, a wild card, and at worst, a liability. Standing all of about 5'6" and slender, this guy had no hair whatsoever on his head, face, or body. That was alarming enough to look at, but he wore this big-ass black cowboy hat that sank down to his ears, old cowboy boots, and usually had a chaw of chewing tobacco packed into his cheek. He had rumbled up to Emmitsburg in a 1970-something Camaro that sounded like a cross between a tank and a Harley-Davidson with a broken muffler. He had broken into a house that was for sale off of Main Street so that we wouldn't be bothered by anyone while we planned, and it had taken him all of five seconds to come to the conclusion, as he put it, that 'this shit is probably gonna take months.' Months we did not have, so I expressed my doubts to Jake openly. Josh apparently wasn't used to being challenged, judging by his immediate hostility towards me.

"It's Eduardo," I said, correcting him.

"Edmundo sounds better," he said.

"It's Eduardo, asshole. You can't understand simple Spanish?" I said.

"Sure, I can. But Edmundo suits you. You never saw *The Wedding Ringer*? You know--that Kevin Hart movie? It's hilarious. Don't you remember the gay Hispanic wedding planner? Edmundo? That's you all the way, buddy," he said.

Jake cracked up.

"What the hell are you laughing at?" I said. Jake couldn't stop the belly-laugh, and that got Josh laughing as well. They actually high-fived each other. Tommy and Vinny were covering their mouths and snickering as well. The truth was I had seen *The Wedding Ringer*, and it was a funny comparison to me and the gay Hispanic wedding planner, Edmundo. But I wasn't about to give this guy the satisfaction. Then I saw Tommy and Vinny lose it, and I started laughing too.

"See? Everybody agrees!" said Josh, slapping me on the back.

"Except about the 'months' part, Josh. Eddie's right. We are here on a rescue mission. We don't know where that Russian cell is or when they're getting here. We don't know how many in the church are aware of what's going on, and we don't

15

know if our friends have been found yet or not. We zoomed up here, and we've got to move quicker than that. Can you adjust?" Jake asked.

"Hell yeah, I can adjust. Why didn't you say so?" Josh said with a smile. I rolled my eyes and shook my head.

"So, first things first. Where are your friends. Do you know that?" Josh asked.

"Eddie?" Jake asked. "You talked to them. Do you know?"

"No. Maureen didn't tell me," I said.

"Can you call her?" Jake asked.

"Text her," Josh said. "Calls can be bugged, traced, and triangulated. Texts are harder."

"I'm not sure texts are working," I said. "Things have been weird."

"Have you spoken with her on that phone?" Josh asked, pointing to my cell.

"Yes," I said.

"Texts should work, then," he said. "They just might take longer. Give it a try."

I texted Maureen and said we were in the vicinity, and asked her where she, Al, Estela and Morgan were hiding. I figured we'd have to wait a while.

"But aren't texts dangerous too? I mean, they're in writing. If somebody finds either of our phones, it's all laid out there for them," I said.

"Hell yeah," said Josh. "Incriminating as shit. Yeah, texts are evidence, bro."

"Then why did you tell me to text her?" I screamed back.

"Duh, Edmundo. So you can find out where they are?"

16

Josh said. He turned to Jake and made a face. "Is she always like this?"

"You have no idea," said Jake.

"I can NOT work with this guy," I shouted. Just then the sound of my notifications came on. It was Maureen's reply.

"Tah-dah," said Josh. "I accept your apology."

"I didn't apologize, dick," I said. "Okay, that makes sense. They're at Kristen's."

"Kristen's?" asked Jake.

"Yeah, you know, Kristen Faust. Our librarian at Hunter's Run. They're best friends. Have been since high school," I said.

"Oh yeah, I know her. She's nice. She's always been friendly to me. Cuts me some favors now and then," said Jake.

"I bet she does," I said. "She's always had a little crush on you." I saw Tommy and Vinny turn their heads, and I cringed.

"Crush? On me? Isn't she married?" Jake asked, suddenly aware of his sons' attention also.

"Separated. Lives right next to her husband on a farm. Weird deal. Great gal, though. Maureen always thought you two would make a cute couple," I said. Vinny and Tommy both scowled at me.

"What? Don't look at me. *I* didn't say they'd make a cute couple," I said. "Take it up with Ms. Kelly when you see her next."

"Can you get an address?" Josh asked.

"I already know it," I said. "I've been there."

"You've been to Mrs. Faust's house?" Vinny asked me. "What for?"

"She and Ms. Kelly love the gays. Adore us. They're both on PFLAG," I said.

"Hey, you're not supposed to use that word, even if you are one," said Josh.

"Not 'fag,' you idiot. PFLAG. It's an acronym. It stands for 'Parents and Friends of Lesbians and Gays.' And they are. Friends, I mean," I said.

"So are we," said Tommy.

"Yeah, but only because Dad makes us," joked Vinny. I gave him a playful smack in the ear.

"Do we have to work with this guy?" asked Josh. "I can feel my manhood slipping away."

"Welcome to my world," said Jake. "And yeah, we do. He grows on you."

I beamed back.

"Like fungus," Jake added.

"Alright, first things first" Josh said. "Let's make contact with your friends and look around to see if they've been discovered. Once we touch base with them, then we'll need to get a game plan going for finding a way to flush these Russians out of the bushes."

"We want them flushed out?" asked Jake. "Isn't that dangerous?"

"More dangerous than hiding in the bushes?" asked Josh. "Able to strike whenever and wherever they want without warning? Come on, dude. Weren't you a Marine? I guess you jarheads all just bust through the door headfirst and shoot until everything's dead, huh?"

"So, you've met Jake before, huh?" I asked.

"Yeah, Dad. This dude knows your style," said Vinny. Jake frowned back at him.

"You make a good point, Josh. Harder to hit an opponent you can't see," said Jake.

"I guess some jarheads can be educated. That's encouraging," said Josh. "So let's drive out to your friend, the cute, separated librarian's house. I'm looking forward to meeting her."

"Are you single, then?" I asked.

"Occasionally," said Josh, smiling with a big new chaw in his cheek. "Be sure and lock the door when you leave."

Josh had decided to meet in a house with a Realtor's "For Sale" sign on the front so that we'd have room to spread out and plan without being bothered. I found his request ironic because of the manner in which he'd "borrowed" the hous, by kicking a hole in the glass side window to unlock the door from inside.

"Lock the door? You broke through the glass to get in," I said.

"Yeah, but there's no need to just invite more people to do that kinda shit. That's just rude. I'll follow you guys," he said. I shook my head and locked the door on my way out. We hopped into the Humvee that Col. Cannaveral had given Jake. It was enormous and painted Army olive-drab.

"That thing is pretty fucking conspicuous," said Josh. "Hey Tommy, come here and blow into the dashboard of my car." Jake's eldest made a face, shook his head, then went over and blew into the mandated breathalyzer that allowed Josh Rimone's Camaro to start up again. His engine was louder than the Humvee.

"Does he know he's like this?" I asked Jake, who was smiling.

"I think he's amusing," said Jake. "We could've used somebody this colorful in Iraq. It would've made the days a lot shorter."

"Colorful. Okay. I guess we can call him that," said Eddie.

"Oh, Eddie, calm down. You're just mad because this guy's getting all the attention instead of you. Don't be jealous," said Jake. Tommy hopped in and Jake backed out of the driveway.

"Where to?" he asked me.

"Head back to Chubby's, it's just off that road," I said.

It was only about a five-minute ride to the farm where Kristen Faust lived in a house next to her estranged husband, whose farm it was. Mitch Faust looked after his parents in the main farmhouse. Kristen lived in the middle house with their teenage daughter, Natalie. A third house, built originally for other farm workers, lay empty, and was currently the hiding place of our friends.

We rolled up to the farm in the Humvee. Kristen came out first, and she looked nervous. Obviously, she didn't recognize the vehicle, as it was loaned to us by Colonel Raymond Cannaveral at the Pentagon. Jake's truck was left in Glenmont at the stables where we had, um, 'appropriated' some horses on our trek to Washington last week. The Humvee was large and drew attention, and that seemed to bother Jake.

"We gotta ditch this thing, Eddie," Jake said. "It sticks out like a sore thumb. Like three sore thumbs."

"Well how do you suppose we're gonna get your truck back?" I asked. "It's at the stables, remember?"

"I don't know yet, but it's on my to-do-list," Jake said.

"Along with protecting our friends who are being hunted by a hidden Russian murder cell," I said.

"Yeah. It's just after that," said Jake.

Josh rumbled up behind us and pulled right up on the lawn with his Camaro. Now Kristen looked completely worried. Two unknown cars had just pulled up, one brazenly on the grass. She looked back and started to head back in the house. I popped my head out the window.

"Kristen! Hey Girl, it's us," I yelled, waving out the window. She offered a sigh of relief.

"Eddie, thank God," she said. "I'm so glad to see you. This stuff is crazy."

"You don't know the half of it," I said. "Has Mo told you about our trip to Virginia?"

"Yeah. All about it. Those orange things sound absolutely awful," said Kristen.

"Big partiers, the mutates," I said. Jake hopped out of the driver's side.

"Hi Kristen," he said, smiling sheepishly.

"Hey Mister," she said, smiling. "What brings you to my doorstep?"

"Um, the five fugitives who called us to save them?" Jake said.

"Oh yeah, that's right," she said with a wink.

It was almost like she was flirting a little.

Vinny and Tommy jumped out simultaneously. "These are my sons, Thomas, and Vincent," said Jake. Both walked up and offered their hands.

"Tommy," Tommy said, correcting his father for the use of his formal name.

"Vinny," said Vinny.

"Nice to meet you guys. Come on in, we'll put our heads together," Kristen said. Then she looked at the Camaro. Josh had stuffed a fresh wad of chaw in his cheek and slipped on the big black cowboy hat.

"Who's that?" she asked.

"The cavalry," Josh said in response, tipping the cowboy hat in greeting. He offered no other explanation, but just walked past her onto the porch and into her house.

"Nice to meet you, Mr. Cavalry," she said.

"His name is Josh, and he kind of is the cavalry," said Jake. "Col. Cannaveral hooked us up with him. He handles problems just like this. He's a little...different. But he grows on you."

"That's what you said about me," I said. "Are you comparing me to that guy?"

"Not yet," said Jake. Jake held the door for Kristen and she walked in. I followed with the boys.

When we entered, we were in Kristen's main house living room. Everyone was sitting there. First was Al DeFillipo, the tall, lean science teacher who was now dating Maureen Kelly pretty steadily. Next to him was Maureen, the Spanish teacher. Maureen and Al were ultra-liberal and two of my better friends. Hard for a gay Hispanic man to make it in a red county, and those two lessened my load considerably by offering a caring heart and a willing ear. Next to them were Morgan Branson, a friend of Vinny's who we picked up at Virginia Tech, and the girl who had become her new love interest, Estela Fuentes. Estela had been working at the Wal-Mart here in Emmitsburg. We had stumbled on her the first days after the bombings had taken place and helped her out when a gang of local thugs had come to do harm to her and her store. She had come with us on the journey and had fallen instantly for Morgan. The two of them had helped discover the involvement of the Church of Many Blessings with the Russians.

And last, but not least, was the most unexpected person on the couch—Mark Longaberger. Mark had been a vocal part of the faction that had 'voted us off the island,' so to speak. The first days after the bombings, Jake had taken the lead in getting us to make a survival plan and work together to prepare for what lay ahead. But a faction of the group broke off and voiced great disapproval with Jake's leadership, and had essentially driven him away. Al, Maureen, Estela and I had joined Jake, along with a couple of students, and we had all gotten aboard a bus to help Jake find his sons at colleges in Virginia.

Mark had played a major role in that dissenting group, and I had trouble forgiving him for that. I knew Maureen had trouble too. She was a big grudge holder, and for her to be sitting in the same living room with Mark meant that something big had happened. She had tried to explain it to me over the phone, but her description of things sounded crazy. I tried not to be overly judgmental about her description of events sounding absolutely crazy over the phone, especially because when she called to tell me of her plight, I was in the process of helping Jake escape from orange-skinned mutates bent on killing and eating him at the direction of his wife, who had become their leader. Times were weird and getting weirder. That much was certain.

"Beg your pardon, but do you have a bathroom around here?" Josh asked, hiking up his jeans. He had a big belt buckle that said "CSA" on it. The letters stood for "Confederate States of America." They were big around here, which I never quite understood. We were in one of the northern-most towns in Maryland, only a few miles from the Pennsylvania state line and Gettysburg. You would think that in a town renowned for bloodshed and an inspiring speech by President Lincoln that the Union Army would be the most popular. I mean, they were winners after all. But for some reason, in nearly every back yard and on every pick-up truck, two flags seemed to be constantly flying together: the stars and stripes, and the Confederate flag of Dixie. As a history teacher, I had trouble reconciling that. The two flags were in complete opposition to one another. You could fly a Canadian flag, or maybe an Iraqi flag and it would raise an uproar from everyone in the area. But the diametrically opposed symbols of the Union and the Confederacy—the flags that stood for the Constitution of America and its once most hated traitorous rebels—were nestled together around here more times than I could count. It was maddening.

"Just down the hall on the left, Mr. Cavalry," said Kristen. Josh smiled at that, tipped his hat again, and wandered down the hall.

"His name, by the way, is Josh Rimone," said Jake. "He doesn't seem to have any social graces that I can detect, but the Colonel swears by him. Kristen laughed.

"He's an idiot," I said.

"Oh yeah, and Eddie hates him already. After knowing him for all of ten minutes," said Jake.

"So how about we address the elephant in the room right off the bat," I said. "Mark? What the fuck are you doing here?"

"Eddie," Jake interrupted.

"No, Jake. This asshole is one of the guys who ran us out, who stole our classrooms, who joined with that fucking Neo-Nazi church. I want to know what kind of nerve it takes now for him to even be here. Hell, as far as we know, he's a spy for them," I said.

"Eddie," Jake said again.

"No, Jake," Mark said. "He's right. I have some explaining to do. Maureen kind of put me through the ringer a little before we got here too, and I have to admit, I deserved it."

"You squared yourself with me last week, Mark," said Jake. "We're good."

"But not everyone else," he said. "I apologized to you, but the truth is I owed an apology to everyone. So, let me offer it now and get it out of the way. Eddie, Jake, Estela, Morgan, Maureen, and Al—I'm sorry. Like I told Jake last week, I let my ego get to me when the bombs first dropped, and we stayed at the high school. I wanted to be the one who was the leader. I wanted to show everyone what I knew, and what I could do. I wanted to be 'the guy.' But I wasn't. Jake was 'the guy.' Jake naturally led in a survival situation that was one that he trained for in the Marines, and he did a great job. I was threatened, I guess. And when Wes and Lou and the others started to push back, I pushed with them. Truly, I didn't think you all would leave. That wasn't in my plan at all."

"Okay, that's a pretty good start," I said.

"It's not all, though. It gets worse. While you guys were gone, I started helping out with the Church of Many Blessings. They were quietly taking over the school, but I couldn't see it. Then little things would come out bit by bit that bothered me. White supremacy. Homophobia. Misogyny. It was subtle at first, and I didn't see it. Father Joe Clarque is a very persuasive man, and he managed to ease my fears every time. He explained it all away so easily. Then, while doing him a favor at the college promoting his big town meeting, I stumbled upon the attempted murder of Estela and Morgan, and the real motives of these people became clear as crystal. I was duped, but I see the light now, and I want to make things right. These people are just what you said, Jake. They're the worst. But I don't even think you would have guessed how bad they actually are. Kristen told us that Father Joe has taken over the town and renamed it New Plymouth, after the Pilgrim colony. He made sure to stress that the reason he named it that was because, like the Pilgrims, we were all White Europeans and Christians, like God prefers it. And if that weren't enough, it turns out he's in league with Russian murderers who somehow are working behind the scenes to establish themselves here in town secretly, I suppose to get a foothold somewhere for their ultimate invasion. It's surreal. But if you'll have me, I'm with you," Mark said. "I want these people stopped."

"He saved our lives," said Morgan. "Flat out superhero-type stuff. He swept in and konked that guy Oleg right on the head and helped us escape. Anything you did before is washed clean, as far as I'm concerned."

"*Para mí tambien*," said Estela. "You are a hero."

"He also helped figure all of this stuff out with us. Al and I have already made our peace with him," said Maureen. "And you know how hard it is for me not to hold a grudge."

"Yes, I do," I said. "I guess that makes it unanimous, Mark." I held my hand out and he took it. We shook firmly and nodded. Mark smiled and looked relieved.

"Well now that we've all shared our feelings and had our group hug, can somebody bring me some fucking toilet paper, and then explain to me what your plan is to get out of this shit?" Josh yelled from down the hall. He poked his head out the door and smiled.

"Please?"

CHAPTER 2--
PERSPECTIVE

"I'm glad to see you're on the mend, Oleg," said Father Joe. "That was quite a bump on the noggin you received last week."

"The Rus are an especially hardy tribe, Father," Oleg said. "You needn't have worried."

The two men were in Father Joe's office at the church. The last time they had been there, Oleg was icing his head after being struck twice from behind by a rock held by Mark Longaberger. That rock had been the difference between life and death for his intended victims, Estela Fuentes and Morgan Branson. More importantly, it had allowed the only people who suspected anything fishy to escape, thus puncturing a hole in the giant balloon that was Father Joe's newly christened town, "New Plymouth," which he had personally changed from its original name, Emmitsburg. That had been days ago, and the fervor that had won Father Joe his new acclaim—and inspired his new constituents to rip down old signs and put up new ones touting the name change—had begun to die down. The revolution was quick and expedient. The business of government remained.

"Lots to do, Oleg," said Father Joe. "Now that we have the momentum in the town, it's important we don't lose it. Law and order is the key, which means a structured leadership system and a proper 'peace-keeping squad.' I am meeting with my generals today. We'll establish things as they should be now, but I will need you to do your part as well. Can you still take care of your side of the bargain?"

"Yes," said Oleg, careful not to speak Russian. "We will handle damage control. Leave that to my team."

"Can your men find the fugitives?" Father Joe asked. Oleg looked perturbed.

"We can find anything," Oleg said. "And eliminate it. It would have been nice if your men could have successfully followed and located them, however."

Father Joe scowled. "Yes, I'm sorry about that. They were right on them and then their tire burst."

"Unfortunately, there is no trophy for such things," said Oleg. "I hope your men are more capable running your town than they were at surveillance."

"They're good men. Good, like-minded men. They're not used to such taxing pursuits as the ones we put them to several days ago, but they will do a fine job at running my city," he said.

"Your city," Oleg said with a wicked smile. "Yes. I suppose it is your city, now. And we will help you keep it...to an extent. It is in our mutual best interests to work together with this. In the end, all our needs are met with this."

An awkward silence followed. Father Joe bit his lip.

"But?" Father Joe said.

"But?" Oleg repeated.

"Everything in your body language looks like it wants to insert something. Something that begins with 'but'," Father Joe said. "Just go ahead and say what you're thinking. I want to hear it now rather than experience it later," Oleg closed his eyes, exhaled through his nose, and pressed his lips together tightly.

"But I am not used to working with soft Americans," Oleg said. Father Joe bristled.

"Now wait a minute," Father Joe protested.

"*Nyet,* Father, you pressed me to speak my mind, and now I will. It is no wonder how we have so easily crippled your country by going after its communication systems first. Your entertainment, your television, your Internet, your precious cell phones. Your country is in complete disarray. You people are so concerned with sharing your feelings, expressing yourselves, and making your opinions heard that you have accomplished virtually nothing in the past thirty years. Your average man cannot perform a dozen push-ups--much less keep track of a car full of fugitives—without checking on You Tube to see how it is done," he said.

"Now wait a minute, Oleg," Father Joe said.

"Your people invented the concept of the influencer on social media. You care that much about how you look to others. Vine. Facebook. Twitter. Snap Chat. Tic Tock. You have more things devoted to showing people what you look like, what you are doing. But it is all fake. None of it is real. Even your own President takes to Twitter to try and change policy, and does photo opportunities that are false, and in spite of his obvious misrepresentations, he manages to keep his followers. America has become a billboard for a place that no longer has any substance," Oleg said. "It is no wonder we found it so easy to manipulate you in the last few elections. Your time has passed."

"America will always be the greatest country in the history of the world," Father Joe protested.

"Hmm," said Oleg. "I have offended you. Your patriotism is touching. But it, too, is fake. You are touting the greatness of your country, while at the same time conspiring with me and my country to bring it down." Oleg chuckled an evil laugh to himself.

Father Joe's face went empty. He stared out the window of his office and said nothing.

"You know, Father, I would be lying if I did not admit that I believe America to be the greatest country in history as well," Oleg said.

"Now you're just mocking me," Father Joe said.

"No, I am serious. You invented and perfected democracy in a time when nobles ran the world. You effectively eliminated the idea of nobility and being born into power. Your inventors created the most important implements in the world, and then created systems for fabrication and distribution of those things. The train, the car, the telephone, the computer. Where would the world be without those things?

"In the twentieth century, at a time when your country was at its most poor, most destitute, and most desperate, you sent your women to factories and your men to war to face Fascism, and helped defeat two of the most powerful armies in history as well. Germany was dominating Europe, and Japan was dominating Asia. If those powers were allowed to continue unchecked, they would be serving sauerbraten in London and sushi in Australia as a national meal. And as much as it pains me to admit, your powerful economy and political maneuvering outplayed the Soviet Union and all of the countries we once had in the grasp of our hands. Nearly twenty communist governments fell to capitalism. Only China remains a real power, and their version of communism is so bastardized as to be barely recognizable as such. Their economy is as capitalistic as anyone's, and their leaders only step in when they are threatened. No, you are correct. America will go down in history has one of the greatest civilizations ever. The Greeks, the Romans, the Mongols. They were impressive. But given the constraints you've had, your influence outdistances even them. There is a McDonald's in Red Square, for God's sake."

Father Joe turned uncertainly to look at Oleg, his mouth slightly agape.

"No, I have always been fascinated with America. How do you think I have come to speak English so well? I was obsessed with your culture. My training was only helped by my facility with language and my fascination with the United States. It is why I have advanced so quickly. But I have seen what has happened to you in the course of my lifetime. You have fallen. You have become obese and sedentary. You have become spoiled and entitled. And you have come to value what looks good over what is real. And that is why you must fall. All of those civilizations I mentioned before? They all became corrupt, soft, and complacent. And then they were demolished. What is Mongolia now? Non-existent. Greece? Bankrupt. Italy? Brought to its knees by its own inefficiency. Their greatness has waned. And now yours has as well."

Father Joe just stared at Oleg. He had never heard him speak so much before. He had simply existed silently in the background, doing the dirty work that Father Joe had sent him to do. But recent events had caused him to alter his status and move from the background to the foreground, and now Father Joe was beginning to see the depth of Oleg Stravinsky. And it was frightening. He was intelligent. Profound. He clearly had deep wells of feeling that he rarely expressed. Most of all, however, Oleg was ruthless. He had made it very clear last week who was in command here. He had allowed Father Joe's powerful personality to take over the city that Oleg would eventually need. But once Joe's ambition had begun to rise beyond its own means, Oleg had checked it quickly and without emotion, reminding him who was really in charge. And it was frightening.

"Don't worry Father. Your work will not be in vain. You can have your city. You have worked hard for it, and it will serve you well. And then it will serve us well. It will survive, when thousands of other cities in what used to be America cease to exist. And it will be your foresight, your vision that has allowed that to take place,"

"Thank you," was all Father Joe could say in response.

"And now, as you say, we must go to work. I will let you meet with your people. You are correct, you must organize with them. My team cannot be your police. We are a trained unit with a specific skill set, and much of our success comes from maintaining secrecy. I will handle your fugitives. They will only need places to stay and establish themselves in this area as I have done. And, of course, the church will need to sustain us. All of my men speak excellent English. We will be part of your new town, members of your church, silent servants in your cause. And as such, we will be able to find and eliminate the small threat that exists, as well as foresee and prevent any others from becoming a problem. At least until we have new orders from Moscow," Oleg said.

"I thought you already had them," Father Joe said.

"*Nyet*. We are on stand-by. The Kremlin is being extremely cautious. We have invested a great deal in this, only to allow it to be sabotaged by our own impatience. No, my men will live here and serve your new cause for a time. Blend in. Then, when we are needed, we will act. And when we are finished, you won't see us again," Oleg said.

"You'll just disappear?" Father Joe asked.

"Yes. Into the wind. As if we were never here," said Oleg.

That day can't come fast enough, thought Father Joe.

CHAPTER 3— PASSING THE INTERVIEW

"Who is this guy again?" Maureen asked.

"Josh Rimone," said Jake. "At least as far as we know. Whenever we ask him if that's his name, he says 'that'll work.' It's a little unnerving."

"It's a little annoying," I said. "How do we know this guy is the real deal?"

"Because we trust the Colonel," Jake said.

"Jake, all due respect, but the Colonel is a fucking chemist," I said. "He works in a lab with another chemist. I mean, he's a great guy. An awesome guy. And he's a great leader. He gets it done. But we need someone who can help us find and take out a fucking Russian cell of killers. This guy can't even start his fucking car without somebody else breathing into it."

"Eddie, there's a lot to the job," Jake said. "And it often requires some rare personalities to do it. And if the Colonel says he's the guy, then we have to trust him."

"I trust the Colonel to solve the mutate problem," I said. "I trust him to set things up in Washington and solve chemical and radioactive issues. But in reality, Jake, he's mostly a bureaucrat. We've only known him to work either in an office or a lab. What does the Colonel know about taking on assassins?"

"Plenty," Josh Rimone said, shaking his wet hands in the air and getting water all over everyone in the room.

"That chemist you mentioned is a decorated war veteran," Josh said.

I didn't have much of a response. So I sat awkwardly and listened.

"Sorry about that hand-towel, ma'am," Josh said to Kristen. Kristen looked confused.

"Nobody brought me toilet paper," he said.

"Eww," said Morgan.

"Ugh," said Maureen.

"It'll wash out," said Josh. "You might want to use it in the barn from now on, though. But it'll wash out."

"You were saying," I interrupted.

"Yeah. The Colonel. Decorated veteran from the Gulf War. He and his men had to cover a stretch of road that was known to be frequented by insurgents. Top brass wanted us more forward, so the Colonel was ordered to get his men down that road and advance. But he didn't feel right about ordering his men to do anything he wouldn't do himself, so instead of relegating the leadership to someone else, he took the lead. An IED blew up his vehicle with him in it," Josh said. "Tore his legs up."

"Jesus," I said.

"Damn," Jake said, looking at the floor and shaking his head.

"He got a Purple Heart and they sent him to work in the Pentagon. He was there for a while, did a bunch of jobs. But then

34

he took an interest in chemical warfare because he had seen so much of it in Iraq, and he wanted to do something about it. He showed a talent for the work, so then they sent him to Fort Detrick to lead the project in defending against some of the newer weaponry headed our way. I understand that's where you all met him," Josh said.

"Damn," Jake said again. "Impressive man. How did you come to know him?"

"We met there, in Iraq. I was part of a private group of contractors assisting with...projects. Our paths crossed a few times," said Josh.

"Private contractors?" I said. "How does being a private contractor in Iraq make you qualified for this kind of mission?"

"I don't know, how does being a social studies teacher who played JV soccer qualify *you*?" said Josh.

"Ouch," said Maureen.

"Now look," I interrupted.

"Eddie, private contractor is a nice way of saying 'mercenary.' Josh is trying to tell us politely that he was a hired killer in Iraq," Jake said.

Everyone in the room froze for a moment. Josh beamed a big smile, pushed up the brim of his cowboy hat with his finger, and nodded.

"That's horrible," said Estela. "Why would you do something like that? It's disgusting."

"Are you really asking?" said Josh.

"Yes. What would make someone do something like that?" Estela said.

"Well first of all, I'm good at it. We all do things we're good at. Some of us are smart enough to get paid to do it. You all are a bunch of teachers. Isn't that what you all and your guidance counselors tell the kids? Find something you love, find a way to get paid doing it, and you won't work a day in your life. Isn't that how the saying goes?" Josh said, lifting the bumps where his eyebrows would have been if he'd had any.

"Um, yeah. That's right," Al DeFillipo answered demurely. Al was a science teacher at Hunter's Run High School and Maureen's new beau.

"So why didn't you just go into the military?" Kristen asked.

"Who says I didn't?" said Josh.

We all looked at each other. Awkward silence.

"Is this the interview?" asked Josh.

More awkward silence. More looking around.

"Okay, fair enough. I went to college nearby and basically wasted four years partying," he said.

"Um, not saying I can't identify a little with that," Maureen said.

"Um, not saying I can't vouch for you," said Kristen. Both of them chuckled.

"What did you major in?" Al asked.

"General Studies," said Josh.

"How is that a major?" said Mark. "You just study 'stuff' in general? Where did you go to school?"

"Can't tell you," said Josh. Mark frowned.

"So, you wasted your education," said Morgan. "That's not an impressive start."

"No, it isn't. But it wasn't a total waste, though, because I competed in wrestling," Josh said. Jake lifted his eyes and smiled and nodded, and Tommy and Vinny looked at each other.

"You wrestled in college?" Jake asked.

"You know that we all wrestle, right?" Vinny said.

"Yeah. You and your brother go to VMI and Virginia Tech. You guys are big time, so I know you feel me," Josh said smiling. "All three of you. But you guys are good. Jake competed for the World Class Athlete Program in the Marines, and you two are both Division I scholarship winners. But I wasn't that good. I wrestled in Division III—so no athletic scholarships—and also I wasn't one of the better guys on the team. I did have a signature move, though. I used to pin D-I boys like you with it all the time. I won a few big matches, placed in some tournaments, but overall I was really only a starter for one season—my senior season--and I had to cut a lot of weight to get the spot. I walked around out of season about a hundred and fifty pounds or so, but my senior year, I cut to one hundred eighteen"

"Damn," Jake said with a scowl. Vinny and Tommy scowled also.

"That's insane," said Maureen. "You could've killed yourself."

"I almost did. But as I'm sure Jake can attest, that was back in the old days, when we weighed-in the night before the match. Back when there were no real rules or restrictions of any kind. A lot of guys did a lot of dumb stuff back then," said Josh.

"They didn't even have weight certification back then, right?" asked Tommy.

"Right," said Josh.

"What's weight certification?" asked Morgan.

"The NCAA, or the high school state association tests your body fat and your hydration and determines what a safe lowest weight could be for you, and it usually has to be above five to seven percent bodyfat. They also restrict how quickly you can descend to that weight, so it is way, way safer these days. Much better than in our day," said Jake. "I feel your pain, dude. I once dropped sixteen pounds in a day and a half for the U.S. Open."

"Right? So, you get it. Anyway, I wrestled. And then I graduated. And with nothing more than college wrestling on my resume, I applied for a job as bodyguard for a Middle Eastern Ambassador of a Muslim nation," he continued.

"Which country?" Mark asked.

"Shouldn't really tell you," said Josh. "But suffice it to say, there aren't too many assassination attempts here in the United States, so I didn't see nearly enough action. So, I decided to enlist in the Israeli army."

"Wait—what?" said Mark. "You're Jewish? And they let you guard a Muslim ambassador?"

"They never asked me," he said. "Besides, do I look Jewish?"

"You don't look human," I said.

"Fair enough," said Josh, grinning. "So anyway, I was in the Israeli army for a few years. Had some tough jobs, too. Had to move Israelis out of Gaza when they gave it up to the Palestinians. Shitty detail."

"I would imagine that wasn't a very pleasant task," said Al.

"You'd be right. Anyway, after my stint in Israel, I moved to the private sector. I was shocked that there even was a private sector, but it's huge. Big business. Steady work," he said.

"What, bombing babies and killing women?" asked Estela.

"Not sure why you think every mercenary is also a heartless murderer. We did lots of jobs for the U.S. military, like rescues of civilians abducted by religious fanatics, and providing food for villages the U.S. technically wasn't supposed to be near. Stuff that they couldn't do because of politics, but you thought they did anyway. Stuff you wanted done, expected they could do, but had no idea that it would have been illegal," he said.

"Like what, specifically?" asked Mark.

"Can't tell you," he said. Mark rolled his eyes.

"But what I can tell you is this. I did some good; I did some bad. Nowadays I am mostly a consultant. Starting to get too old to be a boots-on-the-ground kinda guy. But when I was, I did the job well enough that now I tell other people how to do it. For even more money than I made doing it myself," Josh said.

"So, if you're not a boots-on-the-ground kinda guy, what are you doing here with your boots on the ground?" asked Kristen.

"Fair question. I owe some favors to the Colonel. And to Jake here," he said.

"To me?" asked Jake. "What do you owe to me?"

"Can't tell you. Not yet at least. But I owe you, and I'm paying it back with this," Josh said. Vinny and Tommy looked at their dad, expecting him to drop his expression of wonderment, but he didn't. He was as flummoxed as they were by Josh Rimone's cryptic debt that he owed to their father.

"Well color me curious," said Kristen, smiling at Jake. Jake smiled back. Was I imagining things, or was Kristen trying to send Jake signals? I decided that I was looking too hard and was inventing things in my head that were probably put there the last couple of weeks being around Wendy Yubashiri.

Wendy was the colleague of Col. Cannaveral, and together they were tackling the mutate problem we were having as a result of the new weapon invented by the Russians.

Jake had rescued Wendy from a mutate attack, then fended more off later, and Wendy had definitely shown an interest in her hero. Jake, of course, had the awkward scenario of having a struggling marriage to a woman who had been turned into a mutate—which would have been awkward enough by itself, but made more so by the fact that Wendy was trying to save Laura, Jake's wife, from her mutated state while also exploring her attraction to Jake himself. To make matters worse, Laura had ordered Jake's death at the hands of her fellow mutates before being captured and treated by Wendy.

Yeah, it's hard enough to describe, and it was even harder to watch unfold. I chatted with both of them, and they both admitted it was too complicated to even explore. They both related deeper-than-expected wells of emotion to me during last week's mission, and they had left it at 'not now, maybe later,' and decided not to feel guilty about any of it. Well, Wendy didn't at least. Jake was doing his usual psychological abuse of self. Meanwhile, the mutated form of his wife lay on an army hospital bed at the Pentagon tended by Wendy. Yeah, you really can't make this shit up.

Anyway, I'm thinking that all of this must have been in my head and that was why I was seeing more behind Kristen's friendliness than just friendliness. Like maybe Maureen wasn't kidding about Kristen having a crush on Jake. She was one of the nicest human beings on the planet. That was a scientific fact. And it was also a fact that she herself was in a ridiculously awkward scenario, with her estranged-but-not-yet-divorced husband living next door in another farmhouse. I decided to let it drop, and to stop looking *for* it. But I did wonder just a little if I was looking *at* it.

At any rate, Josh Rimone smiled at everyone, having told his story, and then opened his arms, palms up, shrugged and looked at all of us.

"So, did I pass the interview?" he said.

"You passed," Kristen said, nodding.

"Good. Because everyone else is too fucking busy with World War III to fight, and I'm the only idiot available right now, so this is all you get," said Josh.

"Now," he continued, "tell me who is after you and why."

CHAPTER 4--
BACKSTORY

"Okay, so this is what happened," said Morgan. "Estela and I wanted to see if we could dig up any dirt on this church. We felt like they had brainwashed her father a little bit, and maybe if we could find something bad, I don't know, maybe we could convince him to leave it and maybe have more contact with her. Listen to her. Accept her more. You know?"

"So, her father is in this church, but is not one of the originals?" asked Josh.

"Yes, that's right. He's originally Catholic, but was pretty hardline anti-gay, and he said that the new Pope was being too soft. So, he found this church and joined it," said Estela.

"The Church of Many Blessings?" Josh asked.

"Correct again," said Morgan. "They're the worst. Racist, misogynist, homophobic. Just the worst."

"Okay. And you thought you could dig up worse than that?" asked Josh. "Isn't that enough?"

"Well, no offense Estela, but your Dad is all of those too," said Morgan.

"*De acuerdo*. I'm not going to argue that point," Estela said.

"So, you figured if you could find something that would sour her father—what's his name again?" Josh interrupted.

"Pablo. Pablo Fuentes," Estela said.

"Thanks. So, you figured if you could find something bad enough to sour Pablo on this church, maybe you could reach him," Josh said.

"Yes. That's right," said Morgan.

"And you found more than you bargained for," he said.

"Way, way more," Morgan said. "We snuck into the church, heard Russian being spoken, and followed the voice into a secret room hidden behind a closet panel leading downstairs. In it we found, well, we found tons of crazy stuff."

"Like what?" asked Josh.

"Well, tons of Russian written everywhere for one, the keys to the town water tower for two, and then two big crates full of chemicals. One, REGN-EB3, treats the Ebola virus. The other, PLX-18, treats radiation poisoning. We even found paperwork to a different Russian guy who tried to buy us as sex slaves," said Morgan.

"I'm guessing that's another story," said Josh. "Not related?"

"A little related," Jake said. "Let her finish, then I can fill you in."

"So, this guy Oleg catches us, ties us up, and calls in the pastor, Father Joe," Morgan continued. "They question us, threaten us, even slap us around a little. Then Oleg takes us up to the woods to kill us," Morgan said.

"You know this for certain? That he was going to kill you?" Josh asked.

"He told us so. He had a gun and was making us kneel down. Then Mark here showed up out of nowhere, conked him on the head with a rock, and helped us get away," she said.

"Nice," said Josh, offering Mark an awkward high five. "Did you kill him?"

"I'm not sure," said Mark.

"Anything else you want to add?" Josh said to Morgan.

"Well at this point, Mark should take over," said Morgan.

"Okay hero, what happened next?" said Josh.

Mark smiled at the hero label. Out of the corner of my eye I saw Jake smile too. Jake and Mark had squared up their differences. Mark had sought out Jake and apologized for any part he played in ousting us from Hunter's Run High School weeks ago. Jake said Mark just wanted to be a leader, and jealous that Jake had taken over after those first bombs hit, Mark had joined whatever faction there was that might give him a chance to shine. He said he just got caught up in it. But once the Church of Many Blessings began to show its true nature, Mark had gotten very uncomfortable, though he admitted that the charismatic Father Joe had talked him off the ledge several times and convinced him to help with the town meeting project. Mark found out later that the town meeting in fact was Father Joe's essential takeover plan. He renamed Emmitsburg "New Plymouth" after the Pilgrims' colony, saying that God favored straight, white Europeans and that this town was going to be in the vanguard of the state and the nation once we recovered from the war. Ironically, I saw a hint of pride in Jake's face on Mark's behalf when Morgan mentioned Mark saving their lives.

"Well, it's like she said. Oleg was getting ready to kill them. I hit him on the head twice, and he wasn't moving after the second one. Then we rushed down the trail to the college. Mt. St. Michael's, out near the Grotto. I had some acquaintances there, and they hid us out for the night while we tried to get our shit together. Morgan and Estela explained their story to me, and I called Al and Maureen, and together all of us figured out what Father Joe and the church were up to," Mark said.

"And that was?" Josh prompted.

"Taking over the town, and apparently letting the Russians get a foothold in a country that they are trying to take over," said Mark.

Kristen's face was one of incredulity. She had heard her friend, Maureen, tell this story only a few hours before, but hearing it again in front of new people just hammered home the insanity of it all.

"Are we sure that's really what's going on?" Kristen said. "Or are we just basing it on two crates of medicine and conjecture?"

"Not a bad question," said Josh. "But the attempted murder was real, as was the rescue. And there's no reason a church should have PLX-18 or REGN-EB3. Like, ever. So, I'd say what your friends came up with is right on the money." Al and Maureen grinned at each other.

"Told ya," Maureen said to Kristen, who smiled back.

"Have you encountered any of those chemicals, those medical treatments, in your experience?" asked Kristen.

"Both," said Josh. "Have had to take both at one point and acquire some from an unfriendly nation once."

Several of us looked around the room uncomfortably.

"Does all of this sound plausible?" asked Maureen.

"This is actually kind of a standard playbook in a way," said Josh.

"Really?" I added. "Because this sounds like it's on high levels of crazy to me."

"I'm guessing those orange ape things are on that same level of crazy?" Josh mentioned. I nodded in defeat. "Point taken," I said.

"So, often the way it works is, powers that want to invade an area in which they have little or no influence have to establish a foothold somehow. This is usually done through malcontents, collaborators, and spies. Once that foothold is there, lots of stuff can go on behind the scenes on the sly. In this case, it's kinda brilliant, because they're bombing us from the front, and sneaking in the back window at the same time. Meanwhile, all of the alliances they've made—China, North Korea, Iran, Venezuela—they can keep us busy and misdirected while the Russians move in to run the whole show. When the smoke clears on all of this, Russia ends up on top with the biggest prize. On second thought, it's not kinda brilliant. It's fucking genius," said Josh.

The rest of us looked at each other uncomfortably at Josh's verification of our suspicions. I had to admit, this guy—as weird and goofy as he presented himself—seemed to know his shit. He nodded as if to affirm his theory, then went back to questioning.

"So, what happened next?" Josh asked Maureen. "I hear things got interesting when you got involved."

"That's because I'm the most interesting person here," Maureen joked. "So, we picked up Mark and the girls, and decided to hide out at my place in Taneytown. But we were followed by people from the church. I managed to pop their tires by throwing boxes of roofing nails out the window behind us, and Al was able to lose them, and we came here. Kristen had us hide the car in the barn and has been putting us up."

"Nice move with the nails. You have spy potential if this teaching thing doesn't work out for you," Josh said. Maureen and Kristen gave each other an enthusiastic high-five and smiled.

"So now, you are being hunted by the church, and most likely by a Russian cell operating in secret here in Maryland or thereabouts," said Josh. "You don't know where they are or what they know, but you think that you are safe here for the meantime. Is that about right?"

"Yes. That's it in a nutshell," said Mark.

"So, what do we do?" I asked. "How do we protect them?"

"First off, we need to see how right they are about being safe. I noticed there's three houses here. You live in this one, and the other one is vacant and is for your new guests here. Who's in the main house?" asked Josh.

"My husband," said Kristen. "Er, ex-husband. Sort of. Separated. He and his parents. They're very old and not very healthy."

"Does he know that your friends are here?" Josh said.

"Not yet. He's out fertilizing fields. He'll be back later tonight, though," she said.

"Where does he fall with this church?" asked Josh.

"Well, he did go to the town meeting," Kristen said.

"So, he might be a sympathizer?" Josh asked.

"I don't think so. But I can't be sure. I mean, he's no racist. And he's not that homophobic. I wouldn't have married him," she said.

"What does 'that homophobic' mean?" I said. "Is there a spectrum?"

"Doesn't matter," Josh said. "He can't know they're here. Loose lips sink ships, even if those lips are totally on board with your cause. Is there a way we can get rid of him for a few days or more?"

"Not that I can think of. I mean, his parents are there, and the towns nearby are empty," Kristen said.

"Is there a hospital in town?" Josh asked.

"No. There's one in Frederick, and one in Westminster. But Frederick is a ghost town, right Mo? You said so yourself,"

Kristen said.

"Yes, but I think Westminster might have done okay in the bombings. It's thirty miles from Baltimore, and according to our experts, Wendy and Col. Cannaveral, this radiation doesn't travel that far. Taneytown survived, I think," Maureen said.

"Do your in-laws know these people here?" asked Josh.

"Some of them. Not Mark, and not Jake," Kristen said.

"Okay. Then we have to act fast," said Josh. "Do any of your telephone land lines work?"

"Yes. It's the one thing that has been constant, at least here," said Kristen.

"Okay, then. I'm going to need you to call 9-1-1," said Josh.

CHAPTER 5
— THE LAB

Colonel Ray Cannaveral was in a medical tent outside the Pentagon underneath the summer sun, but the fans and portable outdoor air conditioning units kept the environment cool. There were literally hundreds of rooms inside the Pentagon itself, but this area was cordoned off specifically for use by CBRNE. The acronym stood for Chemical, Biological, Radiological, Nuclear, Explosive Unit within the Department of Defense. The Brigade, as Col. Cannaveral referred to it, was running the mutate project in Washington D.C. They had essentially aided in the capture, retention, and experimentation on mutates in the monument area. More importantly, they had helped Jake Fisher find and capture his wife.

Wendy Yubashiri, the Colonel's research partner from the National Institute of Health, had been working with him for the better part of a year at Fort Detrick to prepare for potential weapons use by foreign countries. Little did they know when they began that they would become two of the most important people in the country. The Russians had combined a newly created radioactive element, Brenerium, with an airborne form of the Ebola virus to create one of the most deadly weapons in history. Brenerium didn't break down like other elements. Its radioactivity was short-lived and less of a lingering threat than its cousins, uranium and plutonium, which plagued anyone who lived within a hundred miles of Hiroshima, Nagasaki, or Chernobyl. What Brenerium did, however, was make Ebola faster, more explosive, and more difficult to eradicate. And most importantly, it did it without destroying buildings. The Russians didn't just want to defeat the United States. They wanted to take it over. Years of living in a frozen world had taken its toll on Russian leaders, and so secret policy by the war hawks had led to the creation of a weapon that would allow for large scale death, but little or no destruction of infrastructure. The Russians meant to move in lock, stock, and barrel to their new country without having to rebuild it.

When the bellicose President of the United States had begun to pick fights with other countries in the East, Russia had sided with China, North Korea, and Iran. Other countries had joined in, of course, but China could provide technology as well as millions of boots on the ground. North Korea could mount cyber attacks and keep the Americans busy on an Asian front. Iran could provide Russia with oil and Muslim anti-American sentiment across the Middle East. Meanwhile, the Russians could end up with the greatest prize of them all: The American continent itself.

Wendy and the Colonel, however, were stuck with solving the problem of an unexpected side effect of the Brenerium-Ebola bombs: the mutates. Mutates. Mutates, as they were deemed at Fort Detrick by the pair of researchers, were mutated versions of former humans. A small percentage of humans are immune to the Ebola virus. That small percentage also had a strange reaction to the Brenerium-based bombs. The special combination created effects that included orange skin and bleach-white hair. For most mutates, their frontal lobe was reduced in size and activity, and they themselves took on a Neanderthal kind of look. They moved like lower primates and apes and had lost the capability to speak. They seemed to behave like pack animals, controlled by alphas—but the alphas were not as devolved as the main pack members. An even more elite group, the alphas walked upright, and seemed to have an inexplicable method of silently communicating with their lower pack members.

Jake Fisher's wife, Laura, was one of those alphas. CBRNE units had helped capture Laura Fisher, and Wendy had prepared to experiment on other mutates to see if her treatment ideas would work to reverse the effects. Those other mutates were lying in induced comas in the tents set up and maintained by the CBRNE Brigade.

"Have you prepped any for the simultaneous treatment, Wendy?" asked the Colonel.

"Yes. The lower mutates on these two tables are ready, and we have one of the higher alphas who should be prepped within the hour. Fingers crossed," she said.

"No luck on the ones where you used both treatments separately, though?" the Colonel asked.

"No. They were no longer contagious with Ebola, but the skin tone remained as well as the reduced brain activity," Wendy answered.

"I've been thinking," said the Colonel. "These creatures were exposed to explosive versions of radiation and Ebola simultaneously."

"Yeah, so?" said Wendy.

"But we are going to treat them with slow-drip medications for both," the Colonel said. "We aren't really mimicking the initial reaction. I worry that we somehow need to."

"Mimic the explosion?" asked Wendy. "How the hell would we do that?"

"I'm not sure," said the Colonel. "But file it away in the back of your head that if these simultaneous treatments don't work, that a catalyst might be necessary."

Wendy's brow wrinkled and she chewed her lip.

"Well," she said, "here goes nothing."

Wendy began to press a number of buttons on the machine that would release the chemicals REGN-EB3 and PLX-R18 into the mutates' systems. The former was a treatment for Ebola; the latter a treatment for radiation poisoning. The two lower mutates, still in comas, did not move. The tubes emptied into their arms silently, and both Wendy and the Colonel looked on with faint hope. Both had become close to Jake Fisher. He had saved their lives when the mutates had pinned them down in a laboratory at Fort Detrick. Later he had helped them escape from criminals who had taken over the town of Front Royal, helping contribute to the gang imploding and letting them go. He had transported them each separately back to Washington—and they had returned to their partnership at the Pentagon. Finally, he had helped them battle, capture, and restrain mutates at the National Mall—including his own wife. Both felt a kinship to Jake, and both desperately wanted to help him in return.

Jake had believed his wife to be dead, his phone call with her cut off when the bombs began to drop on the nation's capital. It had been a rogue video--taken from a drone and broadcast on makeshift television--that had revealed her true status as an alpha mutate in Washington. The Colonel had made available all of the resources that CBRNE could provide. Wendy had worked tirelessly to come up with treatments that might reverse the process. But nothing had worked yet, and Laura Fisher lay dormant in a coma of her own inside the Pentagon.

There was a part of Wendy that was conflicted, however. She had fallen for Jake in the past few weeks and had made her interest known to him when they were together in Washington. She knew that before the war began, Jake's marriage had become rocky, nearing the point of separation. If Laura was returned to her human form, though, it was likely that such a traumatic scenario would produce a spark between her and Jake. Perhaps, a reconciliation, if not an actual affection, could develop. World War III, a near-Apocalyptic United States, a hometown being taken over by right-wing evangelicals, and a reversed status as a carnivorous mutated creature were trauma enough to bond any couple together. And a tiny little selfish part of Wendy was hoping she would fail. It was a part that she had to suppress, but she acknowledged its existence to herself.

The Colonel felt indebted to Jake, even now. He had helped Jake secure his wife, offered the absolute best possibility of her recovery that anyone could, and had the monetary and political backing of the Pentagon to do it. He had even provided Jake with an effective operative in Josh Rimone, who, however unorthodox, was the perfect person to help him solve his problem with his friends and the Russian cell. Despite all of that, Ray Cannaveral knew that in the few short weeks he'd known Jake Fisher and his friends, his life had changed dramatically. He had gone from the last man alive at Fort Detrick—starving, dehydrated, and hunted by mutates—to the very top person in charge of his division at the Pentagon. That would not have been possible without Jake's assistance and intervention. Much of it was timing and luck, perhaps, but it had done the trick nonetheless. He had a desperate need not to fail Jake now, but so much was experimental and out of his hands that he felt a powerlessness, and it frustrated him.

Hours went by, and the lower mutate that Wendy had treated with the double-serum had not changed color or any physical aspect. A brain scan showed that his higher-level cognitive skills were still below normal and operating at a sub-human level. The only change was his level of Ebola, which had dropped to non-contagious, just like the rest. Wendy looked at the Colonel and shook her head solemnly. Then she looked over at the table where the other alpha was laying.

"We only have one alpha left?" she asked.

"Just one—besides Laura Fisher," the Colonel answered.

"We need to see if this works," she said.

"And if it doesn't, then what?" the Colonel asked.

"I don't know. Maybe your idea about adding some type of explosive approach would work," she said.

"Wendy, we don't even have any ideas for that yet, much less the means to implement them," the Colonel said.

"Well maybe we should be getting on that. Can any of your physicists in the CBRNE brigade come up with something?" she asked.

"They are the best in the world at what they do. I can take it to them, but in truth, we need another alpha to experiment on. Otherwise, if your current treatment doesn't work, Laura Fisher will have to be the experiment. I'd like to avoid that," the Colonel said.

"We all would. Can't we just go get another one?" Wendy asked.

"They don't grow on trees. We were lucky to find these two groups. We do have eyes in the air over Washington, though, and they're already on the lookout. If there are any out there, we'll hear it first," he said.

"Colonel," a young man in a HAZMAT suit shouted from the other side of the room. "Look!"

Wendy and the Colonel turned around and glanced at the table where the lower mutate Wendy had been treating was laying. Something was happening. It was stirring from its coma, making a groaning noise and thrashing on the table.

"Check the restraints," the Colonel said. The young man tugged on all four of the restraints holding the mutate as it writhed.

"They're good. They're holding, sir," he said.

"What's happening? Did you bring him out of sedation?" asked Wendy.

"No, ma'am. I didn't do anything. This is happening on its own," said the young man.

The mutate arched its back and howled. It came off the table in a kind of back bridge, as if it were in pain. Muscles strained, and the restraints were tugged almost to their limits.

"Oh my God, Ray. Look at its coloration," Wendy said.

The mutate's skin tone was fading right before their eyes. It went from a deep orange to a normal flesh tone, the color draining away into nothingness. It thrashed to and fro as the process continued.

"The hair, look at the hair," the Colonel said.

The mutate's hair began a stark white, but flowing from the roots, slowly and steadily, was a grayish-black, almost as if ink were being added from the skull itself. Within about five minutes, the mutate had a normal human's coloration, with salt and pepper hair. It writhed and moaned, and it almost looked to Wendy like the shape of its head was changing ever so slightly.

"Get that portable brain scan over here pronto," the Colonel said. The young man in the HAZMAT suit sprinted to the corner of the building. He reached for a machine that looked like a giant, metallic daddy longlegs spider on wheels. It was a low-field MRI, developed for battlefield use, that can record a magnetoencephalography with surprising accuracy and low risk to patients. Put into development around 2015, the portable MRI had taken various shapes as it had evolved. Some held patients in a chair and surrounded the head. Others are smaller and allow beds to ride up beside them. This one was designed to ride over the bed, surrounding it on either side. The long, thick power cords started to unravel and the young assistant tripped over them, catching himself on the machine before he fell. The Colonel frowned at him, but the young man got the machine over the mutate with surprising dexterity after righting himself.

"How will we keep it still, sir?" he asked.

Just then, the mutate went limp. No movement, no noise, just stillness.

"I think it just heard you, soldier," the Colonel said. "Get an image on it as soon as you can."

The machine made a deep whirring noise.

"These portable units are awesome and getting better every day," the Colonel said.

"How long until we know something?" asked Wendy.

"Half an hour at least," the soldier said. "That's optimistic."

"I guess we just wait, then," Wendy said.

"We may not have to. Look at him," the Colonel said. "He's reverting."

Right in front of their eyes, the mutate's orange coloration began returning. Its hair simultaneously began to fade back to the stark white it began with, and the skin around its head began to tighten. Within a couple of minutes, all of the changes had gone back to the form the mutate had begun with when he was brought into the tent.

"Oh my God," Wendy said. "That's unbelievable."

"Did we get any pictures of it before it turned back?" the Colonel asked.

"I think so. It will take a little time to know for sure," the young man said.

"We have 'before shots' of the brain. It would be crucial to have the 'after shots' as well. I wish I knew why the results faded so fast," the Colonel said. "Wendy, your idea was a good one. It seemed to work. I wish I knew why the treatment didn't take. I guess we could try again with a higher dose."

"Sir, there's something else you ought to know," the young soldier said.

"What is it, son?" the Colonel asked.

"The mutate, sir. It's dead."

CHAPTER 6—A BALANCE OF POWER

Oleg was waiting on a bench in front of the church in the sun. He had the keys to the van in his pocket and was watching and listening for any traffic that might be approaching. Father Joe was inside the entrance to the church. Oleg ran his hand over the back of his head, gently feeling for the lump that Mark Longaberger had put there with a rock. The lump had not receded much at all in the week or so that had followed. Oleg wondered if the rock had cracked his skull at all. In this post-bombing world, open hospitals were few and far between. There was none in Emmitsburg, or New Plymouth, as Father Joe was now calling it. The hospital in Frederick was useless. There was no one alive in Frederick to man it. Oleg speculated that the hospital in Westminster, some thirty miles or so to the southeast of Emmitsburg, might be operational. It was far enough away from other targets that the Russians had hit, including Baltimore, Washington, Frederick, and Columbia.

Oleg laughed silently to himself. Even if the hospital were operational, it wasn't like he could go there now. There were witnesses to his murder attempt, and they were locals. By now they had begun to spread the word, and Oleg had no plausible backstory to counter what they would say. No, now he would have to melt into the shadows again, just as his team would when they arrived. He realized the difficulty of what he was doing. Right now, the United States was in flux. Some towns were dead. Others were completely untouched with only a few communication challenges. Still more were without power, though otherwise safe from the dangerous bombs the Russians had sent.

Without its precious media, the U.S. was crippled, just as he had said to Joe Clarque. No one could tell the Americans what to do, where to go, or how to live their lives—and that would be their undoing. Apart from some pioneer types in Alaska or a few homesteaders scattered around the country, he surmised, most Americans were either dead or simply lost. This town that they had spared was one exception. It was partially functional. Day-to-day operations continued once the novelty of the bombings was over and people realized that they could go on. But as he had predicted, they were lost sheep without a leader. The Russians had chosen their alliance well. Father Joseph Clarque was charismatic, intelligent, cunning, and utterly ruthless. Like most propped-up puppets, he could occasionally become full of himself, but he was no danger to them in any way. As soon as Oleg had reminded him of his true status, Clarque had cowered just as he expected he would.

"Well, hello there Oleg," said Wes Kent, sauntering up to the front of the school. "How is your head feeling?"

"Better Wes, thank you," Oleg said.

"Is Father Joe inside?" Wes asked.

"Yes. He was in his office when I left him," said Oleg. "Why are you not at the school?"

"Well, Father Joe called and suggested that I might be of some help around here. Apparently some of your friends are coming to town and need a place to stay? I was just wondering how many, so that I could clear out some of the classrooms for you," Wes said.

Wes Kent had been a math teacher at Hunter's Run High

School when the bombs dropped. Being a native of Frederick, he had been made aware of the high concentration of bombs dropping there, so like several others, chose to stay at the high school to hunker down and survive the barrage. He had been there when Jake Fisher took over things and began training everyone for survival mode. He also had been the one to rally a large portion of the other survivors against Fisher, driving him away.

"That won't be necessary," said Oleg. "My friends will find places in town. But thank you."

"Are you sure?" asked Wes. "It's certainly no trouble. We've done it before."

"Frankly I'm a bit surprised that you even know about it," said Oleg. "What has Father Joe shared with you?"

Wes pressed his lips together for a moment and considered the question. Oleg furrowed his brow at the pause and cocked his head as if to add emphasis to his query.

"Well?" Oleg asked. Wes remained silent. Oleg stood up from the bench. Just then, Father Joe came out the front door.

"It's alright Oleg," Father Joe said. "Wes knows."

"Knows what?" Oleg said uneasily.

"Everything," Father Joe says. "Absolutely everything."

"Father, that was not wise. I cautioned you about informing too many others. You endanger the project," Oleg said.

"Did you think I could do this alone, Oleg?" Father Joe asked.

Actually Oleg was counting on it. Much of Oleg's presumed leverage on Father Joe was that his takeover of the town—however bold and unprecedented—was at least acceptable to a majority of the townspeople. Oleg had known that this portion of the state harbored a large percentage of the extreme political right. He calculated that they would be on board with a church that discriminated against people of color and the aberration of homosexuality. But these rural people were also patriotic to a fault. They were the kind who assaulted anyone who did not stand for the playing of a national anthem or a pledge of allegiance, and most of them flew flags from their pick-up trucks. The leverage Oleg hoped for was the secrecy of Father Joe working with enemy Russians to infiltrate the country. With Wes Kent knowing the plan, not only was that leverage threatened, but the talkative school leader could possibly endanger everything by saying too much.

"Father, this is a big problem," said Oleg.

"Calm down, Oleg. It's not as big a problem as you might think," said Father Joe. "There are a select group of individuals who have been on board with this since the beginning, working behind the scenes to help bring it all about. I couldn't have done it alone. And neither could you."

Oleg frowned and shuffled uncomfortably.

"How many others know?" said Oleg. "I need to know exactly who."

"Me, John Segen, and maybe his wife by now," Wes said.

"You have got to be kidding me," said Oleg. "This is unacceptable. There is no way that you can justify this. This endangers everything."

"Let me explain Oleg. Wes has been with me from the beginning. He shares my vision of a new country. We have always seen eye to eye in terms of what God had planned for us. Your intervention was both timely and convenient. Your bombing of large cities across the country will permanently alter the demographic of this nation. It will bring us back much closer to what we were when this country was at its greatest. When it first began," Father Joe said.

Oleg stared at him for a minute. Then he looked at Wes.

"But you understand what our final objective is, yes? Russians will transplant to this country. We will live here, settle here, and combine with those who survive to make it an entirely new country," Oleg said.

Wes and Father Joe lifted their eyebrows and smiled at each other.

"Russians are white Europeans, right?" said Wes.

"You are willing to trade your nationalistic patriotism for a shared racism?" Oleg asked.

Father Joe and Wes just looked at each other, eyebrows raised.

Oleg's face wrinkled from incredulity. He shook his head.

"Very well. Even I didn't expect this," he said. "But this John Segen. I have concerns."

"Don't," said Wes. "He's completely on board as well."

"But," Oleg began.

"He feels exactly the same way," said Wes. "And he's popular. He knows a lot of people. When the time comes, you will need to know someone who can help the people in this area assimilate to the new normal. John can provide that."

"But he is an idiot. He babbles incessantly. He cannot possibly keep this a secret long enough. You even mentioned he's spoken to his wife," Oleg said.

"Most men in America tell their wives everything. John can convince Addie of whatever he needs to. And he's not as dumb as he plays to be. A lot of that is an act. He can be calculating and nefarious, and he knows how to use social networking to get things done," said Father Joe. "His biggest issue is his ego. And that can be controlled. He's not going to be the most important man in any room that any of us here occupy."

Oleg stared back at the other men after that comment. The veins in his temples were showing, and he ground his teeth in thought.

"Consider this, Oleg," Father Joe began. "I needed Wes to get me the school. I needed John to get me the people. That's been done. This town is in my pocket and headed in the right direction. We have a base of operations second to none in Hunter's Run. In this town it is clearly the greatest conquerable resource. Taking over the college was never realistic, but the high school--which is by all accounts is a phenomenal campus-- is ours. The only possible rival for it was Jake Fisher, and he is gone. With any luck he died in Washington D.C. looking for his wife. The college has sent most people home and is officially closed. Our only concern is finding and eliminating the people who interfered with you. Five people. And they're huddled together somewhere soiling themselves out of fear. We know what they were driving and at least two routes they were taking. You are panicking for no reason, other than the fact that you realized that perhaps your grip on me just loosened a bit."

Oleg turned quickly and stared at the pastor. His nostrils flared and his jaw clenched. The veins in his arms began to pump and his hands formed fists. The look in his eyes was almost reptilian.

"Yes. That's what I said, Oleg. Your grip on me just loosened. Now that you know that I'm not alone and powerless, things are a little different now. We have more of a balanced relationship, don't you think? And I think it's well that you remember that. It's a relationship. And those are never one-sided. I needed you to help me implement my changes. You needed me to get this town. But I am no one's fool, and I am no one's puppet. You would do well to remember that. A history teacher bested you, and two frightened girls escaped your grasp. You are the only reason this plan wasn't flawless.

Your country's weapons have taken out the major cities in Maryland, maybe even the East Coast. But you can't obliterate the entire population of the United States. So, if you want this plan of yours to go through, you will need to acknowledge the importance of my side of it. This is a part of the state, why, even a section of our country, that owns and loves their guns. They have no trouble assembling at the snap of a finger if they're properly motivated, and I believe I've shown the effects of my motivational abilities."

Oleg was speechless. His hands kept gripping into a fist, and his teeth ground, and his jaw clenched.

"When your men arrive, they will live at the school. Wes has rooms provided. There are showers, food, access to things. The back story will be the same. You are Ukrainian. You hate Russia. You and your friends emigrated here because America provided freedom and opportunity. These men are friends and relatives of yours who have been driven out of their Baltimore homes, and they found out through you that Emmitsburg—excuse me—New Plymouth, was safe and untouched by Russian attacks. No one in this town will question that, especially if I back it. You will find and eliminate our young conspirators, and then you can go about whatever business you choose. But your veiled threats will get you nowhere. Not now."

Father Joe smiled calmly at Oleg. Oleg stared back emotionless. Wes was clearly enthralled by the exchange. His eyes were wide, and his heart was pounding, and there was a tiny trace of excitement in his smile.

Just then a Jeep pulled up, driven by John Segen. The top was down and the sides were off, as was usually the case on these types of summer days. He was wearing a baseball cap with a mesh backing, a Jimmy Buffet shirt, and was chewing a large wad of tobacco, spitting into a Gatorade bottle. In the front seat next to him was a large twelve-gauge shotgun.

"Oleg, how's it goin' buddy," he said enthusiastically. "Your homeboys get here yet?"

An awkward silence followed. Oleg looked at the seat next to John, then cut his eyes back to the satisfied smiles of Wes Kent and Father Joe. Finally, he turned back towards the Jeep.

"*Nyet,* John. Not yet. But it won't be too long," Oleg said.

CHAPTER 7—
GAME PLAN

"Say what again?" Kristen said. "You want me to call 9-1-1? Why on Earth am I doing that? Is there anyone even there to answer?"

"There wasn't when the bombs first hit," said Al DeFillipo. "Remember when Jake fought those looters? I couldn't get anybody then."

"That was weeks ago, Al. We have some television back and some phone service now. Even moderate internet," Jake added.

"Try again," said Josh.

"And just what, pray tell, am I going to say?" Kristen asked.

"You're going to tell them that your in-laws are having heart trouble," Josh replied.

"What? Why? What's the benefit in that?" Kristen asked.

"We need them, and your husband, out of here for a few days, free and clear. You're going to call and say that your mother-in-law is behaving strangely and may have suffered a stroke. Then you're going to say that your father-in-law started complaining of chest pains after that. When the ambulance arrives, you'll verify that. Your in-laws are old enough that if you tell the first responders that they're forgetful or have dementia and sometimes lose track of reality, it would be believable. You will calmly reassure the first responders that you have been unable to reach your husband on his unreliable cell phone, but that you will go out in the fields and get him from his tractor and that both of you will go to the hospital to follow up. Think you can do that?" Josh asked.

"Holy shit," Maureen said. "Kris, can you do that?" Kristen looked nervous. "You acted in every play we ever had in high school and even did one in college. You can do that," Maureen reassured her.

"Okay, I can do that. Then what?" Kristen asked.

"That depends. What mode of transportation does your husband have right now?" Josh asked.

"He's on the big tractor, but he had to drive to the field to get it. So, he has his pick-up truck with him down at the field," she said.

"Okay. That's actually even better. Then we tell your husband that his parents were taken to the hospital in Westminster for the exact reasons you mentioned, and that you'll follow the ambulance down and meet him there," Josh said.

"And then?" Kristen asked.

"And then you don't meet him there. Folks in that age category are high-risk. They'll keep them there for a while and do tests. Stress tests often can't be performed on the same day, so unless your in-laws want to drive back here, only to go back again tomorrow, they'll likely stay overnight," Josh said.

"But what will Mitch say when I don't show?" Kristen said.

"You will have an excuse, like car trouble. And as erratic as communications are these days, it won't be weird when you never pick up the phone when he calls. It will buy us some time, and nobody gets hurt. They're only inconvenienced. And if we get lucky, you can convince him to stay there for another day. Maybe even two," Josh said.

"Okay. I'll do it," she said. "I'll call right now from the kitchen land line. Maureen, come with?" she said.

"Gotcha," Maureen said. "Al, come with us, unless this guy needs you." Josh waved her off as if to say it was fine for Al to go along.

Jake was smiling and nodding at Josh. I had to admit, as much as I hated him, this guy was pretty good.

"Kristen—any chance your husband could come home and look around here before he heads to the hospital in Westminster?" Josh asked.

"Maybe," she said. "He can be a toe-dragger sometimes."

"Then we probably need to hide these five," Josh said, gesturing at Al, Mark, Maureen, Estela, and Morgan.

"Wait just a second," Josh said. "Let me think out loud a little more. Jake, I need you to lose the Hummer for the time being. It's too visible. Not enough cars on the road up here, so it stands out like a sore thumb. We might need it later, though, so I need it hidden, not gone. I'm guessing you left your usual vehicle somewhere in D.C. if the Colonel lent you this?" Josh asked.

"Yeah. At the stables. We left my truck at Glenmont Stables, so we could ride horses past the military blockade on the Beltway last week," said Jake.

"Horses? Pretty smart," Josh said. "You may have some potential yet, jarhead. We should have time for you to go get your truck and ditch the Hummer somewhere. Do people around here generally know where you live?"

"Yes and no. I mean, it's no secret, but nobody really cares. It's a little out of the way, in the country. A little farmette," said Jake.

"Perfect. So, here's what you're gonna do. Take these five with you in the Hummer to go get your truck. Fewer eyes on familiar faces while the first responders and maybe Kristen's husband are here. Give me directions to your place, and make sure to have sissy-boy with you. I have his number on my phone and can reach you if I need you in a hurry," said Josh.

"Hey," I said in protest. "I'm not a sissy."

"Still undecided," said Josh dismissively. "That's seven people in that Humvee, which will be tight. No room for these two," Josh said, pointing at Tommy and Vinny. "So, you guys are gonna come with me. You alright with that, Jake?"

"I guess. It depends on what you're doing," Jake said.

"We're gonna raise a little hell," said Josh. Tommy and Vinny both smiled.

"They're good at that," I said. "They beat up their father in a jail cell at the Pentagon."

"Nice," said Josh, offering each boy a fist bump. "We won't be doing anything quite that attention-getting. We're gonna do some recon, and maybe a little vandalism if the occasion calls for it. I'll keep them safe. I won't put them at any overt risk. Not yet at least."

Jake nodded.

"And we all meet back at my place? What time?" Jake asked.

"That is gonna depend a lot on the first responders, but I'm gonna say three hours," Josh said.

It was already early afternoon. This would have us meeting back a little after dinnertime. Jake looked at me for confirmation, and we both nodded.

"So, you're leaving Natalie and me alone?" Kristen said. "What if my husband shows up and wants me to drive with him?"

"You won't be here," Josh said. "We're going to get the first responders here, you're going to tell them you're off to get your husband, then once you drive out and let him know, you can come out to Jake's farm with your daughter, too. Once we're sure the coast is clear, we bring everybody back here and squirrel them away for Phase II."

"What's Phase II?" I asked.

"Whatever the fuck makes sense after we see how Phase I goes," Josh answered. I rolled my eyes and shook my head. Jake and his sons laughed.

"Sounds like a plan," Kristen said. "Okay, Mo, come join me in the kitchen so I can lie to a hospital."

Kristen and Maureen went in the kitchen and dialed Carroll County General to see if anyone was there. Someone did pick up. Kristen asked a few questions about what medical facilities were open and what options for transport there were. The operator confirmed that Westminster hospital was open and operating at two thirds capacity. She also said that an ambulance was not authorized to come out to Emmitsburg because that was a different county. Then Kristen's acting chops kicked in. She panicked, cried, explained that everyone in Frederick was dead, and that she was just as close to Westminster, she started talking about her poor, sweet, in-laws and what a crime it would be to have healthy people die due to neglect all because of a county line. Finally the operator relented and said she would send a memo to her supervisor, and that he would direct the ambulance to Kristen's husband's farmhouse, but that she would have to dial 9-1-1 officially once they were finished. She high-fived Maureen after she hung up.

"Woo-hoo," Kristen said. "I feel like a spy!"

"You are a spy," said Maureen. "Nice work with the crying part. It almost convinced me."

"I feel bad about involving Mitch's parents, though. They're innocent in all this," Kristen said.

"The worst thing that's going to happen to them is the ambulance ride," said Josh. "They're gonna get a very good check-up at a hospital. It's like an expensive hotel, with doctors. You're a teacher, right? The only thing good about being a teacher is the insurance. This won't cost you anything."

Kristen smiled and shook her head. "Still," she said.

"Look, this is a small price to pay to stop the absolutely horrific shit that's coming down," said Josh. "Invading Russians collaborating with a Nazi preacher who took over a town and tried to kill friends of yours?"

"Well, when you put it that way," Kristen said.

"Seriously. So well done. Now, two more acting jobs: One for the responders. The other for your husband. Ex-husband. Separated, estranged husband. Whatever," Josh said.

Morgan, Estela, Mark, Maureen, and Al all got in the Hummer. There was one more spot left for me in the front, and of course Jake behind the wheel. Jake went over to his boys for a second before getting in.

"Boys, do what this guy says. He's a little out there, but it's obvious that he knows his shit. Keep your heads low, and I'll see you back at the farm," Jake said. Vinny and Tommy shook his hand and nodded. Then we were off.

"Alright boys," Josh said. "Time to find out what we're dealing with. Tommy, can you blow into this breathalyzer for me? The goddamn thing won't start otherwise."

"Sure thing," Tommy said with a smile.

"Cheap way to get shotgun," said Vinny.

"You can get it next time," Josh said. Vinny climbed into the back seat of the old Camaro.

"Slobbering after him on that thing? I'll pass. Um, there are no seatbelts back here," Vinny said.

"Yeah, I know," Josh said. Tommy laughed derisively at his brother while searching for his own. He reached up, back, down, and swiveled around in his seat looking for his own.

"You don't have one either," Josh said.

"Whoa, so what are we supposed to do if we're in an accident?" Tommy said.

"Duh. Don't get in one," Josh said, firing up the car and spinning wheels as he drove onto the road.

The car hit the pavement and Josh headed into town, past the rural "Four Corners" section of the area that lay in the middle of fields all around. He pulled past Chubby's Barbecue, then turned right and headed towards Hunter's Run High School. Vinny was scrutinizing Josh as he leaned forward between the seats.

"Mind if I ask you a question?" Vinny said.

"Shoot," Josh answered.

"How come you don't have any hair, like anywhere?" Vinny asked.

"Dude," Tommy said. "Don't be a dick."

"I'm serious. I mean, is that a thing? Like being an albino or something?" Vinny asked.

"Dude, dick question. He's young, sorry Mr. Rimone," Tommy said, scowling at his brother.

"It's alright, I don't mind. People ask me that all the time," Josh said. "And call me Josh, Mr. Fisher." Tommy smiled and nodded.

"When I was in high school, I was a bit of a hellion," said Josh.

"Could've fooled me," Vinny joked.

"Yeah. No surprise, huh? So, after a few hundred trips to the principal's office, the counselors suggested I get therapy. After a few therapy sessions, the therapists suggested I be medicated," Josh said.

"Medicated? For what?" Tommy asked.

"They said I had emotional disorders, attention deficit, anger issues. The whole nine yards," Josh said.

"What did you do?" Tommy asked.

"Nothing. My parents and I agreed that we didn't want medication," Josh said. "But the court ordered I be institutionalized after the whole thing with the dumpster and the airplane, so once I was in the institution, they medicated me by force."

"Whoa, court order? What was the thing with the dumpster and the airplane?" Vinny asked.

"Can't tell you. That settlement was pretty clear about not discussing that. But I can tell you that I did not like being in the institution," Josh said. "And I got pretty good at getting out of straight-jackets."

"What? You can get out of a straight-jacket? Like, how many times were you in one?" Tommy asked.

"A lot. Just a lot. It's actually a pretty good party trick when things get boring. Straight-jackets are kind of easy. But I hated the fucking burrito bag," Josh said.

"Burrito bag? What's a burrito bag?" Vinny asked.

"Well, first they put you in a straight jacket. Then, before you can get out, they put you in a giant canvas duffel bag with grommets on the top. Then they chain the grommets together. God damn, I hated that!" he said.

"Jesus," Tommy said.

"How long were you in the institution?" Vinny asked.

"About a year and a half. And whatever cocktail of drugs they gave me made all my hair fall out. My parents were pretty pissed," he said.

"I bet. Weren't you pissed?" Vinny asked.

"Still am. They said it would grow back," Josh said.

"How long ago was that?" Tommy asked.

"I was in high school, so you two weren't born yet," Josh said.

"Damn," Vinny said. "I'd be super pissed. So, what did you do?"

"What did I do? I spent a lifetime honing the craft of murdering people," Josh said with a chuckle.

"Oh," Vinny said. "Yeah. That."

"So, what are we doing now, besides raising Hell?" Tommy said.

"We're gonna find out what these fuckers are up to," said Josh.

CHAPTER 8—BACK TO THE STABLES

"Wow, this thing is massive. There are seven of us in here and I don't feel cramped," Maureen said.

"Your government tax dollars at work," I said. "I can't believe the Colonel just gave you this."

"I don't have any papers on it, Eddie. I'm sure it's a loan. I'm not planning on keeping it," Jake said.

"Just sayin'. Must be nice to have that kind of influence at the Pentagon. The Colonel is a pretty big cheese," I said.

"Big cheese indeed," said Jake. "He practically had all of the CBRNE brigade working for him. That's a big deal."

"What's CBRNE?" Morgan asked.

"It's one of those four billion ridiculous military acronyms," I said. Jake laughed.

"He's right. And it stands for Chemical, Biological, Radiological, Nuclear, and Explosive. As in, these are the people who handle all of that. They're pretty amazing. They can do just about anything," Jake said.

"Pretty much," I said. "I guess we're gonna see just how much they *can* do, won't we?"

I shouldn't have said it. I regretted blurting it out seconds after it left my big mouth. I was just trying to sound cool, and in my mind I was referring to Wendy and the Colonel's attempt to deal with the reversal of the effects of the

Russian weapon on the mutates. But let's be serious here—the reference was to Laura Fisher. And Jake stiffened the minute I did it. You could see him tense up. He sat up straighter, and the veins in his forehead started to bulge. You could hear him breathe, and he pressed his lips together tightly. Maureen and Al instantly looked at me with a frown. Morgan, Estela, and Mark weren't quite sure what the tension was about. I felt like a dick. An awkward silence followed for about thirty seconds, then thankfully Maureen started talking.

"So where are we going again?" Maureen said.

"Glenmont. It's near Wheaton, kind of close to the Montgomery and Prince George's county lines. There's a stable there. We went there to get horses so we could ride past the military blockade on the beltway and major roads," Jake said, obviously relieved to be talking about something else.

"Wow. That's actually brilliant. Was it effective?" Mark asked.

"Slipped by the military easily. We were able to stay within parks and along the rivers. There were, uh, other obvious challenges, of course," said Jake.

"Like what?" Mark asked.

It was just then that I realized that Mark was the only one in the car that had never seen or even heard of a mutate. He had stayed in Emmitsburg when we rode down to Virginia to get Tommy and Vinny, and he was still there when we were in Washington trying to wrangle mutates ourselves. The rest of us had encountered them while on the bus, both times in Frederick, but at different spots. Everyone else's eyes bugged a little and they looked at Mark.

"What? Did I say something wrong?" he asked.

"Holy shit, you don't even know about this, do you?" Maureen asked.

"About what?" he said.

"Mutates. Orange and white mutated people that have become, well, some kind of thing that eats flesh," Maureen said. "You seriously don't remember me talking about this? About, about Jake's wife?" Jake stiffened again.

"You said that you had to hang up with Eddie because Jake's wife was trying to kill him. I thought it was a joke. It was serious?" Mark said. Jake was clearly uncomfortable, and Maureen noticed it.

Another awkward silence.

"Alright, I'm already the jerk on this bus, so I might as well reprise the role. Mutates were people who, for some unknown reason, proved to be immune to the Russians' weapon that fused radiation and Ebola," I began.

"Yeah. I know about the Russian weapon," said Mark.

"Well, a portion of the population actually devolves into like a caveman-type-ape-creature, complete with bent over motion and a weird-shaped cranium," I said.

"Jesus," said Mark.

"I'm just getting warmed up," I continued. "They are orange. Like, orange-orange, and their hair is stark white."

"Holy shit," said Mark. "Really?"

"Really. But not all of them totally devolve. There are an even more select few who remain upright and control the pack somehow with noises, and pheromones, and physical cues, as far as we can tell. Jake's wife, Laura, is one of those 'alphas' as the Colonel calls them now," I said.

"Good God," Mark said. "And where are they?"

"As far as we know? Everywhere. At least everywhere that the Russian bombs hit. The news is only barely returning now, and not on a national level yet by any means, but I remember the first couple of days, back when we had news. The North Koreans hit Japan and U.S. islands and territories in the

South Pacific. China hit our allies in Australia and New Zealand, and maybe some of Europe. But as far as I can tell, only Russian bombs hit the Eastern half of America. It's like they called dibs on us. If they used only those kinds of bombs, then nearly every big city in the country statistically has mutates in it. We know that means Baltimore, Annapolis, Frederick, Columbia, and Aberdeen in Maryland. Of course, Washington has them, and in Virginia probably folks in Northern Virginia and the Tidewater areas near Norfolk got hit at the very least," I guessed. "The Colonel wasn't really sure of the range of the effects, but all of Washington and most of Northern Virginia were blanketed. They have their hands full down there."

"Jake, if you don't mind my asking, what happened with your wife?" Mark queried. Jake stiffened a bit.

"We were able to capture her and contain her. She's currently in a lab at the Pentagon. They're experimenting with some possible treatments, maybe even a cure," Jake said.

"I hope it works out alright for you," Mark said diplomatically.

"Thanks. Me too," said Jake.

What he really meant by that, only God knows. Jake's wife had eluded us successfully at first, and then directed an assault that led to the capture of Jake and both sons by a new pack of mutates that Laura commanded. In the end, she had defied the odds and found a way to speak. None of the other mutates that we encountered—even the alphas—had been able to form speech in any way. And the words she chose were to instruct her pack to kill Jake. Jake's already rocky relationship with his wife took on a whole new level of estrangement with that scene. If I hadn't been there myself, I probably wouldn't have believed half of it.

We pulled up to Glenmont Stables, and we could see Jake's truck parked right where we left it. He had hidden the keys in case of our return. I suddenly had a flashback of our first arrival here weeks ago. The owners of the stables had been killed by the bombs, and their bloated corpses were lying in the yard. It was that memory that led me to scan the yard and prepare our guests with a proper warning. I couldn't quite remember exactly where the bodies were. I leaned out the window, looking in all possible directions. I knew we weren't planning on walking around or taking a tour, so I figured if I couldn't see them in plain sight, then there was no need to warn the others.

"Eddie, what are you doing?" asked Jake.

"Nothing. Just looking around," I said.

Jake pulled up next to his truck and put the Humvee in park.

"So, now we have to decide who's driving what," Jake said.

"I always wanted to drive a Hummer," said Eddie.

"I'm not even gonna touch that one, Eddie. Too easy," said Jake.

"You are a sick bastard, you know that?" I said, smiling and shaking my head.

"Besides, it's a Humvee, not a Hummer," Jake said.

"What's the difference?" I asked.

"Not much, really. Humvee is another one of those acronyms. Stand for High Mobility Multipurpose Wheeled Vehicle. I think Hummer is just what the company calls the civilian version, to be honest," Jake said.

"So, in other words, another occasion when one of your know-it-all corrections for obscure trivia is completely worthless," I said.

"There is always an occasion for obscure trivia," said Jake, grinning.

Everyone got out to stretch their legs. All walked around fairly close to the house and the nearest fencing, looking around at the green grounds and attractive setting. The grass was a bit overgrown, but that was becoming the norm in places near where the bombs had gone off. I looked at the corral where we had selected our horses before. There were five of us: me, Jake, Wendy, and the boys. We had over a dozen horses to choose from, and they had all come up to see us when we arrived, hoping to get a treat, or a handful of grain, and some fresh water. This time, however, there was a difference.

I didn't see any horses.

"Jake?" I called.

"What is it now, Eddie? Do you have to pester me incessantly with questions?" he said.

"These might be a bit more important," I said.

"Alright, what is it?" Jake said, feigning impatience.

"The bodies of the owners. Weren't they here in the yard last week?" I said.

"Yeah," Jake answered, "they were right over—"

Jake spun around and looked at the empty spaces on the grass.

"Wait a minute. I'm sure they were here," Jake said.

"And weren't there at least a half a dozen horses we left here?" I asked.

"Yeah. We only took five," Jake said. "Why?"

"Where are they?" I asked.

An empty pit in my stomach formed as I looked at Jake's face. His thoughts were the same as mine. Dead flesh removed. Live animals gone. There could only be one answer.

"Everybody, get in a vehicle now. Now! Eddie, you take the Hummer," Jake said.

Maureen, Al, Estela and Morgan were all closer to the Hummer, so they jumped in and buckled up, not sure why the panic showed in Jake's face, but knowing it was no small thing to see. Mark Longaberger was closer to Jake's truck, so he reached for the passenger's side door and started to open it.

"What's the hurry all of a sudden?" asked Mark.

That's when the first mutate flew out snarling from the stables and sprinted towards us.

"Holy shit! What the fuck is that thing?" Mark yelled.

"That, my friend, is what we were talking about. Get inside, fast!" Jake said.

But it was too late. The mutate had already closed in on Mark and grabbed the truck door with one hand and Mark's arm with the other. Muscles powered by radiation and a brain that was slow to process pain locked onto Mark's arm and he screamed in surprise. From the stables two more lower mutates emerged, intent on finding us.

"Shit," Jake said. "Eddie, tell Al to reach in the back and toss me Tommy's katana sword."

Al did just that, leaning over the seat and perusing the strange collection of weapons in the back that we had packed last week on our journey to Washington. Jake, Tommy, and Vinny had fought off two packs of mutates with them successfully, and though a gun might be more powerful and efficient, it also required unpacking, loading and aiming—all of which required time Jake didn't have. The mutate yanked Mark over next to it and reached for his shoulder and bit down hard.

"Agghh," yelled Mark, trying to push the mutate off ineffectively.

Al tossed the katana over to Jake, who unsheathed it, ran up behind the mutate biting Mark, cocked back, and swung hard. The swing took the back half of the creature's skull off. The front was still clinging to Mark when it slumped to the ground.

"Jesus," Mark said.

The other two were sprinting toward Jake, who was helping Mark get the dead mutate off his arm. Jake couldn't see them approaching, focused totally on helping Mark. I looked back at Al to see what weapons I could grab. Realizing there was no time, I slammed the Hummer into drive.

"Fuck it," I yelled, jamming the accelerator. The vehicle lurched forward like a rhino beginning a charge. I slammed into the other two mutates hard, their heads cracking against the chassis as they went down.

"Thanks Eddie," Jake said. "That was quick thinking."

"Looks and brains. I'm the full package," I said. "How is he?"

Mark was in shock. His arm was bleeding, but his psyche was worse. He wasn't expecting the attack, and it clearly rattled him. Jake reached into the glove compartment and pulled out a rag and gave it to Mark.

"Apply pressure on the wound," Jake said. "It's not that bad."

One of the mutates I hit wasn't killed, and it was just now coming back to its senses and stirring to life, wriggling on the ground slowly in an attempt to stand.

"No time," Jake yelled. "Get in."

Jake spun wheels and was out of there before we were. I followed suit, and within minutes we were on the highway headed back to Emmitsburg. I could see Mark leaning back in his chair holding the rag on his bite wound.

"You okay?" Jake asked.

"I think so. It caught me by surprise. Those damn things are strong," he said. "But you were right, the bite wasn't that deep, and it's already stopped bleeding, so I'm in good shape."

"Well," said Jake. "I'm not sure I'd say that."

"What do you mean?" Mark said.

"Well, unless I miss my guess," Jake said, "You just contracted Ebola."

CHAPTER 9—
ALL FOR ONE

Father Joe welcomed John Segen and Wes Kent inside his office. The two of them looked wary, eyes darting back and forth with one another as they entered. Father Joe looked out into the halls, then shut his door behind them and locked it. Inside the room waiting already were Lou Orville, Billy James, Emery Butler, and Pablo Fuentes—four of the most instrumental men in the church, the school, and now the town as well.

"Now then, gentlemen. Let's talk," Father Joe said.

"I think we need to talk about this business with Oleg first," said Billy. "This whole story about the girls spying on the church, him taking them to the police station, then getting hit on the head and almost killed by Mark Longaberger? It's insane. I think we need some answers."

"I'll be very frank. Oleg frightens me," said Emery.

"Everything frightens you, Emery," said Lou.

"He should frighten you," said Father Joe. "He's dangerous. But then so are we--when we need to be."

"So, let us in on this. Who is Oleg—really, and what friends does he have coming to visit that John told us about?" asked Billy.

Wes scowled at John, and Father Joe cut his eyes toward John and frowned. Then he nodded resolutely and turned back to face Billy.

"Oleg is *Spetsnaz*. Russian special forces. He is in charge of a cell that has been stationed here in the United States for nearly a decade now. We met some time ago. When it became clear that our two countries were about to be at war, we got into a philosophical discussion about the direction of things. We kept it hypothetical and between friends, but it became obvious that very few moves would be made by our two countries that we 1) couldn't predict, and 2) would be powerless to stop. We realized that we, as people, were just pawns in a game played by much more powerful individuals. We began talking about what our visions were, our dreams of the future, and how we could embrace the inevitable and do something with it," Father Joe began.

"Holy shit," said Lou.

"With Russia? What do you mean, Father?" Billy said.

"Take a breath, Billy. For you to understand this, you need to open your mind a bit past its predisposed suppositions and limited vision," Father Joe said.

"Okay," Billy answered meekly.

"Russia has called dibs on the United States. No other country in this World War allied to them is allowed to touch us. The Russians want to move in here, take over. They love our country so much, they want it for their own," Father Joe said.

"That's bullshit," Billy yelled. "They can't have it!"

"Stop reacting with your heart for a moment, Billy, and use your head. What usually happens in a war? Destruction of everything. Lives lost, history destroyed, decades erased. Think about what we did to Hiroshima. What the Nazis did to France. What the Japanese did to Pearl Harbor. What Al-Qaeda did to the towers. The Russians don't want that. They want to move here," Father Joe continued.

"Well that's not gonna happen!" Billy said.

"I'm not crazy about that idea either," said Lou.

"Your patriotism is commendable," Pablo said. "But please listen to the Padre. Billy, Lou--let him finish."

"Thank you, Pablo. As I was saying, Russia is going to continue to bomb us. They are doing it now. They have eradicated every living being in about eight cities here in the mid-Atlantic region already. They have a new weapon that takes massive human toll, but does no damage to buildings, roads, churches, or any infrastructure. We can't stop them. It's already happened, and it will happen again. Now Billy, it doesn't necessarily mean that they will win. I grant that, and I'm certainly not rooting for them. But I am a shrewd man, and I want the future of our church, our congregation, and our new city to be solidified *no matter what ending occurs.* Do you understand me? I don't want to be any man's pawn, any country's slave. I want to lead, no matter what the flag of the country that survives this Cataclysm looks like. I want to insure that for my flock as well."

"Okay," said Billy, his eyes wide and his mouth agape.

"I guess I can get behind that notion," said Lou.

"I love America. I love what it stands for. I love our freedoms. I love everything about it. Well, that's not quite accurate. Not everything. I don't love that America recently has abandoned the God that helped it win its own independence. I don't love it that godless individuals tell us how to speak, what to think, and how to worship. I don't love that my religious freedom to believe what God's word says is no longer legitimate because it doesn't serve their needs for feminism, miscegenation and homosexuality. And that has been way too prevalent of late. But now we have a chance to change all that. With all other large cities in Maryland—and who knows where else—devoid of life, we have been spared to recapture the purity of God's vision here on Earth. Here with New Plymouth, and beyond," Father Joe thundered.

"But Father, God blesses *America*," said Billy.

"God isn't American," said Father Joe. "He is without a defined country. He is every country and every man. Ask your friend Pablo about that. He is from Spain. Is God not there as well? Or in Mexico, where he used to live?"

"But God spared our town," said Emery. "The others died, but God spared us. You even said so."

Father Joe closed his eyes and put his clasped hands up to his forehead for a moment to think.

"Tell him," said Wes. "Tell him the truth."

"God didn't spare us, Emery. I did. I spared us. I worked out a deal with Oleg to provide us with prophylactic chemical treatments in our water that would allow us to live through any Russian attack in the area. In exchange, I allowed Oleg's forces to move about this area without alerting their presence to the authorities," said Father Joe.

"But that's treason," said Billy.

"Is it? If it was engineered before we declared war? By definition it can't be. It's merely an alliance. And let's be honest, Billy. One small rural Maryland town is not going to either win or lose this war. Neither is one small handful of Russian soldiers. No one is using it as a staging area for a campaign. It's just a base of operations, for all of us. But the alliance I made—it has allowed us to create New Plymouth, and it's allowed us to ensure the continued existence of the Church of Many Blessings and its congregation no matter who wins this war. And most importantly, we ensure--by virtue of the targets selected by the Russians themselves--that the survivors, no matter what language they speak, will be white, European, heterosexuals. Just like Jesus himself. I can never regret doing that."

You could have heard a pin drop. Everyone stared at each other with wide eyes. They were at once incredulous and completely rapt.

"Let me get this straight, Father," Pablo said. "You are choosing your ethnicity and your religion over your nationality?"

An awkward silence followed. Wes and John both stared at Father Joe.

"Yes," he said.

"Then it is exactly what God would ask of you. This is directly from the scriptures. 'Render unto Caesar that with is Caesar's.' And that is what you are doing. God and your tribe over flags and anthems. I am with you. One hundred percent," said Pablo.

"I am as well," said Emery.

"Okay," said Lou.

"I guess so, yeah," said Billy. "I think that's right, you know?"

"Of course it is. And when these Russians lose, as they're sure to do, all we've done is make sure we're not like Frederick or Washington. We are alive and will carry on our great country into the next era," said Father Joe.

"Do you mean that?" asked Billy.

"I am not *for* the Russians, Billy. *We* are not for the Russians. But we're not afraid to use them to our advantage to make this world a better place. One God wants us to live in. Can you get on board with that?"

"I, I guess so," Billy said.

"We are still Americans. Patriotic, God-fearing Americans. We are doing nothing to counter that. We are not aiding and abetting a group of people plotting to destroy our country. They happen to be citizens of a country that is currently at war with us, but the only thing they have done is spared us an early death, and the only thing we have done is allowed them to stay here unmolested. That relationship will continue. America wins wars, and when we win this one, we will be better set to lead our new country into the 21st Century with honor. Do you understand me?" Father Joe asked.

"Yes," said Billy.

"Sí," said Pablo.

"I do," said Emery.

"But in the off chance, the very slightest possibility, that things do not go our way in this war, we are still in good standing to continue God's mission the way He wants us to. Are we together on this, then?" Father Joe said.

Everyone stood and clapped for him.

"Excellent," Father Joe said. "You are my chosen disciples. You are my Knights of the Round Table. Together we can do anything."

More shouts, claps, and hoots followed for a moment. Then things went quiet.

"So, since you've brought it up, Padre," said John Segen. "Just what are we doing right now?"

"Oleg's *Spetsnaz* colleagues will be coming here soon," Father Joe began. "He wants to house them all over town to avoid being too conspicuous. I want them housed at the school so that we can keep an eye on them. If it looks like they are going to betray us or do something we don't like, we will be in a better position to stop them."

"Yeah, I knew you weren't some kind of Commie traitor, Father," said Billy.

"Russians haven't been Communist since 1991, Billy, and I've never been a traitor," Father Joe said.

"But what could we possibly do to stop them?" Emery asked. "They're Russian Special Forces. We're just regular people."

"We are regular people in a rural county where every-one owns half a dozen guns," said Wes. "And all of those people have been eating out of Father Joe's hand all week. And we out-number them 100-1 on our worst day. We can do plenty."

"Bet yer ass we can," said John, pulling out a large .44 magnum pistol.

"Good God, John," said Wes. "Where did you get that monster?"

"Ebay," said John, laughing and patting Wes on the back. "It cost me a lot, but it'll put a fist-sized hole in a guy's chest if you use magnums. Let those fuckin' Ruskies come at me."

"Shhhh," said Father Joe. "They are not our enemies right now, John. And talk like that will go nowhere at all. It could wreck our delicate relationship and endanger us all. I in-sist you put that thing away, and don't let me see it again until I tell you."

"Alright, Padre. You're right. It might be a little over the top," John said, putting the gun back in a hidden holster. "I'll leave it in the Jeep, like you want. Besides, I got a switchblade with me at all times anyways," he said with a grin.

Father Joe nodded in acknowledgment.

"Now then, Wes, are the new group's accommodations ready?" asked Father Joe.

"Yes, they are," said Wes. "They are all in one of the art rooms, in an area nearer the gym and locker rooms, in a part of the school that is away from everyone else. They'll be fine with that, I'm sure."

"Well done," said Father Joe. "And their first job—they're only job right now—is to find the people who spied on us, broke into our church, and assaulted our people."

"And then what?" asked Pablo.

"We'll burn that bridge when we come to it," said Father Joe.

CHAPTER 10—RECON

"Aren't we a little too close?" Vinny asked.

"Yeah. I can practically see their faces," said Tommy. "Which means they can see mine."

"Have any of them seen you before?" Josh asked.

"That guy on the end. Oleg, I think his name is. He may have seen me once, but not for more than a second," said Tommy.

"Then stay well out of sight," Josh said. "They don't know me, and they don't know this car, so let's just pay attention and watch for a while."

Tommy slumped down into the seat a little more and put his binoculars away. Vinny scrunched down in the back. Josh smiled to himself and spat some of his tobacco juice outside onto the pavement. They were outside Hunter's Run High School, across the street and near the Wal-Mart parking lot watching Oleg's six new friends unpack their belongings.

"So, it looks like there's six of them. Seven counting Oleg. They are Russian, probably *Spetsnaz* or *Spetsnaz*-trained, to be more accurate. Two bags each, one big, one small. The smaller one will be the weapons. They're mostly young guys, probably in their 20's. That's good at least," Josh said.

"Why is that good?" Tommy asked.

"Because younger guys are easier to fuck with. Twenty-somethings think they know it all, but they're usually not old or experienced enough to know much of anything. Easier to fuck with that mentality," Josh said.

Tommy, who was twenty-one, pressed his lips together tightly and looked at the floor. Vinny was grinning in the back like a cat and pointing silent taunts at his big brother behind his head.

"I can hear you taunting your brother back there," Josh said.

What? How? I was totally silent, said Vinny to himself, frustrated. *How the hell did he do that?* thought Vinny. *This guy's like a demon or something.*

"Oh, and in case you're wondering, old teenagers think they know it all too," said Josh. "And to answer that other question you want to ask, the answer is 'rear view mirror.' Duh."

Tommy grinned and turned around and smirked at his brother.

"We are probably going to need some help," Josh said.

"What do you mean? What kind of help?" Vinny asked.

"The kind that can handle an opponent of this caliber. These guys are not like some backward-ass third world warlord. These guys are trained. They can shoot, they can run, and they usually don't falter under pressure. And there are six of them," Josh said. "Again, seven if you count Oleg."

"So? We got numbers too," said Vinny.

"No, we don't," said Josh. "We have me and your father. And to be honest, your father might not be up to this."

"What are you talking about? How about us? We killed mutates. We know how to fight, wrestle, and shoot. We can fuck those guys up," said Vinny.

"All due respect boys—no, you can't. You can fuck regular guys up, sure. I won't question that. Wrestlers are usually

JAY VIELLE

tougher than everybody else, and most of us know how to fight. Some of us even know how to shoot a little. I'm guessing you guys can, having grown up in the country. These guys, however, are specialists. They're on a totally different level— one that we can't compete on. We are going to have to take them out of their game. At the moment, we don't know how long they're going to be here, where they're staying, or what their mission is. We know they want to kill your Dad's friends. And we're pretty sure they don't know where those friends are. Yet."

"We know more than that," Tommy said. "We know they have a weakness for sex."

"What makes you think that?" Josh said.

"These are the same guys we got a glimpse of in Front Royal when we were taken hostage that day. We were all going to be sold into slavery, and they were gonna buy four women for sex slaves. The deal went crazy bad, and two of them ended up getting killed when the gang imploded and had a shoot-out," Tommy said.

"How do you know that?" Josh asked.

"Morgan told us she found a sales slip with that guy, Sergei's name on it among the stuff they found in the church office. He was part of this group. So was the guy with him," Tommy said.

"You're right, kid," said Josh. "I remember that. I even asked your Dad about that after Morgan mentioned it. You say two of them got killed there in a shootout?"

"Yes," said Tommy. "I'm sure of it. We were right there."

"So if two of them got killed in Front Royal, that means that two of the four of these guys are brand new. Which means they're completely unfamiliar with the territory here. Moscow wouldn't send a commander with Oleg already here. Not during a war, and not unless they had a very top-secret mission. And this ain't that. These dudes are here to kill a handful of civilians and get the fuck out."

"Does that make the odds a little better?" Vinny asked.

"It does, just a little. Your dad and I have seen combat. You two are capable and you have balls. I don't know if you can take orders or not, judging by the number of brawls I hear you get in with your old man. That's four of us and seven of them. Mark got lucky on Oleg. He might be useful. He apparently has some balls too, and thinks quick in a tight situation. So that's five of us versus seven of them. Not great, but better, especially if they have a couple greenhorns with them. I still would like some help, though," said Josh. "And we're gonna need a much bigger arsenal. Much bigger. Last of all, I think we're gonna need to get them off balance."

"Off balance?" Tommy said. "What do you mean?"

"We need to flush them out. If they're dug in at the school, they'll be hard to get to. But not if we kick the hornet's nest a little," Josh said.

"What do you mean?" Vinny asked.

"Fuck with their supply line. Make them feel vulnerable instead of safe in their nest. Give them a reason to leave the nest in a hurry, less prepared," said Josh.

"So how do we do that?" Tommy said.

"Not sure yet. I have a few ideas, but I need to reconnoiter with your Dad and his people. Find out some things about the church and the school. First, I want to see if we can get some help. Get a little supply of our own, and maybe an extra hand," Josh said. "Your Dad still has keys to this place?"

"Yeah. To a lot of rooms in there. And the other teachers will, too. Mr. Longaberger, Ms. Kelly, Mr. DeFillipo. Even Ms. Faust," Vinny said.

"Good. We're gonna need 'em. We also may need to

sneak into that church," Josh said.

"Morgan and Estela have already done it. And Mr. Longaberger was invited. They'll know a little about that," Tommy said.

"Alright. Good place to start," said Josh.

"So, what do you mean, fuck with their supply line?" Tommy said. He kind of swallowed the curse word, still in that awkward age when you aren't quite comfortable cursing around adults.

"Armies gotta eat. They need food, water, a place to sleep, and weapons of some kind. These guys brought their own weapons. But all of their ammo is confined to a bag, so even if they have a lot, it's not an endless supply. And either the school or the church has to be feeding them. We know now that they're sleeping at the high school. If we can screw up their supplies, they can't stay put and feel comfortable. They'll have to come out, and they won't be as prepared when they do come out," said Josh.

"So, we have a plan," said Tommy.

"We have a plan," said Josh. "Sort of. We have the beginnings of a plan. But I need to find an old compadre to help us out first. Excuse me."

Josh grabbed his phone. It was a satellite phone and worked immediately. He dialed and waited.

"Hello?" said the voice on the other end.

"Colonel? Josh Rimone here," Josh said.

"Josh! Where are you? Did you rendezvous with the Fishers?" the Colonel asked.

"Affirmative, sir. And I can verify the situation. Seven Russian *Spetsnaz* operatives here in Emmitsburg," Josh said.

"Seven? Damn! What are they doing?" asked the Colonel.

"Nothing yet, sir, but they are looking for Fisher's friends. The ones on the bus with you, sir. They're hiding out. I have them meeting me within an hour to discuss what I've seen and to formulate a plan," Josh said.

"Do you have a plan?" asked the Colonel.

"Affirmative, sir. But I'm going to need more firepower and maybe a hand or two," Josh said.

"I can't help you there, son," said the Colonel. "Forward teams have been pulled out. All I have access to is the brigade, and they're not really fixed for combat, undercover or otherwise."

"I figured that, sir," said Josh. "I was wondering if you knew how to get a hold of Boo Andrews."

The Colonel was silent for about fifteen seconds.

"Sir? Did you copy that, sir?" Josh asked.

"Roger that, Josh. Copied loud and clear. I'm not sure I'm supposed to tell you that information," the Colonel said. "By whose request?" Josh asked.
"His request," the Colonel said.

"Sir, I don't understand. Boo and I are in good standing. We've worked together a bunch of

times, and I know he's not forward yet or occupied at the moment. I just don't have his new number, and you do," Josh said.

"It's not you," the Colonel said. "Boo already knows what you're working on. I've been in contact with him. He said under no circumstances would he come up there, and he wanted me to discourage you from even asking him."

"He owes me, Colonel," Josh said.

"He knows, Josh. He's hoping you don't call that debt in this time," the Colonel said.

"Well in case he's got fucking glaucoma, sir, we're in a goddamn World War right now, and

we're not doing particularly well. You're in a fucking zombie-infested dead zone, if you'll pardon my French, sir, and I have intel on invading agents of our enemy state. I'm not sure there's gonna be a next time for him to wait for," Josh said. "And if there is, he may have to brush up on his Russian alphabet."

Another fifteen seconds of silence.

"I'm texting you his new number now," the Colonel said. "And I've passed your concerns up the

ladder here at the Pentagon. Right now it's not deemed a credible threat."

"Colonel, I've seen them sir," Josh said.

"And how's your standing with the U. S. Military right now, son—present company excluded?" the Colonel asked.

This time it was Josh's turn to be silent.

"So, you understand your predicament, yes?" the Colonel said.

"That I'm on my own?" Josh asked.

"Affirmative, son," the Colonel said.

"Then tell Boo Andrews his options just got limited to one," Josh said. "I'm calling in that debt."

"You tell him, Josh. His number should be coming up now. God speed," the Colonel said.

"Thanks, Colonel," Josh said.

"What's the word?" Tommy asked. "That conversation didn't sound too great."

"It wasn't. I'm gonna have to force my buddy up here. He doesn't want to come for some reason. And the Pentagon will not be sending in the cavalry. Apparently, I'm *persona non grata* with the U. S. Army at the moment."

Josh sent a text to the number that the Colonel sent him. It was short and simple:

Boo. I'm calling it in. Grotto, Emmitsburg, MD, 0900. Vici package, low profile.
--Pineapple

So now, we can't count on the army, we may not have help, we may not have proper ammunition or weapons, and any help or ammo we might get-- we will have to wait until tomorrow morning to find out."

"Well, that sucks," said Vinny.

"It does, indeed, suck," said Josh. "But we gotta adapt, improvise, and overcome."

"That's a Marine saying," said Vinny. "I hear my dad use that all the time."

"Marine saying," said Josh. "Why do the goddamn Marines think they are the first to invent everything?"

"If the Marines didn't invent that saying," asked Vinny, "Then who did?"

"I'm thinking it was Clint Eastwood," Josh said.

CHAPTER 11 —GETTING TO KNOW OLEG

The Russian agents had been sent to a portion of Hunter's Run High School that housed the Fine Arts Wing. The Fine Arts Wing was directly across the hall from the main and auxiliary gymnasiums, themselves flanked by locker rooms, a weight room, and the wrestling room that Jake Fisher had made famous. The Fine Arts Wing's rooms were large, spacious, and there was ample access to water and showers in the theater's dressing rooms. Wes Kent had ordered beds to be put there with mattresses—seven to be exact—one for each of the new men, and one for Oleg, should he choose to bunk with them. Wes wasn't sure exactly how Oleg was going to interact with his new compatriots.

The men had carried their gear to the wing and set up their room. Large cabinets that had once been filled with art projects were now filled with duffel bags full of weapons, clothing, and toiletries. It was a handy make-shift barracks, and the men were remarking how nice their accommodations were in comparison to some of the other places they had been forced to inhabit. Four of the men had been with Sergei and Dmitri in Front Royal before. They had been observing Washington D.C. and Frederick—two major targets of the new Russian weapons--from a distance. Their orders were to establish themselves, blend in, keep a low profile, and observe. Then they were to await new orders as news of the outcome of the bombings started to become clear to the generals and leaders in the upper echelon of the Kremlin.

The four that had been with Sergei and Dmitri had become well-accustomed to the United States and were obviously more relaxed than the two new arrivals. Maharbek, Buvaisar, Aleksandr, and Anatoly joked casually with one another and experienced a camaraderie built on shared experiences in a very niche business. The two newest additions, Valentin and Arsen, were both a bit stiffer and more regulated, having just arrived in the United States a day or two ago. All six of them were settling into their rooms as Oleg, the newly appointed leader of this cell, oversaw their accommodations.

"Remember, English only at this point. Even in our rooms. We will be raising enough suspicion as it is with our arrival and our accents," said Oleg. "Limit your Russian to vehicles, and even those may be problematic."

"At least your friends were kind enough to put us in a place to ourselves. We can make plans here and stay out of sight from the rest of them," said Anatoly. "It shouldn't take long to find these people, yes Oleg?"

"It is a small town. I can't imagine there are too many places to hide," Oleg said.

"First we settle in, yes? Then we make teams. Then we start to look for the targets," said Valentin.

"That was the memo we got in the text, Valentin Valentinovich," said Buvaisar. "Is this your first mission?" he said, mockingly.

"*Nyet*," said Valentin. "I am simply new here, that's all. I want to verify things."

"Are you sure? I don't want you to embarrass me when the girls come," Buvaisar said. "If you look like a little virgin, they won't be impressed."

"Girls?" Aleksandr said. "Girls are coming? Tonight?"

"Why not?" said Buvaisar. "Oleg has been here for a year. He's had plenty of time to meet girls and get them here."

"I want a slut," said Maharbek. "I want a girl who knows what she's doing. I think we should hire professionals. The last time we used locals it was a disaster. My girl cried and I didn't even get to finish."

"I don't see why not. Oleg has access to a deep bank account here," said Anatoly. "Isn't that right Oleg? These people have money, no?"

"Quiet you idiots," said Oleg. "There are no professional escorts around here. This isn't Washington before the bombing. Everything has changed. This tiny town was spared, thanks to the alliance I made with the local pastor. There is no one in this town. And since the bombs have dropped a few weeks ago, everything nearby is gone. Professional prostitutes work in cities, and we killed everyone in their cities. Baltimore, Annapolis, Columbia, and Washington. Nothing is even close by. Not even Frederick survived. You need to focus on the job. Get it done, then leave. Be professionals yourselves."

"But Oleg," said Maharbek. "It's been hard being here. We are bored. No television, no movies, very little Internet. There is no place to train."

"You can train here. They have a big gym and a wrestling mat. You can do sambo with one another. But this school is tied to a church, and I'm pretty sure the church doesn't rent out whores. And the girls in this town are country bumpkins and members of the church. They are too stupid and too religious to sleep with you. Put your things away and assemble for the meal in half an hour," said Oleg.

"Sergei would have understood," Marhabek half mumbled.

"Sergei is dead!" Oleg yelled. "And he is dead because he got sloppy. He did business with a criminal who couldn't control his people, and Dmitri is dead as well due to his sloppiness. Do you understand what is at stake here? There are at least five people who know what we're up to. If they find a platform to get word out, the entire plan Moscow has in place could fall through. These people we are looking for were actually the girls that Sergei was trying to buy when he got killed. Did you hear what I said? The same girls! Do you even believe that? Fate, gentlemen, is a cruel bitch. She mocks us at every turn, and to best her you must be crueler still. These people escaped me once. They left me with a concussion and a taste for vengeance and blood. And you--you six are my instruments for that vengeance, make no mistake about that. I am not sloppy. I will not make a second mistake, especially just so that you can satisfy your lustful weaknesses. The younger agents these days are full of weakness, and it sickens me. I wonder how we will ever conquer this country if we are softened by it. So, unpack and meet me in the cafeteria, and don't let me hear you speak of Sergei again," he finished.

Oleg stormed out and slammed the door behind him, leaving the six soldiers wide-eyed, mouths agape staring at one another.

"*Bozhe moi*," said Anatoly. "*Mudak!* What an asshole."

"Who does he think he is?" said Maharbek. "Treating us like children."

"When this job is finished, I may have to beat some respect into that old bastard," said Anatoly.

"You would do well to keep your mouth shut," said Valentin. "That old bastard would drop you in a minute's time. Then he would wait until you were sleeping, walk in this room and cut your throat, and then butter his toast with the knife. And none of us would even know he was here."

"Hummph, *derrmo*" said Maharbek. "You are full of shit, Valentin."

"*Ty che, suka, o'khuel blya?* You really don't know who he is, do you?" asked Valentin.

"And you do?" asked Buvaisar.

"Yes, we do," said Arsen, finally speaking up.

"Oleg Andreivich Stravinsky is a legend among the *Spetsnaz.* As a twenty-year old the SVR sent him into Chechnya when they were causing trouble. There was an organization just getting off the ground, and they had rioted and burned buildings in the town square, rallying the people. Within a week, Oleg had discovered who the source of the agitation was. The man just disappeared. They never found him. The group tried to meet again without their leader. Another week later, four more disappeared. No bodies were found."

"That's not true," said Aleksandr. "That's a myth."

"It is true. And a few years later, when Ukraine was complaining that they had been invaded by Russia in Crimea, some of their complaints got headlines and caught the attention of the United Nations. Again they sent Oleg. Within two weeks, the government denied the complaints, saying they were sent by a radical faction and that Russia was guiltless of all charges," Valentin said.

"That I remember. I thought it was strange, how they recanted," said Buvaisar.

"That was Oleg?" asked Maharbek.

"That was Oleg," said Valentin.

"The last time I remember hearing about him was at Sochi. At the Olympics. The entire world was watching and complaining that Russia was unfairly persecuting homosexuals. There was even a documentary movie they put out about the jailing of the band called *Pussy Riot.* A dozen people had interviews lined up with the American news outlets. They even announced that the interviews would be played live. Putin got tired of the press. So, he called in Oleg. None of them —not one—showed up for an interview, and none were heard from after Sochi. The news people were left fumbling with empty chairs, the world forgot all of it, and Oleg is the reason," said Valentin.

"*Bozhe moi,*" said Aleksandr. "My God."

"He is the most dangerous man in the history of the post-Soviet SVR. The fact that you don't know that is one of the reasons it is true," said Valentin.

"You are serious?" asked Anatoly.

"Yes. And so is Oleg. I suggest you do as he says and don't piss him off," said Valentin. "Like I said before, I may have just arrived, but this is not my first assignment. Do your homework. Then do your job."

Valentin finished packing up his duffel bag and threw it on his bed, then walked out the door towards the cafeteria. The others just stared at one another in silence. When Valentin entered the cafeteria, he was met my Wes Kent and Lou Orville, who met him with cordial smiles and hands out.

"How do you do?" said Wes.

"A pleasure to meet you," Valentin answered. "My name is Valentin Valentinovich Jordanov."

"Wow, that's a mouthful," said Wes. "Do all you guys have such long names?"

"They just seem long to you. My middle name is actually a nickname of sorts. It means that my father's name was Valentin as well. So Valentinovich means 'son of Valentin.' Jordanov is my last name."

"Okay. I get it now. Your name is Valentin, and so was your father's, but your last name is Jordanov. Very good. Well, nice to meet you too, Valentin. I'm Wes Kent. Much shorter name, right? I'm in charge of the school and the facility here. I trust you like your room?" said Wes.

"The accommodations are spectacular," said Valentin.

"As is your English. Do all of you speak English in Russia?" asked Wes. "We Americans are not very good linguists here. We have trouble just learning Spanish."

"Many of us speak English, but obviously some of us are better than others. Everyone here among our group is exceptional in English. My travel partner, Arsen. He is not as confident with his English as the rest of us, but he knows it well enough. He should be along in just a moment or two," said Valentin.

"We're all about to sit down for a nice meal," said Wes. "Your places are off to the right at that table."

"*Spasibo*," said Valentin. "Ah, excuse me. I meant to say, 'thank you.' Oleg told us to speak only English here. It's more polite."

"And Oleg is nothing if not polite," said Wes. "There he is now."

"Of course, Wes," said Oleg. "I am a model of courtesy. Nothing—if not polite."

CHAPTER 12— THE RIDE BACK

"Ugh," said Mark. "Those things smell bad."

"Yeah, you know I never really thought about that, but they do. I guess that's what not bathing and spending all your time eating live and dead flesh will do for your personal body odor," said Jake. "Then again, I've been a little sidetracked on my interactions with them. You know, ordinary every day distraction--like your wife trying to kill you, being ripped apart while suspended in mid-air, shooting them in the head before they eat Eddie. Shit like that."

"Yeah, those things can be distracting, I guess," said Mark.

"How you feeling?" asked Jake.

"Rough. Besides my shoulder aching like a sonofabitch, my neck and back are all tight and sore for some reason," Mark said.

"That thing hit you hard from behind by surprise. You weren't ready for it. Your body is letting you know that now," said Jake.

"It sure as hell is," said Mark. "Um, were you serious about me having Ebola?"

"Unfortunately, yes," said Jake.

"So, does that mean you have it too, now? Because of me?" asked Mark.

"No. I've actually gotten inoculated. I can't get it now," said Jake.

"So what does that mean for me?" said Mark. "Am I gonna die a horrible death now? Ebola is some nasty shit. I've seen people with it on television. I, I don't want to die just yet."

"You know, I just had a thought that might cheer you up. If I'm not mistaken," said Jake. "The town's drinking water has been loaded with anti-Ebola medicine. You are probably going to be okay."

"So, I'm like you?" said Mark. "I mean, you drank the water for a while yourself, right?"

"Yes and no. A vaccine is not like a treatment. I actually got vaccinated at the Pentagon. You've basically been drinking the medicine they use to treat it on a regular basis. You may still get it, but you're already kind of protected from getting it bad, or suffering symptoms," said Jake.

"Oh Jesus, thank God," said Mark.

"Thank God, sure, but also thank Father Joe. He's the one that loaded the town with antiviral medicine and radiation sickness treatments," said Jake.

"That son of a bitch is evil, Jake. I've seen it," Mark said. "He's slick. He speaks well, he has a very calming effect when he talks to you, he sounds very reasonable, but deep down, he's the devil. You were right. All those weeks ago when you warned me, you were right. They are the worst of people."

"I wish I wasn't right," said Jake. "But anytime you see people twist the truth to gain influence, power, wealth, or anything for themselves—that's the definition of evil. Think about the Seven Deadly Sins. What letter do they all have in common?"

"Let's see, Wrath, Pride, Lust, Gluttony, Greed, Sloth, Envy. Is it…no, it's not that. They don't all share a letter," Mark said.

"Actually, they do. I. They all share the letter I," said Jake.

"How do you figure? Lust, Sloth, Gluttony—they don't have an I," said Mark.

"I want what you have. I don't feel like doing anything. I want sex with that person. I want to vent my anger on you. I want more money. I want more food. I am better than you. All of them start with I," Jake said.

"I see your point," Mark said, nodding. "That's clever."

"It's also true, if you think about it. All of those sins put the self in front of others. Those so-called churchgoers who took you in? They are interested in one thing more than any other. The person in the mirror," said Jake.

"A couple of them are okay," said Mark. "That guy Billy. Pablo…a little. I mean, nobody's perfect."

"You said they changed the name of the town to 'New Plymouth,' right? So, let's see how many of the good ones decide not to follow Father Joe now that he's the new self-appointed mayor. Conscience doth make cowards of us all," said Jake.

"I guess that is the test," said Mark. "If they follow him in changing the town, knowing that it's blatantly set out as racist, homophobic, and misogynist—well, that's very telling."

"I wonder how many of them know about the Russians," said Jake.

◆ ◆ ◆

In the other car, I was following Jake, who was starting to drive like a madman again. Maureen, Al, Morgan, and Estela were all with me. It was kind of a heady feeling, driving something this big and powerful. I always used to call big, powerful vehicles like this 'compensation machines,' alluding to a guy having to compensate for having a small penis. I still think that. I'm not sure I'd buy one for what they cost, and I imagine the gasoline bill for this thing is like a small mortgage. But for now, I felt kinda cocky.

"Think the Colonel would let me rent this?" I asked Maureen.

"You want to keep one of your famous penis compensation machines?" Maureen said back, laughing. "That's a real advertisement for your next boyfriend. He'll know you have a little package."

"What I lack in size, I make up for with enthusiasm and coachability," I said back, laughing. Al got a kick out of that and leaned back for a big laugh. Morgan and Estela just rolled their eyes.

"Nothing we need to worry about," said Morgan, smiling.

"So, Eddie—now what? We've got both vehicles. What does that guy Josh want us to do now?" asked Al.

"He said to meet him at Jake's. He's doing recon with Tommy and Vinny right now. Depending on what he finds, he's going to make a plan of action to see if we can draw the Russian cell out and make them more vulnerable."

"You don't like him very much, huh?" Al asked.

"Not my style. He's a little too cocky, a little too weird for my tastes. Jake finds him way too amusing," I said.

"That's not jealously I'm hearing, is it?" said Maureen.

"Oh stop. It's not like that. I'm not hot for Jake. He's my friend. Besides, he's straight anyway. As a goddamn arrow," I said.

"People can be jealous for lots of reasons," said Maureen. "Friendship, professional, collegial. Hell, you can be jealous of my wardrobe."

"Girl, I've seen your wardrobe. Nobody is jealous of that," I said. We both laughed at that.

"But I see what you mean," I said. "And maybe you've got a point. I kind of got used to being Jake's, I don't know, sidekick or something. Now Josh is. I don't know. Maybe I am jealous."

"We gotta get you a boyfriend," said Maureen.

"Great. I decide to be single during the fucking Apocalypse," I said.

"Well, anybody who said they wouldn't date you if you were the last man in the world is getting closer to making good on that threat," said Maureen. "I know a few guys who are free, though, and always looking for someone new."

"Really?" I said. I couldn't imagine who she could possibly be talking about. We both knew everyone in this little town, and they didn't fit my bill in any way.

"Really. But they have standards. For one, you can't be racist," said Maureen.

"Are you kidding? I don't have a racist bone in my body, Mo. You know that. For Christ's sake, I'm a gay Hispanic in a redneck town. I can't afford to be racist. What do these guys look like, anyway?" I asked.

"Well, they have orange skin, white hair, and they're very touchy-feely," she said, laughing out loud.

"You bitch," I said. "You are not fixing me up with a mutate."

"Racist. Like I said," Maureen chuckled.

"That's more like, *'species-ist'*," I countered.

"Fair enough," said Maureen.

I laughed out loud for a while. It was good to joke around with friends again. Tiny pieces of normal. That's what we had to live for. Tiny pieces of normal. I smiled and thought to myself. Here we are, driving a big old Humvee with the windows down, laughing it up, kind of enjoying ourselves. But we just narrowly escaped the closest thing to zombies we're ever likely to encounter. And we were riding to meet with a paramilitary mercenary who was trying to concoct a way for us to defeat a team of trained Russian assassins who were being housed, fed, and armed across town by a megalomaniacal preacher. A preacher who had convinced an entire town to make him king and to ban anyone who wasn't white and straight. Oh, and if that wasn't enough, World War III is our backdrop, and our enemies have demolished our communications and flat out killed millions of us, leaving some towns empty and others facing lawlessness and uncertainty.

It's been a weird month to say the least.

I thought about poor Morgan. Here was a girl going to school far enough away to be unharmed by the bombs, but whose parents were now almost certainly dead, living on the outskirts of the nation's capital. Her only contacts were Vinny, a friend she had made at Virginia Tech—and Estela, a new lover she had known for a little over a week, in whose company she had been physically beaten and nearly killed. And now she was with us, riding in the Humvee, hiding from mutates, plotting against Russians. How crazy was that?

Estela wasn't much better. Cast away and disowned by her homophobic father who had also driven away her former girlfriend—the only other contact she had, having lost her mother years ago. She was trying to make ends meet by working at a Wal-Mart, when the bombs dropped all around us. Left with nowhere to go, she was forced to defend her life from armed thugs twice. The second time, luckily for her, Jake was around to handle them. Now she had tied her wagon to us as well. I couldn't imagine how strange things must have seemed to both of them, and I suddenly wasn't skeptical of why those two had become so close in such a short time. They truly didn't have anyone else to turn to.

And finally, I started to think about me. How I had been without romance now for over a year, and there was nothing likely on the horizon. I had tied myself to Jake, but at least I now knew that my parents were alive and okay, and I planned on visiting them once we got this Russian thing out of the way. Funny, I was brimming with confidence that we would find a way to succeed, but that was simply because since the bombs dropped, that's all we had done. We had found ways to win, to survive, even to thrive—in most cases despite serious odds against us. Here I was presuming we would do it again. But the truth was, we were outnumbered seven warriors to two. Al and I weren't fighters, and despite their wrestling training, neither were Vinny and Tommy. Not yet at least. But even counting them, at best we were outnumbered seven to four. They had done a decent job against mindless mutates, that was true enough. But mutates didn't shoot guns, or plot tactics, or work in coordinated teams. These Russians were specialists at what they did. They were the best at what they did. In actuality, we not only had little chance of winning, we had little chance of living out the week.

Suddenly I thought I had better visit my parents soon.

CHAPTER 13—
BOO ANDREWS

We all pulled into Jake's driveway at the same time. Jake and Mark were in Jake's Honda Ridgeline, Josh had pulled up with Tommy and Vinny in his loud old Camaro, and I was bringing up the rear in the Hummer. But waiting for all of us, parked under a tree, was a silver Dodge Durango. There was an African-American man sitting behind the wheel, motionless. He was obviously a big guy, broad in the shoulders and tall enough that his head almost reached the interior upholstery on the roof of the vehicle. At first, I was worried that one of the Russians had found us. Then I thought that it was highly unlikely that a Russian was black. Then I felt like I was racist for even thinking that way. Then I thought of the drink called the Black Russian, with Kahlua and Vodka. This is what it's like to have ADD in your twenties.

The African-American man opened the door of the Durango and stepped out. Turns out appearances were correct. He was big. Very big. Like 6'3" and heavily muscled. He looked like an NFL linebacker. And he was not smiling. In fact, he looked quite put out to be here. I looked over at Josh, who by now was getting out himself. He had that permanent smirk I saw him wear when he was really pleased with himself. I was guessing that this was the help that he mentioned we needed.

Then I looked at Jake, and I saw something I had never seen in his eyes before. Fear. It was like nothing I'd ever witnessed in him. I had seen Jake tear into a pile of mutates without hesitation, wade through a handful of armed gangbangers without so much as flinching and stand nose to nose with guys much bigger than him and make those other guys blink. But I had never seen him scared before. Vinny and Tommy noticed it, too. Their faces were full of disbelief. They had fought with their dad numerous times in my company, and it was clear that they did not suffer from the same kind of hero worship that many people did who spent time around Jake. But this was something different on their father's countenance. It was a kind of dread that immobilizes you. All of that I could see through the tinted windows in Jake's truck. What I didn't see was him getting out of it.

"Boo Andrews," said Josh. "Long time no see. Glad you made it."

"That makes one of us," Boo said. "You called in your debt, and I'm a man of my word. I'm not happy about being here. So once this is over, we are square. You got me?"

"Sure thing, dude. But don't get too cocky. I wouldn't have called in the debt if I was 100% sure we were gonna get out of this at all," Josh said.

"Whatever. Where is he?" Boo said.

Josh nodded towards Jake's truck. Boo turned his head towards the Ridgeline and waited for what seemed like minutes. Finally, Jake moved to open the door. He got out very slowly, took a deep breath, and shut the door, finally turning towards the stranger in his driveway. But he didn't move, and he didn't say anything.

"What the fuck is going on?" Maureen whispered. "Have you ever seen Jake like that?"

"Nope," I whispered back. "Who the fuck is this guy, and what kind of history do they have that Jake Fisher is rendered unable to move or speak?"

"Jesus. I don't know," said Al.

We watched them for a while. Neither one of them moved or spoke. They just stared at each other. Josh was intrigued. His brow was furrowed in confusion. He sidled over towards the new person in his old cowboy boots.

"What the fuck's going on?" Josh said. "You two know each other or something?"

"You know we do," Boo Andrews said.

"Jesus, Dude, I didn't know it was like this. This looks like *High Noon* for Christ's sake. Like you're Doc Holliday and he's Johnny Ringo or some shit. What's this all about?" Josh said.

"Ask him," said Jake.

"I'm not the one not speaking to me, so don't fault me," said Boo Andrews.

"Well it sure as fuck wasn't Richard Nixon's fault," said Jake. "I'm not sure who else there is to blame."

"We've been over this. I'm sorry it worked out like it did. I've said that before. But blaming me isn't going to solve anything. It is what it is," said Boo Andrews.

" '*It is what it is*?' That's what you're going with?" said Jake.

"Jake, it was over twenty years ago. We've both had entire lives since then," said Boo.

Jake just stared back at the man in front of him.

"What are you doing here, anyway?" Jake said.

"He sent for me," Boo said, nodding towards Josh.

"Does he know?" Jake asked.

"Not really. He knows we used to know each other, and that we haven't spoken for decades. I don't think he knows the extent of it," Boo said.

Josh just stood there grinning, enjoying the show, with wide eyes and his cowboy hat tipped back and his hands on his hips.

"Does he have anything to do with Blackbird?" Josh asked. Boo's head went back, and he threw his hands up in frustration and grunted.

"Ugh! Here we go," said Boo.

Jake saw red. He turned on Josh, stomped over toward him, grabbed him by the shirt with both hands, lifted him up and threw him back on his ass onto the hood of his Camaro, boots up. His hat fell off and he spit his chaw out to keep from choking on it. Jake stared down at him in fury like I'd rarely seen from him. I'd seen him go to that 'dark place' he spoke of when he was literally killing attackers with his bare hands. I'd seen him fight his sons when they were being rowdy. But this was new, even to me.

"You planned this, you little son of a bitch," Jake said, pointing at his chest.

Josh put up a hand and sat up.

"Whoa, hold on a second. I don't know anything. All I know is, I needed help, and this guy is the one I needed. The Colonel put me in touch with him, but we've met before. I knew he didn't want to come up here, and I knew it had something to do with you. That's it. Nothing else. What the fuck is going on with you two anyway?" Josh said.

"I don't want to talk about it," Jake said.

"Dad, what the hell? What's the matter? What's going on with this guy? You're acting crazy," Vinny said.

"Shut your mouth, boy. This was before your time," Jake said.

I was incredulous. I'd never seen Jake this mad or this stubborn. He refused to speak about what was bothering him, and he was instantly furious at the idea that it was a set-up. Josh's face rang of innocence. He truly didn't know what trouble he had caused by summoning Boo Andrews here. Whatever it was, one of us had had enough of it.

"Alright, all of you, just calm the fuck down and stop acting like teenagers!"

It was Maureen. She had gotten out of the Hummer and was storming into the middle.

"You," she pointed at Josh. "You called for him (pointing at Boo) to come up here and help?"

"Yes," Josh said.

"And you didn't know they had bad blood before asking him here?" Maureen asked.

"No, ma'am. Not like this," said Josh.

"And you," she said, pointing at Boo again, "You came here because he asked you to, even though you knew you were coming to Jake's house?"

"Yes," said Boo.

"If you knew it would be like this, why did you come?" she asked.

"Because I literally owe Josh Rimone my life," said Boo Andrews, "And he literally called in the debt right now."

Maureen's eyebrows raised and she nodded.

"Okay," she said. "And you," she said pointing to Jake. "You need to calm the fuck down and talk this out right now."

"I'm not talking anything out," Jake said.

"The hell you're not," said Maureen. "My life, my friend's life, my friend's daughter, Estela and Morgan, Eddie and your sons. What is that? Seven? Eight lives? All on you right now. You are the lynchpin. You're what's holding us together, like it or not. We are here because of you, we are alive because of you, and we are being threatened with murder because of you. You are the key to fixing all of this."

"You are not in this all because of me," said Jake.

"No? Then tell me what every one of those people I just named, plus these two guys has in common. It's one thing. Just one. You. You are the common thread. Some of us threw our lot in with you a month ago, and like it or not, you have responsibilities. Now march your ass in that house and sit down in the living room. It's time for me to go Oprah on your asses," Maureen said, stomping up the driveway towards Jake's house.

Vinny and Tommy looked wide-eyed at each other in a combination of fear and amusement. I imagine I looked like they did. Estela and Morgan had the same look. Al was grinning. He'd seen this before. Josh was sitting on the ground with his bottom lip stuck out, his eyebrows raised, nodding to himself.

"Impressive," Josh said.

"I think I'm gonna like her," Boo said, turning and walking into Jake's house.

As for me, I couldn't wait to hear this one. While it isn't as riddled with nostalgia, emotion, and awkwardness that Jake and Boo recounted it with, I will do my best to re-tell it in my own inimitable style. Looks like you'll just have to go with my version:

◆ ◆ ◆

As it turns out, Jake Fisher and Beauregard "Boo" Andrews were best friends at William & Mary University in Williamsburg, Virginia. They had met as freshmen on the wrestling team, become immediately close, and done everything together all of the time. Boo was from urban Minnesota, Jake from a rural tidewater community, but those differences only seemed to strengthen what was an instant and profound friendship. They soon became inseparable. They hung out in the locker room; they worked the same summer wrestling camps together at the Naval Academy. They stayed at each other's houses on breaks. They even joined the Marines together. They went through Officer's Candidate School together, and after serving in forward locations—Jake in Iraq, Boo in Afghanistan—they both wrestled together on the All-Marine team. They did, indeed, have more than a little history in common. The two of them ended up inseparable for the better part of a decade. That is, until Maria.

Maria Jones was a waitress and bartender at The Palms Bar and Grille in Quantico, Virginia. At that time, the World Class Athlete Program trained in Quantico. Since then, the program has moved to North Carolina. But Fate had placed the three of them in the same dive on the same night, and Fate had wound her threads into a knot. Jake fell for Maria. Hard. He was completely smitten with her. He told Boo that she was "the one" a dozen times. They went back to the Palms dozens of times to see her. It was where they spent the majority of their free time. They laughed, drank, ate, and told stories. The three of them were seen enjoying each other's company all the time.

Lots of the guys on the team had gotten to know Maria on a first name basis. Jake's girl. Two of the guys on the team back then, Keith Wilson and Jay Antonelli, even used to make it a regular habit upon entering the bar to ask Maria if she thought she was going to marry Jake, and her answer was always "probably." They would joke and call her "Mrs. Fisher" all the time. But the other guys on the team called Jake something else. Blackbird.

You see, Maria was black. Strike that. That's not correct, either factually or politically. Maria was bi-racial. Her father,

Fred, was an African American man from Pittsburgh. Her mother, Carmen, was from Spain. Maria was beautiful. Like, Halle Berry beautiful. I saw pictures of her after that, and in every single one she looked like a movie star. She had a dazzling smile, a great figure, and just flat out beauty for miles. And Jake was head-over-heels, ass-over-teakettle in love with her. It looked indeed like one day she would end up being Mrs. Fisher. Until that one fatal week in Las Vegas.

Back then, the U. S. Open Wrestling Championships was the first round of the Olympic Trials. Since then, Jake tells me, they have altered the format. But back when Jake and Boo were on the Marines team, anyone who placed top six in the Open was considered "All-American" and would automatically qualify for the Final Trials in Colorado. The U.S. Open was always held in the Las Vegas Convention Center, a location so physically large, that it could hold several other convention centers inside of it. It had multiple massive rooms, and in one of them, it was full of mats. Thirty wrestling mats, each one 40' x 40' stretched out over the floor with bleachers, scoreboards, and vendors everywhere. Jake showed me pictures of it. It was hard to imagine anything that big. And Maria had come along to see it all for herself and support her man.

The tournament was three days long. The brackets were so large, that it took three days to get through them, even at double elimination. In some weight classes there were sixty to seventy opponents. The last two years in a row, Jake and Boo had not fared very well. They had both lost twice on Day 1, and thus had been eliminated. Of course, Semper Fi to the bone, the whole team stayed to watch some of the more talented guys like Antonelli—a multiple All-American, and Wilson, a national champion, finish their tournaments. But this year, both Boo and Jake had survived Day 1 and had made it to the quarter finals.

In the first match of the second day, Boo badly sprained his ankle and had to default. The ankle had swollen and turned purple almost instantly, and it became obvious that Boo's tournament was over. A visit to Sunrise Hospital and Medical Center, however, showed that the ankle wasn't broken. Boo was sent back to his hotel room on crutches. Jake, on the other hand, lost his quarterfinal match to the wrestler who would eventually become national champion. Since placing in the top six was now the next best goal, Jake would have to wrestle back in consolation rounds. Depending on when he lost, he might even compete to the point of triple elimination. He would be at the tournament all day long. Maria, on the other hand, would not.

After Jake's loss, Maria said that she had a migraine and told Jake she was heading back to the room to take a nap and maybe get in the hotel pool to see if that helped. Jake, who tended to wrestle better when he wasn't distracted, silently felt relieved, and kept on winning matches the rest of the day. He survived to compete in the final "blood round" the following day. Losers in the blood round were out. Winners would be named All-Americans and be invited to compete in the Final Trials for the Olympic Team. That was Jake's dream. He never thought that he was good enough to make it all the way to the Olympics, but he desperately wanted to be considered among the best in the country. Just to be in that company, Jake said, was his lifelong goal.

He was brimming with optimism, eager to share with Maria and Boo his good fortune of the day and get a good night's sleep to rest up for the biggest match of his life the next day.

When he arrived at the hotel, however, he found Maria and Boo together in bed.

Jake was so distraught that he left the room and didn't

return all night, finally collapsing on a park bench in the middle of the city. He barely woke up in time to catch a cab to the Convention Center for his match. Still dressed in the singlet uniform and sweats he'd had on the previous day, Jake trotted into the Convention Center to hear his name being paged for a final call to Mat 25, with a two minute warning for disqualification. Sore, exhausted, broken-hearted, and disillusioned, Jake took the mat in the last seconds, hastily tying his wrestling shoes before shaking hands. He lost. Bad. In addition to being defeated by "technical fall"—essentially the mercy rule in wrestling—Jake was flung multiple times on his head. It added insult to serious injury. Jake was in a neck brace for three days afterward.

There is a throw in Greco-Roman wrestling that begins from the mat called innocently, "a lift." The simple, unadorned name is deceiving. It involves straddling your opponent's body in a squat position, grabbing him around the waist or above, hoisting his uncooperative body to hip height, and then flinging him over your head in a back arch with a suplay —or as the WWE guys call it--suplex. The opponent lands on his head and shoulders, cushioning the eventual fall of the thrower. It is violent, frightening, and looks like it could cripple you pretty easily. Jake showed me some on You Tube once. Jake's opponent did it to him three times in that match. Jake no longer had the heart to defend himself.

The effect: a sprained neck, a broken heart, a shattered friendship, and an unpleasant ending to what was the closest Jake ever came to reaching out and touching his dream. The long flight home was silent. Jake, in his neck brace, didn't speak to anyone. Maria took a different flight home later on the next day. Jake refused to discuss anything with Boo. A few days later, when Boo was off his crutches and Jake was freed from his neck brace, the team met to get in a workout. Boo and Jake were expected to be there, even if they were too injured to join a full practice. The coach had told them to get in a light workout with weights, do some stretching, and join the team. In the locker room after practice, Wilson and Antonelli approached Jake to try and lift his spirits. They meant well, but the gesture went horribly awry.

Keith and Jay tried to explain soothingly that Jake was better off without Maria, and that she was far from the kind of girl he wanted to marry. Knowing Jake to have been blinded by his feelings for her, they had kept the truth from him for months, but decided to tell him the truth for his own good. Maria had been with nearly everyone on the team. She had even earned a racist nickname among the Marines at the base: "Blackbird"—not only because of her ethnic background, but because she flew from one Marine to the next in Quantico. To make matters worse, the nickname followed Jake around, even being used by people who had no idea where it had come from.

The well-meaning gesture of Antonelli and Wilson, though intended to lessen Jake's burden, only served to send Jake deeper into depression, and after a few more weeks of practice, Jake took a medical leave to get recommended hip surgery. Everyone knew that meant his career as a Marine and a wrestler were over. His tour of duty ended while he was in a hospital bed recovering from surgery. He never spoke to any of his Marine friends again, and despite attempts to reconcile on Boo's behalf, Jake just buried the entire incident deep in the basement of his own despair.

"Jesus," Maureen said, after hearing the story firsthand. "I think now I know why you two are a little dysfunctional."

CHAPTER 14— KRISTEN FAUST

Having just finished perpetrating the persuasive con on her in-laws that they were, indeed, in need of medical attention, and also earlier having convinced Carroll County General Hospital that their 911 services should cross county lines to treat her in-laws, Kristen summoned up her courage, picked up the phone, and dialed 9-1-1 directly.

"Hello, 911 Emergency response," said the voice on the other end.

"Oh, thank God. I wasn't even sure you guys would be there," said Kristen. "Is the hospital there even open for business?"

"We're still here, ma'am. But I hear that lots of places aren't. Carroll County General is open, and it's staffed about to seventy-five percent," she said.

"Wow, that's, that's almost normal. See, we live in Emmitsburg, and nobody is picking up in Frederick," said Kristen. "I called Westminster earlier."

"Yes ma'am, they sent us a memo. We've heard that Frederick got hit pretty hard, too, ma'am. I don't think they even have a skeleton crew there yet. Word has it they're working on it, but lots of people there died," the 911 operator said. It was almost as if she craved conversation. These days, that wasn't so egregious a sin.

"I heard the same," Kristen said.

"Well, how can I help you? What's your emergency, ma'am?" the Operator said.

"Well, it's my in-laws. Or rather my, well, they're not. Okay, okay, they're my in-laws. My mother-in-law is showing some symptoms like she might be having a small stroke. Confused, only occasionally responsive. In and out, kind of thing," Kristen said. She felt horrible having to lie.

"How old is she, ma'am?"

"Seventy-seven," said Kristen. "With no underlying conditions to my knowledge."

"Okay, I'm getting an address on this call. Are you calling from the location where they're at right now?" the Operator asked.

"Yes, yes. They're here. But, but that's not all," Kristen said.

"There's more?" the Operator asked.

"Yes, my father-in-law is a little anxious about all this, and he's having indigestion and maybe even chest pains as a result," Kristen said. "It could be his heart."

"Okay, ma'am. I'll send a unit out to you right away. Do you have any baby aspirin there?" asked the Operator.

"I think so," Kristen said.

"Give each of them a baby aspirin for now until the first responders get there. Do you want me to hold on the line to stay with you?" the Operator asked.

"No, no thank you. I'll be alright. I don't think they're doing that poorly, but I will do as you suggest, and give them each an aspirin. Thank you, thank you so much. I'll keep a lookout for the unit," Kristen said.

"Okay ma'am. I may call back if they have trouble

locating you," the Operator said.

"Okay, no problem. But tell them we're the first farm on the right past the Four Points. The biggest house of the three in a row. If they've ever been up here, they'll know where that is," Kristen said.

"Thank you, ma'am. I'll pass that along. Good luck," the Operator said.

Kristen hung up the phone, went to her kitchen, and grabbed two baby aspirin from the cabinet. God knows how old they were. She had probably bought them for Natalie years ago. Then she bowed her head, smashed her face into her fist and squinted. *What am I doing?* She thought to herself. About twenty minutes later, several ambulance crews pulled up to her front lawn. The crews got out, spoke to Kristen briefly, then entered her in-laws' house. About fifteen minutes later, they were wheeling them out towards the ambulances. They looked none the worse for the wear, but there was an anxious and slightly confused look on each of their faces.

Kristen looked like she swallowed a frog. She was standing in front of the house as first responders were wheeling her father-in-law outside on a gurney. Her mother-in-law looked confused and upset. She felt terrible. She had done as Josh Rimone had said. She had called 911 and told them that her mother-in-law had suffered what appeared to be a small stroke, and her father-in-law was having some chest pains and indigestion. She told them both in a calm, caring voice that it was probably best if they got checked at the hospital, and that the one in Westminster was the only one in the area functioning at nearly full staffing. She assured them that she would find their son, Mitchell—probably somewhere in the fields at the moment—and send him to the hospital to see them, and that she would follow after later on. She had played her part well.

And it made her almost vomit from guilt. Once she

gave the first responders all of the proper contact information—which was essentially Mitchell's number—she got in her car with Natalie and headed out to the field where Mitch was fertilizing that day.

"Mom, it's gonna be alright," said Natalie. "I mean, I know you lied and all, but Grandma and Grandpa are gonna be fine. The doctors can check up on them, and Dad will bring them home. Remember, you're doing this to keep your friends from getting murdered."

"I know, I know," Kristen said, quietly proud of her teenage daughter for showing such wisdom at such a young age. "It just makes me feel like a jerk, that's all."

"I can see why it would, but that bald guy with the cowboy hat said nobody can know that they're here, and you know that Daddy will blab it all over town. It's just his way," she said.

Kristen smiled and mussed her daughter's hair.

"I'm glad I have you around to keep me sane," she said. "I know it hasn't been easy for you, with me and Dad separating and living in different houses and all."

"It's not that bad. I mean, you live right next to each other," Natalie said. "It's not like you're in Long Island or something."

Kristen smiled again at her daughter, patted her shoulder, then waved good-bye as she hopped in her car. Natalie would hold down the fort for a few minutes while Kristen headed out to the fields to find Mitch. Natalie's comment had helped her. These days, Kristen felt a pang of guilt each day having separated from Mitch. She didn't want Natalie to have to pay the price for her inability—no, that wasn't right—her unwillingness to continue living with her father. But Nat was right. The two were barely separated as it was. It wasn't like she was in Long

Island.

Long Island. Kristen's hometown. She wondered if it still existed. If her parents were still alive. If anybody in the greater New York area even survived this long. Nobody answered when she called them, but that could have something to do with the cell tower, or their phones, or a satellite or something. Kristen had learned, as we all had, that during this crazy time, you just never knew what was happening anywhere. It might be fine in one town and devastation in another. She couldn't be sure who was alive and who wasn't, who had electricity, or cable, or old Internet. It was completely unreliable.

We had told her about Lexington, Virginia—which had rolling brownouts for electricity, but in general was operating at nearly normal. We told her about Front Royal, Virginia—which (when we had visited it) had been taken over by ex-convicts who had turned it into a Mad Max Fury Road stopover, complete with drug and human trafficking.

And now, of course, there was her home here, in Emmitsburg—or New Plymouth, as Father Joe had renamed it. What was going on here was still a mystery. Cable seemed to work, and some local stations were attempting to put together reports. It was one of those half-hearted reports that had originally led us to Laura Fisher in Washington. Some people's phones were able to access previously posted Internet, though nothing recent. It was a Mt. St. Michael's student's phone that had helped Mark, Maureen, Al, Estela and Morgan to figure out the mystery of the Russian connection with the Church of Many Blessings. But for all intents and purposes, Kristen was wallowing in a Purgatory of communicational ignorance.

Her job as Librarian and Media Specialist at

Hunter's Run was suspended, along with everyone else's. Her status in town was questionable, because as a free-thinking woman not prone to brainwashing, she chose not to follow the Aryan-like Father Joe and his mission to remake the world in the image of White European extremists. Even her status here, on the farm, was awkward at best. Her estranged husband, Mitch, lived next door, and that provided her with access to numerous agricultural advantages. Mitch's farm was diversified. Not only did it include such cash crops as feed corn and soybeans, but it also had orchards, a greenhouse, and livestock. If there was a place for her to make it through a war-time Apocalypse, she was already living there. But she was also struggling for independence from her spouse. That was tough to do at a time when she had nothing to offer but dependence.

Even her notion of a divorce seemed to be put on hold. How important could it really be to separate from your spouse when your country is being decimated by Russian weapons in World War III? The idea of moving back in with Mitch was unthinkable now. She had crossed that line and didn't want to cross back. Yet there she was, living off of the farm teat—both literally and fig-uratively--if you counted Mitch's dozen or so dairy cows. Right now, Natalie was her focus and her everything. Her bright fifteen-year-old daughter was her sun and moon. She selfishly relished the fact that the war had shut schools down. Teens don't take long to grow up and leave the nest. That usually began with going out with friends, trying new things and meeting new people. Very little of that would take place now. Not for a while at least.

She pulled up to a large field with rows of short, green growth sitting in dry, hard-packed earth. She could hear Mitch's tractor in the distance, and see his truck pulled off to the side of the field in the shade. The tractor was headed towards her. When he arrived, he'd see her there. She was rehearsing lines in her head, trying to figure out what to say and how to say it. She figured if she looked distraught, she might not be able to sell it. So, she decided to undersell it. She would say she was sure they would be okay, that she was just being cautious, that she didn't know how long he would have taken to make it home, and that if they needed sending to a hospital it would be easier on everyone if it was done in the daytime at a leisurely pace, with plenty of time to prepare bags and such.

The tractor eased its way to a halt about ten yards away. Mitch left the big diesel engine running. Diesels liked to run and responded poorly to being turned off and on in a hurry multiple times, at least more so than a standard gasoline engine. The tractor's engine kicked up dust, and he kicked up more of it when he dropped down to field level and began walking towards his estranged wife.

"Hey," he said. "What brings you here?"

"It's your parents," Kristen said with a lump in her throat. "Now, I'm sure it's nothing, but your Mom was acting a little strangely, like maybe she was having a small stroke. And then your Dad got a little anxious and had some indigestion, which is one of the symptoms of a coming heart attack. Just to be safe, I called the hospital in Westminster, and they came to get them."

"What? Why the hospital in Westminster? That's out of the county!" Mitch remarked.

"There's a world war going on, Mitch. Frederick took a direct hit. There's nobody in that hospital. Westminster is almost fully staffed. To be honest, it's not more than five- or ten-minutes' difference driving anyway," said Kristen.

"Well, will Westminster take our insurance? It's not in-county," Mitch repeated.

"I'm sure they do, Mitch. The 911 operator said as much to me. And there are no other clear options for people here, especially since Frederick Hospital has nobody there. Plus, it's your parents. You would want them to get care if the insurance didn't cover them, right?"

"Yeah, I guess so, sure," said Mitch, scratching his head with his cap in his hand.

An awkward silence stood for about ten seconds. Kristen waited patiently.

"So, what are we doing again?" asked Mitch.

"You are going to park the tractor and drive down to Westminster. I am going back to the farm to make sure Nat's alright, and then maybe we can follow you there," Kristen said.

"Nat didn't go with them?" Mitch asked.

"No room. Two gurneys, one big ambulance. Besides, I told them I was getting you. They have your contact information, so you'll need to go up there," Kristen said.

"Okay. Do I need to fill anything out?" Mitch asked.

"Probably. When you get there, most likely," Kristen said.

Another awkward silence with only the diesel engine's roar in the background.

"There is nothing to fill out in this field, Mitch," said Kristen.

"Yeah, I know. I just, I'm not sure what I'm supposed to do," said Mitch.

"I told you. Go to Carroll County General Hospital. Find out where your parents are and support them.

The fields can live without being fertilized for a few days. If it turns out to be nothing, you can bring them home. If it turns out you have to stay," Kristen began.

"Wait, I have to stay?" Mitch asked.

"You'll find out when you get there, Mitch. Now go park the tractor, get in the truck, and head down to Westminster. I'll call you to see if Nat and I will follow you there," Kristen said.

"Okay, okay. I'll do that," Mitch said. "Thanks."

Mitch climbed back up into the tractor's cab and started heading towards a grassy spot alongside the rows of crops where he could leave it. Kristen waved good-bye to him and hopped back in her car, backed out of the field, and headed back to the farm.

"Nope," she said out loud. "I cannot go back to him. He has made a career out of learned helplessness and the sympathy of others to do his jobs for him, and I am no longer going to enable him like that. I'm done pulling up men's pants on boys. He's gonna have to learn to pull up his own big boy pants by himself."

Kristen smiled at her own monologue, as if she'd said it to the therapist. She took in a deep breath, leaned her head back, and let out a long, cleansing exhale. She felt much better now that the entire deception—however necessary—was behind her. She pulled up to the driveway, hopped out, and walked into the house. She looked upstairs, checked both bathrooms, then went outside to peek around the barnyard. She looked in the shed where Al's car was hidden, then she went next door and looked around her in-laws' house. Then a chill went down her spine when she exited the house and looked across the street and noticed large-wheeled tire tracks in a place where none of them ever parked. She shook her head trying to remember where Jake had parked the Hummer and remembered it had been behind the house. Then she remembered that Josh had literally driven into the front yard. The ambulances had been in front of Mitch's parents' place.

Suddenly a deep, long dread descended upon her as she came to fully realize what had happened.

Natalie was gone.

CHAPTER 15—
MENDED FENCES

"So now what?" Vinny said.

"Yeah," Josh chimed in, "That's one hell of a story. I swear, Jake, I didn't know any of that. I called Boo in because he owed me, and because I knew he was what we needed right now. The Colonel is the one who gave me the code name 'Blackbird' for you. Apparently, he'd been talking to some of your old Quantico buddies at some point too, and your name came up. Then the Colonel heard someone else call you that at the Pentagon. I don't think he knew the story either. I mean, no wonder you got pissed. You thought I was rubbing it in your face. I'd have been pissed too."

"Jake, you're gonna have to let this go," said Maureen.

"Jake, for the millionth time, I'm sorry. I did you wrong. She did you wrong. I was weak, vulnerable, and I gave in. One time. I know you loved her, but she was the devil, man. Did you know she's on her fifth divorce? Fifth! I think you dodged a big bullet, man," said Boo.

"So that makes it alright?" said Jake.

"No. It doesn't. I apologize with no conditions. Period. Jake, we were best friends. Maybe we can't be best friends again, but we shouldn't be like this. This is wrong," Boo said.

Jake was silent. He was staring at the ground now. Huge awkward silence, with all eyes on him.

"Jake, let me tell you what you're thinking, and then I'm gonna tell you what's gonna happen," said Maureen.

All eyes turned to her now.

"You are more upset that your vulnerability is showing. I think that's what's bothering you the most. This is your Achilles heel. Your old friends saw it, your best friend helped cause it, you felt betrayed and exposed at the same time, and powerless to help yourself. You fell in love with a she-devil, and the part that hurts most is allowing yourself to be taken in. It's humiliating, and you can't stand the idea of being humiliated—especially in front of people," she said.

"Oh, so other people actually enjoy that?" Jake said with a sneer, still looking at the ground.

"Of course not. But for you—you who have to be the hero, the savior, the white knight—it's much worse for you. You can't stand for anyone to see a chink in your armor, and you have to go through a whole 'thing' just to allow yourself to ask for help," Maureen said.

"Now you sound like Wendy," Jake mumbled. "She said the same thing."

"Smart girl. Of course she did. She's a doctor, right? PhD? So, of course she did. Now here's what's gonna happen. You are going to forgive your best friend. You are going to allow him and Josh to help you prepare for this challenge, and you're going to do it because you are still the white knight, still the savior, still the hero. All of our lives are at stake here, Jake. All of us. Your friends, your family, your town, everything. And you are the key. Again. Somehow, a small-town middle-aged History teacher who can't stop wrestling people despite his fake hip is in the position of being the fucking hero during a World War, for Christ's sake! Don't ask me how, but here we are. But this wallowing in your moody, self-pitying bullshit is not helping any of us, do you hear me?" Maureen said. "Now pick yourself up, go hug the guy who should have been the best man at your wedding to Laura, shake Josh's hand as he forgives you for throwing him on the ground, and let's go kill some fucking Russians!"

I was speechless. Maureen's pep talk was amazing. She Oprah Winfrey-ed, Iyanla-ed, and Doctor Phil-ed the hell out of Jake just then. We all looked around, wide-eyed, cautious smiles on our faces, all of us suddenly ready to kick some Russian ass. Vinny and Tommy looked ready to go right then, grinning madly. Josh had a big smile on his face and spat a giant wad of chaw on the ground next to him. Boo was brandishing a tight-lipped, guardedly optimistic smile himself. Then I looked at Jake. He was sitting on a stump, hunched over, looking at the ground and hugging himself. Then I saw him start to shake. I suddenly got worried that he was going to have a breakdown. His body started to rumble like a motorcycle trying to start up. *Oh shit*, I thought. *It's over. He's done. He's going to have a nervous breakdown right now, worse than the one in the Pentagon bathroom.*

And then I heard the laugh. Jake was laughing. Honest, deep laughter. He closed his eyes, threw his head back, and the laughter came from deep inside his bowels. His arms dropped to his sides, and tears started streaming down his face. He stood up, still squinting, still teary-eyed, and walked over to Boo Andrews, who by now was wondering what the hell was going on. Jake reached out his arms, and Boo flinched backwards a bit. Then Jake opened his eyes, still laughing, looked at Boo squarely, and hugged him. Hard. Boo was startled a first, not sure what to do with his arms. Then he leaned in and the two shared a hug that was twenty-five years overdue. After almost two full minutes of laughing and hugging, they separated, Jake patted Boo on the shoulders, and walked over to Josh. He reached out his hand, shaking his head.

"Sorry," said Jake.

"No sweat, dude. No sweat," said Josh. "You're still

pretty strong for an old fucker."

"*Porque es un tejón*," said Estela. "It's because he's an old badger."

"Yeah, I can see that," said Josh. "Got that grey-around-the-temples, Dad-bod, scrappy thing going for you. A lot more badger than blackbird, huh?"

Jake scowled and eye-rolled at Josh.

"Too soon?" said Josh.

"Everything you do is too soon," I said to him.

"It's part of my charm," said Josh.

"It's *all* of your charm," I answered. He nodded and gestured at me for having scored a point.

"So, what did you see?" Jake asked Josh. "Are the Russians there yet?"

"Hell yeah they are," said Josh. "Six new ones came in, and it looks as if your pal Oleg is their leader. What's interesting is that two of them seemed to separate themselves a bit from the others. Those two also looked a tad younger than the others. I'm thinking maybe they're new replacements."

"What difference does that make? Why wouldn't the group be different ages anyway?" I asked.

"Because this unit has had to be here and work together in extremely dicey situations. They are an enemy cell during a time of war. They have to be like the fingers of a hand, operating together. Any dissension, any splitting and that connection is broken, making them more vulnerable. There are a number of programs that operate that way. If I'm right about what I think I saw, two of them are new," said Josh.

"Wait—we *know* two of them are new," said Morgan. "Because we watched the previous two die."

"How do you figure that?" I asked.

"We found notes and bills to someone named Sergei in Front Royal, Virginia connecting him to Oleg and their operation in the church basement. That's the same Sergei that those convicts in Front Royal were going to sell us to. We know that. And we also watched them die. It totally makes sense that they have two new guys," said Morgan.

"Okay, I remember that. And it's a weird coincidental tie-in. But I still have to ask why that matters," I said. "A terrorist group is a terrorist group."

"But a team is not a team," said Boo. "Chances are, the other four were loyal to their leader, Sergei. These two new ones are going to be getting their orders directly from Oleg, having just gotten here. That may only be a small rift, but when you're operating at the kind of deficit we are, you have to exploit any potential rift any way you can."

"No offense, Mr. Andrews, but how is it that you know all this?" I asked.

"Because that's what I do. It's what I've always done. I assemble teams, and I take out other teams. I did it for the Marines, now I do it in private. In fact, now, I supply those teams and act as a consultant. So, what I am doing here, now—it's what I do best. It's why Josh called me," Boo said.

"Has he briefed you on any of this?" I asked.

"A little. But I can read between the lines pretty quickly. That's something else I do," Boo said.

"You're operating on assumptions, though," I added. "Morgan's story, Josh's quick observation. You can't have verified either one of those."

"People assume all the time," said Boo. "We have to assume to live. And in our business," he said, pointing back and forth to himself and Josh, "those assumptions and decisions have to come fast and be accompanied by action."

"But don't you 'make an ass out of you and me' if you

assume?" I said.

"If you assume all black men operate a certain way, or all gay men believe a certain thing, or all Hispanics do something else? Yes. You're an ass. But assuming pieces of intel in order to make a quick battle strategy? Standard operating procedure," said Boo.

"So, what's your thought on getting them separated?" Josh asked.

"Have they seen you?" Boo asked.

"Nope. You neither. Everybody else here, though, has been seen or is known from previous interaction from someone in the church, and therefore is quickly verifiable," said Josh.

"So, it's gotta be us," said Boo.

"It's gotta be us," Josh agreed. "My thought is, infiltrate the high school, assess, then improvise."

"Why the school?" asked Boo.

"It's where the Russians are staying. The head guy there, Wes Kent, has something of a homeless shelter going on there. He moved people in at the behest of the church, in part to legitimize the operation and in part to make sure *they* didn't come back," said Josh, pointing at a bunch of us.

"Who? Us?" Maureen said.

"You represent contention. You represent numbers. You all have a leader who has been seen taking the lives of dangerous criminals, and whose back you have. Eliminating you physically, by killing you, even with Russians—that's a problem. That's a lotta death to be dealt on the sly. Somebody would notice, and even though this prick has the town by the nose, it's a tenuous grip right now. But having you choose to leave because homeless people are in your classrooms? Fucking brilliant. Problem gone, façade of community service created and verified. I wonder just how long they've been planning this," said Josh.

"Scary to think," said Jake. "Okay, so you and Boo are gonna go infiltrate and do a better piece of recon. What do you want us to do? We're too visible a target to help."

"People know where you live, and they know you're all tied together, so the longer you stay here the bigger the risk. Get back to Kristen's house and hide out. As far as we know, they don't know any of the connection there," said Josh.

"Um, there's a huge problem with your plan," I said.

"What's that?" said Josh.

"You forgot that they're a White Supremacist church," I replied.

"And?" Josh asked me.

"Um, Boo is Black," I said.

"Oops," said Josh.

"Oops?" Boo answered. "Who says 'oops'?"

"He already told you about the church?" said Jake.

"He already told me," said Boo.

"So how the hell are you gonna infiltrate this place?" Jake asked.

"I'm guessing Josh has a plan to bring me in, like on a bounty or something," said Boo.

"Something like that," said Josh, "But now you've given me an idea."

"Glad I could help," said Boo. "Do we need back-up?"

"Maybe, but probably not," Josh said. "If we play it right, and stay away from Oleg, we could pull it off. I'm thinking we can play off of the some of the disconnect between the Russians and the church people a little. How's your acting chops?"

"Better than yours, mini Vin Diesel," said Boo. "Don't worry about me pulling my weight. But what if we do run into Oleg?"

"Then you're fucked, amigo," said Josh.

"Then let's try hard *not* to get me fucked," said Boo.

"If only you'd said that to the waitress twenty-five years ago in Vegas," said Josh grinning and looking at Jake.

Jake rolled his eyes and scowled at Josh. Boo cringed. I cringed. Maureen cringed. Everybody cringed.

"Too soon?" asked Josh.

CHAPTER 16— KIDNAPPED

Jake had me pull the Hummer into something he called a "corn crib." It was a large shed that had some roofing over one side and a closed in area on the other, apparently for corn. The spot was large enough for a tractor, so the Hummer fit just fine, and I pulled in as close as I could to make it less visible. Jake drove his truck up to the back of Kristen's house. I had five people with me, Jake had four. Nine of us disembarked and started to go into the guest house that Kristen had set up for us.

Suddenly, Kristen came running out of her house in tears. She was red-faced and breathing heavy. She ran up to Maureen and grabbed her shoulders.

"What's wrong?" asked Maureen. "What happened?"

"Natalie," she said. "They've got Natalie. I did everything he said. I called 911. I sent Mitch's parents to Westminster. I drove out to the field to get Mitch and sent him to Westminster. I left Nat here to hold things down, in case somebody came back. But when I came back, she was gone."

"How do you know someone took her?" Maureen asked.

"Tire tracks. On the wrong side of the road, where nobody parks. They're fresh, imbedded in the dirt. Nobody goes there. Anyone I know who ever comes here parks on this side of the road, in one of the three driveways. Delivery people, utilities people. I looked everywhere for her. All three houses. She's gone, Mo. Gone! What am I gonna do? I can't lose her!" Kristen said frantically.

Jake walked over and put his hand on her back. She turned to him, crying, and put her face in his broad chest and grabbed his shoulders. He patted her with his left hand gently.

"We'll find her, Kris. We're not gonna let those bastards do anything to her. I swear," Jake said.

Kristen looked up through teary eyes with a look of desperation. But there was something in Jake's tone, in his bearing, that lent her a confidence. Her expression changed.

"I, I believe you," she said.

"You *can* believe me," said Jake "Now, show me where those tire tracks are."

She walked us across the road to the other side. There was nothing there but field, and no shoulder to speak of. She was right. Nobody would come over here. If you did, you'd be hanging out in the middle of the road with one wheel and practically in a ditch with the other. A total stranger would naturally pull over to the side of the road that had the farmhouses on it. There was plenty of room, tons of parking spots, and a few pullovers. Nobody in their right minds would park on the other side of the road.

Unless they were up to no good.

It must have looked weird, ten of us walking over to the other side of a country road, but there we were. Jake and Kristen led, the rest of us stayed back. Kristen pointed out the tire tracks, embedded in the soil outside the pavement, practically in the ditch. One of the wheels actually had been in the ditch at one point, but had ridden out and spun a little.

"Yeah," said Jake. "There they are. Whoever did this had a four-wheel-drive vehicle. That ditch is too deep on that side of the road. You can also see the front and back wheels spinning on this, not just the back."

"Pretty observant for an old fart," I said. "But did you notice this?"

"What?" Jake asked.

"The treads. As they start to lead out to the road. Look at them. Three of them have the exact same pattern, but one of them doesn't. This one here has a different tread. Like it was a new tire, or a spare tire or something," I said.

"Nicely done, Eddie. Not bad for a pain in the ass," Jake said.

"Holy shit, the Jeep!" Mark blurted out.

"What? What Jeep?" I asked.

"We were being chased by a Jeep, and Maureen threw out several boxes of roofing nails. I remember it. Al complained that it would mean they couldn't ride home the same way. Then the Jeep was speeding after us, and they blew a tire and went into the field. That's how we got away. I bet they got that tire changed with a spare, like a snow tire or something, and that these came from that Jeep. He could've figured out we were here. These back roads have very few places on them, and this farm has 'Faust' on the sign. They could've figured out this was Kristen's place, and that we were hiding here," Mark said.

"But kidnapping? That's a leverage move. Whoever did this is trying to force our hand, make the five of us they're specifically targeting come out into the open, or get Kristen to tell them where you all are," Jake said.

"Oh my God," Kristen said. "If they hurt her."

"They won't. Not yet at least. She's the guarantee that you'll give them what they want. That means they're gonna contact you somehow," Jake said.

"But not everybody's phone is working," I said. "They can't count on that."

"No, but it'll be their first attempt. Whoever it is knows that Mo is involved, and that Kristen is her friend and would likely know how to find her. They'll need Kristen on board and compromised to make this work, so they'll make sure she gets the message," Jake said.

"But how?" I asked. "We don't even know who did it, and they can't just call and tell us."

"They'll likey have to come here in person. Think about it. Whoever it was came here, looked around, and found nobody but Natalie. So, until they get some answers they can use, they have to assume that you all are not hiding here. At least that is to our advantage. But if Kristen was gone, they'll probably assume that she is helping you all hide somewhere, which is why they took Nat. And they probably don't know that we are back yet, either," said Jake. "Otherwise they'd be here right now. Which means they don't know that there are actually five more of us in the mix. They won't think to add to their own numbers."

"Do you think it was the Russians? Or that guy Oleg?" I asked.

"No. Tommy and Vinny were with Josh, watching them when this took place, while Kristen was gone. Boys—was Wes Kent at the school? Did you see him there at all?"

"Yeah. He met them in the cafeteria. At least a couple of them. He was there. It couldn't have been him. That big guy, Coach Lou, the football coach. He was there too," said Vinny.

"So was that pastor, Father Joe," said Josh. "We saw him outside."

"So, if it wasn't the big cheeses, that means this is somebody who is not a main player—but who wants to be. It's someone who's trying to gain favor by finding you...who's trying to toady up to Wes or the pastor, trying to score some points," said Jake.

"It wouldn't be Billy, or Emery, or Pablo. They're not kidnappers. They're not that sleazy, they're just misguided. And they're all pretty wimpy," said Mark. "I'm not even sure Wes would stoop to this. He doesn't like to get his hands dirty."

"Who is it then?" I asked.

"John Segen," Mark answered. "It's gotta be him. He's a total slimeball. Slap-happy, tries to be on everybody's good side, but slippery as a snake."

"You think he's bad enough to do this?" I asked.

"I think he's capable of anything. I think he raises or lowers himself to the levels of the people he's trying to get in with," said Mark.

"And those people right now are Russian assassins and a megalomaniacal preacher who just took over a town," said Maureen. "Not good. Are we sure it's him?"

"It's him," Al said. "He's got a Jeep. The newest, fanciest Jeep in town. I saw it."

"How'd you see it?" Maureen asked.

"Facebook. He plastered it all over Facebook before the bombs dropped. And he was bragging about it at the sports boosters meeting a couple of months ago," Al said.

"What were you doing at a sports boosters meeting?" Maureen asked.

"I'm the faculty liaison to them. Plus, the whole tennis thing. They were trying to get me to coach tennis," Al said.

"But you don't play tennis," Maureen said.

"Apparently that's not a deterrent," Al replied. "Now that I think of it, that's the Jeep that was following us. I should've known. It's him. It's John. He's got Natalie."

"So, what's our next move?" I asked.

"We get her back," said Jake. "Al, would he do this alone?"

"He might take her by himself, but how would he get word to Kristen? Wouldn't he need somebody to run interference? To get Kristen to come to the table?" Al asked.

"Not necessarily. Not if he could hide the girl somewhere in the meantime," Jake said.

"He wants to impress Father Joe, and Wes, and the Russians. He won't tell anybody until he has the information, so I think he'd do it alone if he had a preference," said Mark. "Which means he's got her tied up or locked up somewhere."

"But where?" I asked.

"We know where," said Morgan. "We've been there. It's a secret room in the church. Nobody knows about it except for Oleg. Even Estela's Dad didn't know about it until he found it by accident."

"That's right," said Mark. "I was there when he did. I think I saw it too."

"But if Pablo didn't know, how would John?" Jake asked.

"He's part of the inner circle," said Mark. "Father Joe used him for projects that he didn't even give to me or Pablo. John knows where that room is. I'd bet on it."

"And you don't think he'd use someone else to come for Kristen?" Jake asked.

"No. He's too full of himself. He'd think he could do it alone. And he's insecure enough that if he blew it, he wouldn't want anyone to see it. I don't even think he'd have her guarded. As long as the room is pretty sound-proof," said Mark.

"It is," said Morgan. "If we hadn't left the sliding door open, Estela's dad wouldn't have intervened, and Oleg would have taken us earlier. Before Mark got there. We might be dead by now."

"Holy shit. Do you think you could get back in there?" asked Jake.

"Yes. I'm sure of it," Morgan said.

"*Sí. Podemos hacerlo*. We can do it," said Estela.

"Okay, then here's how we play it," said Jake. "Listen carefully."

CHAPTER 17— TRAINING DAY

"Come on," said Valentin. "Training session."

"What?" said Maharbek. "Why do we need a training session?"

"Oleg says so," said Anatoly, frowning. "Get dressed."

"*Piiiiz'dets, blyaaaa!* This is bullshit," said Buvaisar. "I don't want to do this. We don't need training."

"Where are we going to train? We'll draw attention. This is stupid," said Aleksandr.

Arsen silently pulled out his duffel bag and began changing into his sweats. They were plain gray sweats with no markings and ample padding. The others slowly started to do the same.

"Maybe this is the chance we want," said Anatoly. "You ever think about that?"

"What do you mean?" asked Buvaisar.

"I know what he means," said Maharbek. "We get Oleg to train with us."

"Ah, I get it," said Aleksandr. "Then we teach him a lesson. Show him who should be making decisions around here."

"I can't believe you all are talking like that," said Valentin. "Moscow gives the orders, and they say Oleg is in charge. What is wrong with you?"

"What is wrong with you, babyface? Moscow isn't here. Nobody from Moscow knows what this is like, and nobody from Moscow has the balls to come here and do what we do. We have been on this assignment for a long time now. We know how to do our job. I don't care how scary you think Oleg is; he shouldn't be telling us what to do like he does. We should be telling him. That's our way. The best man is king. The best man has the say. All we have to do now is show him who the best man is," Maharbek said.

"I like how you think," said Buvaisar. "But maybe that's just because I'm the best."

"You? I don't think so," said Anatoly. "You have clearly forgotten my skills,"

"*Otva`li, mu`dak, b`lyad!* Ha! I say fuck to all of you," said Aleksandr. "Anatoly, you are like little squirrel. I am like Russian bear. Skills don't help when bear is eating you."

"Buvaisar, are you hearing this?" said Maharbek. "I am big, strong, and skilled. Biggest one there is. Why do Aleksander and Anatoly Vladimirovich think they can last one minute with me?"

"Because they won't need to. After I have knocked you out, they will have to face me," said Buvaisar.

"We'll see about that," said Maharbek. "Arsen, you aren't saying anything. You just sit there getting dressed. What's wrong?"

"Nothing," Arsen said. "Boss says to go to training, I am getting dressed for training."

Just then Oleg burst through the door of the room. Everyone went quiet and looked at each other, and the light-hearted mood in the room dropped immediately. Oleg looked at Valentin and Arsen.

"Well, did you tell them?" Oleg said. "Are you all ready for training?"

"Da, spasibo, Oleg," said Buvaisar, pulling on his shirt. "We're ready. What are we doing?"

"Training. Sambo. Fighting skills. I have training weapons as well. And stop speaking Russian. The door is open, and we are going past a common area," Oleg said.

"Sorry," said Buvaisar. "I forget."

The seven men walked down the hall and through the gymnasium to the wrestling room. Like most wrestling rooms, it had to be shared with other activities—like dance, Physical Education classes, and cheerleading practices. But now that school was out and Wes Kent was in charge, Oleg had the mats left down permanently for training.

In Russia, there is a combative style of grappling known as sambo. Sambo originated in the Soviet Union as a training method for law enforcement and soldiery in the earliest days of the new socialist republic. The word sambo is an acronym of the romanization *samozashchita bez oruzhiya,* which translates to "self-defense without weapons." It looks a little bit like a cross between judo and wrestling, complete with chokeholds, submissions, and holds designed to restrain and harm the opponent. There are sport versions that have yearly championships, and there is a more violent version used for hand-to-hand combat in training operations. Informal workouts occasionally blurred the lines between the two. Oleg was planning to do just that today with his new team.

Traditionally, sambo practitioners wear something resembling a judo-style *gi* on top called a *kurtka,* and either shorts or sweatpants on the bottom. Each of the seven men was wearing his *kurtka* as part of the provided training materials on his way to the Hunter's Run wrestling room. It was simply part of the culture. The younger Arsen and Valentin were wearing sweatpants. All of the others wore tight wrestling shorts. Oleg's *kurtka* and shorts were black, unlike the usual traditional red or blue.

"Where do you even find a black *kurtka*?" Buvaisar whispered to Maharbek. "I've never even seen one before. I thought they only came in red, blue, or reversible."

"Yes, and the reversible ones are too hot," said Aleskandr.

"He's showing off," said Maharbek. "It doesn't matter. He will get what's coming to him.

The next ten minutes, the men all warmed up leisurely. Each one did something a little different. Some did jumping jacks, some stretched, others lightly practiced throwing and submission techniques, but all at a lower level of intensity, with a lightness and ease that belied the violent roots of the sport. Soon, the six grabbed a partner and all began doing quicker and stronger versions of the techniques. Oleg chose to stay by himself, "shadow wrestling" and stretching. Every once in a while, Anatoly or Buvaisar would glance over at him to see what he was doing. Maharbek and Aleksandr, however, were trying to get his attention by performing explosive, violent, high-arching throws that usually ended with one of them bouncing off the mat. Oleg didn't even turn his head.

After about a half an hour of mid-level intensity technique, the six newcomers were all sweating profusely. Oleg clapped and informed them that they had two minutes to get a drink or relieve themselves in the bathroom. Then live competition would ensue. Maharbek went to the water fountain. Arsen went to urinate. Aleksandr poked his head out the door to get a breath of fresh air. Valentin and Buvaisar stretched. A few minutes went by, and when Arsen had returned, Oleg stood up.

"Okay. Match-ups. We will do what the Americans call, 'King of the Mountain.' The person who gets the takedown, bringing his opponent from feet to mat, wins the bout and stays in the middle. The rest will rotate in for about ten minutes, but the winner always stays," Oleg said.

"We're not doing any submissions on the mat?" asked Valentin.

"Not yet. Just on your feet for now," said Oleg. "Valentin, you and Arsen first."

Valentin and Arsen circled one another before latching onto each other's *kurtka*. They each tugged and pushed, trying to unbalance the other. Then Valentin lowered his level and reached for Arsen's right knee. Arsen swept Valentin's advancing foot while twisting his shoulders. The result was a quick and violent drop to the back for Valentin."

"Nice foot sweep, Arsen," said Oleg. "Anatoly. You're next. Arsen stays in the middle."

Anatoly immediately attacked Arsen's legs, latching his arms around both of them. He tried to lift Arsen up, but Arsen dropped his hips and sprawled backward. The two struggled, nearly immobile in that position for a few seconds, then as Anatoly started to raise up, Arsen headlocked him and threw him to his back.

"*Derrmó*," said Anatoly. "Shit! Nice throw."

Arsen bounced back to his feet, ready for the next attacker. Oleg pointed to Buvaisar, who was about twenty pounds heavier than Arsen, yet rippling with lean muscle.

"Okay little man, let's see if you can throw me," said Buvaisar. Arsen lept forward and tried to do just that. His right arm around Buvaisar's waist, and his left tugging on Buvaisar's left forearm sleeve, Arsen strained to throw the larger man with a hip toss. It looked for a moment like he would succeed, then Buvaisar lowered his hips, locked around Arsen's body, and back arched him to the mat with a thud. The observers' reactions, despite their attempts to look unimpressed, showed a great appreciation for Buvaisar's technique and athleticism.

"Not today, little man," said Buvaisar. "Who's next, the

bear or the gorilla?"

Oleg pointed at Aleksandr, who walked out onto the mat with his massive size and height.

"Ah, the bear. Well soon I will have a new rug," said Buvaisar, who then launched himself toward Aleksander's leg, struggling to lift it. Aleksandr defended, grabbing Buvaisar's shoulders. A scrum ensued, with both men losing and regaining footing in the same hold, neither able to get the advantage. Finally, the enormous Aleksandr, the largest of the seven, leaned in and locked around Buvaisar's body, and with sheer brute strength, lifted the lighter man into the air and slammed him on his back. The air left Buvaisar's lungs in a gush, and several of the men winced at the scene.

"No rug for you today," said Aleksandr. Buvaisar rolled over in pain, holding his back. "No one left but gorilla," Aleksandr said.

Maharbek strolled onto the mat. If Aleksandr was a bear based on his sheer size, Maharbek was a silverback gorilla. His chest and back were enormously broad, and his arms were freakishly thick and long. He was hairy too, and had a slightly darker complexion like the men of the south of Russia near the Muslim stans. He nodded his head silently and lay hold of Aleksandr. The larger bear tried to force a body lock right away, but Maharbek, an expert at technique as well as a frightening physical specimen, met the attack with a quick deflection, and then seamlessly transitioned into his own throw. With his right hand, he grabbed the back of Aleksandr's *kurtka* behind the neck. With his left, he reached into his crotch. He stepped behind the larger man, straddling his near leg, and then popped his hips and launched the bear into the sky and ultimately on his head.

"Metzger throw, *harasho*," said Valentin. "Very good. Beautiful."

"Looks like I am king of mountain," said Maharbek,

flexing both arms.

"Not yet," said Oleg. "You must defend your mountain first."

Oleg strolled onto the mat. Maharbek grinned visibly, then cracked his knuckles, which made Anatoly laugh.

"You going to come for a try, old man?" Maharbek said. "I might break you in half. You sure you want to do this?"

"Let's go," said Oleg.

Maharbek instantly slammed both hands hard onto Oleg's shoulders. The noise was enough to alert the crowd to a higher level of intensity. There were unspoken protocols in all martial training, and slaps like those meant Maharbek was deadly serious. Oleg pushed forward, seemingly trying to do a desperate throw, but with his opponent so much larger, heavier and stronger, the attempt was overtly a failure. Maharbek grinned at the futile gesture, confident in his size and ability... which was just what Oleg wanted. In the moment that Maharbek relaxed ever-so-slightly in his confidence, Oleg grabbed the top of his kurtka with one hand and whipped one of his legs inside and tripped Maharbek, reaping the leg to the sky. The result was a frighteningly fast slamming down of Maharbek's back to the mat, knocking some of the wind out of him. Oleg landed on top with his face a few inches away in a smile.

"The king is dead. Long live the king," Oleg said with a grin.

Oleg stood up but offered Maharbek no hand. He rolled over slowly and groaned. Oleg started to walk off the mat.

"New king must defend his throne, *nyet*?" said Anatoly.

Oleg looked at Anatoly and smiled. He bowed and made a sweeping welcome gesture with his hand, like a waiter at a French restaurant about to say 'voila.' Anatoly walked onto the mat and faced Oleg. He got into a wrestler's stance and gritted his teeth in readiness. Oleg casually strolled up to him standing upright and relaxed. Then in the blink of an eye, Oleg's right hand came crashing onto Anatoly's head in a smack, while Oleg's left leg swept Anatoly's right foot. It was a similar move that Arsen had used earlier on Valentin, but this one was much faster and much more violent. Anatoly dropped like a stone, visibly shaken by the speed and force of the move.

"*Bozhe moi*," said Valentin. "My God! Did you see that?"

Arsen just shook his head incredulously with his mouth open.

"Next?" Oleg said, looking at Buvaisar.

Buvaisar sneered and stomped onto the mat, then drove in for a double leg tackle, his legs pumping like a running back. Oleg back-pedaled quickly, but it looked as if Buvaisar would triumph, his legs moving faster now. As they got to the edge of the circle, Oleg set his feet, then reached over the top to the belt of Buvaisar's *kurtka*, across his hunching back. With his other hand, he grabbed Buvaisar's lapel, then set both feet, popped his hips and arched his back and flung Buvaisar completely off the mat into the wall.

"*Blyad*," Anatoly said. "*Piiizdets, blyah.* Holy Fuck! He threw the shit out of you, Buvaisar!"

Buvaisar lay on the edge of the mat upside-down, feet on the wall, neck crumpled, groaning.

"*Aleksandr Medved*?" said Oleg. "Your turn."

Mouths dropped at Oleg's comment. "*Medved*" had a clear double meaning for the men. It literally means "bear" in Russian, which is what this Aleksandr had called himself. But the famous Aleksandr Medved was a three-time Olympic champion wrestler, considered perhaps the greatest of all time. He was a national hero, was flag bearer for the Soviet Union in the Olympics, and even had tournaments and training centers named after him. Oleg's comment was ironic in that Aleksandr considered himself a bear—*medved*--and thus indirectly compared himself to the great Aleksandr Medved as well. But Oleg's sneering comment was clearly done sarcastically as an insult, a point not lost on his opponent, as his scowl demonstrated. The enormous man walked out onto the mat. Maharbek might have been nearly as large and much more skilled, but the sheer size of Aleksandr was impressive. Oleg was smaller by at least forty pounds if not more. The sight of the two together provided an almost comical juxtaposition.

"Ready?" Oleg said. "Buvaisar, you should watch how it is supposed to be done."

With that, Oleg stepped between the larger man's legs in a crouch, slapping his hands behind Aleksandr's calves. Oleg's head and shoulders were planted firmly in Aleksandr's chest and stomach. As he drove forward with his feet, his head pushed Aleksandr backward, but Oleg's steely arms held the big man's legs stable. The result was a crashing table-top spear-tackle that sent Aleksandr down hard and fast on his neck and shoulders, with Oleg still holding his legs. Oleg unceremoniously dropped his opponent's legs to the mat as he groaned, then walked off.

"Don't forget to shower before you eat," said Oleg. "Even squirrels, bears, and gorillas start to stink after a practice."

Arsen and Valentin looked up with obvious reverent awe. The others, battered and beaten, scowled and looked at the ground.

"And try to remember who is king," Oleg said as he left.

CHAPTER 18—NIGHT AT THE IMPROV

On the other side of the Hunter's Run campus, Josh Rimone and Boo Andrews were walking through the school. Josh had a pistol aimed at Boo's back. They had entered through the main entrance but had no idea in what part of the school the Russians were specifically being housed. Josh, Vinny, and Tommy had watched as they arrived and then entered but knew very little after that. Josh was hoping he could stumble his way into them.

"And exactly what is your story on this again?" said Boo.

"I'm a white supremacist, and I caught you sneaking around the church trying to steal," said Josh.

"Why would you assume that I was stealing if I was just sneaking around the church," said Boo.

"Well, you're black," said Josh.

"God, you are such a racist. Assuming any black man walking around the place is a thief," said Boo.

"See? My cover is working already. I make a great White Supremacist, don't you think?" said Josh.

"You do look the part," said Boo.

"Why would you assume I'm a racist White Supremacist just because I'm White?" asked Josh.

"It ain't just because you're white, dude. It's the cowboy hat, boots, and big ol' chaw in your cheek," said Boo with a smile.

"Point taken," said Josh.

"And no need to even bring up that totally-hairless-Hills-Are-Alive look you got going on there. It reeks of some kinda Marvel Universe super-villain or something," Boo said.

"No need to be cruel," Josh replied with a chaw-filled grin.

The pair walked down the hall, glancing occasionally into the classrooms that had become makeshift apartments. They each had a family in them and were set up comfortably. Now weeks into the project, the rooms were starting to sport some decorations and personal style for the families.

"These are nice," said Josh. "These people are living kinda large for being homeless."

"These people are selected and being propped up by a power-mad racist church breeding new drones," said Boo.

"True, but they have a nice sense of style. I mean, look at what they did with that bookcase. Very classy for a public-school classroom, don't you think?" said Josh. "And is that a fucking Harley-Davidson over there in the corner?"

"I'll be damned," said Boo. "So it is."

Just then, Lou Orville walked around the corner. He looked at Josh and Boo and immediately got a confused look on his face.

"Uh, who are you guys, and what are you doing here?" said Lou.

"Well, I'm Billy Joe Johnston and I caught this here hooligan sniffin' around the church, up to no good. The fella there told me if I brought him here, I'd get a bounty paid for him," said Josh.

"What fella where?" asked Lou.

thing."

"What is it?" asked Aleksandr.

"The two new guys are double agents," said Josh in a low voice.

"What? I don't know what you are talking about, I'm leaving," said Aleksandr.

"Shhhh. They'll hear you. Listen to me. The two new guys? They are CIA. They are not Russian," said Josh.

"Who are you?" Aleksandr said, grabbing Josh by the throat. "What do you want here?"

Josh put his gun to Aleksandr's head and pulled the hammer back.

"I'm the guy who can end your life in two seconds. Now shut up and listen before they get wise. *Menya zavout Yuri.* But I go by Josh in English. I am a double agent from Pripyat. I came here to tell you that the two new arrivals are not Russian. They are American CIA agents. *Vi ponimayetye, chto ya govoryo?* Do you understand what I said?" Josh said.

"Yes, yes," said Aleksandr. "*Bozhe moi!* My God! What should I do? Does Oleg know?"

"No. He doesn't know. What are their names?" asked Josh.

"Arsen and Valentin. They arrived yesterday. You mean that these two are impostors?" asked Aleksandr.

"That's exactly what I mean. Arsen and Valentin were supposed to meet you here. These two killed them and took on their names, but they are agents with the CIA. You need to take action and eliminate them immediately. They are here to infiltrate your operation. And I have endangered myself and my own cover to tell you this. Now get back in there and tell your comrades what I told you. Find an opening, and finish them before it's too late," Josh said.

"Shouldn't we capture them and see what they know?" asked Aleksandr.

"Everything you have said and everything they have seen since they arrived is what they know, you idiot. And they have been communicating it back to the Americans the entire time. Were they ever separated from the rest of you?" asked Josh.

"Yes. Yesterday. At a meal. They were alone," said Aleksandr.

"Oh God, it's worse than I thought," said Josh. "You need to kill them. Quickly and discreetly. Don't let people see."

"What about Oleg?" asked Aleksandr.

"I'll go talk to Oleg now, but I have to hurry, or my cover is blown. *Vi ponimayetye, chto ya govoryo?*" Josh whispered, asking again if he understood.

"*Da, spasibo,*" said Aleksandr aloud. Josh slapped him in the face.

"In English, you idiot," he said. "Otherwise whisper."

"Sorry. Yes, thank you," said Aleksandr. "But what about the black man? Didn't you shoot him? Don't you need my help?" said Aleksandr.

"I don't even know him. I paid him $200 to come in and do as I told him. He took the money and ran, and I missed him on purpose. And now I'm leaving. Don't blow my cover, and don't let these two get away," said Josh.

Aleksandr nodded and walked back in the wrestling room. Josh went around the corner and grabbed Boo.

"Come on, let's get the fuck outta here. Damage done," said Josh.

They started running down the hall, when Lou Orem started walking out of the coaches' office where Oleg was taking his shower. Josh spotted him and dropped to the ground holding his groin. Boo looked behind him and Josh winked. Boo nodded imperceptibly and picked up speed. As he ran by Lou, he shoved him hard into the office, sending him sprawling onto a teacher's desk.

"God damn, he got me. Don't let him get away," Josh yelled.

As he yelled, Boo took the cue and shifted into another gear entirely. He saw an exit at the end of the hall and made a beeline for it, slamming into the door and running outside.

"What the fuck is going on?" said Lou.

"He hit me in the nuts and took off running. God damn, I think I'm gonna puke," Josh said.

He offered a couple of fake heaves and aimed his chaw right at Lou's pants.

"Oh God that's nasty. What the fuck, dude? What's your problem?" said Lou.

"The problem is my bounty is running away," said Josh.

"Oleg said he didn't know anything about any bounty," said Lou.

"Well that's what the preacher man said," Josh repeated. "He said take that man to Olaf and he'll pay you handsomely for it. I'm not sure what handsomely is, but it sounded good."

"Well, we will now have to take you back to him to find out what he meant," said Oleg, coming out of the locker room drying his hair. Perhaps Father Joe can shed some light on this. And you are coming with us."

"But my bounty is getting away, I can still catch him," said Josh nervously. "Just let me go after him."

Oleg grabbed Josh by the shirt and held him.

"He is gone, my friend. But you are still here, and we will get to the bottom of whatever this is," said Oleg. "Come Lou, help me escort this man to Father Joe, and he will clear things up for us. But first, take his gun from him."

Lou put his hand out and Josh slowly handed him the weapon and smiled. Just then a darkly clad figure turned the corner and entered the office.

"And just what is it, then, gentlemen, that I need to clear up?" asked Father Joe.

CHAPTER 19—
THE RESCUE

"It's too dangerous for you to go alone," said Jake.

"But we know how to get there, and we snuck in before," said Morgan.

"And you got caught before, and were on your way to be executed until Mark saved you," I said.

"No, too much is at stake here," said Jake. "We need to think it through a little more. If you get caught, we're all sunk. All of us, including Nat."

"You really think John Segen will come here?" I said.

"Yes," said Mark. "I'd bet my life on it."

"You may be doing just that," Jake said. "What we need to do is get enough of us in that secret room to sweep in like a flash and bug out. They won't be expecting us, and the Russians aren't even settled in yet. Hell, none of them probably know Segen has done this, and that's to our advantage. But we also need somebody here to grab him, turn the tables on him."

"I have an idea," said Kristen.

All heads turned toward her. She was wiping away tears. Her cheeks were stained with dust and teardrops, but she was calm and lucid now.

"I can turn them in," Kristen said.

"What? We're not going to let you do that," I said.

"No, not for real. They know where the room is, right?

So, I go with them, bring them in tied up, and tell the people at the church I'll trade them for my daughter," Kristen said.

"But they don't know this is going on. They'll suspect something," I said.

"Maybe so, but maybe not," said Jake. "You may be onto something. We can exploit this a little. I like it. Kristen, you take them in, tell them you're trading them for your daughter. If anybody is in the church, they'll be confused, but they'll go along with it, because you have the fugitives they've been looking for. When they go to get someone, you can run down into the room and rescue Natalie."

"Are you kidding me?" I said. "I am the least sexist guy here; can we agree on that?"

"Agreed, twinkle-toes, what's your point?" said Jake.

"You can't send in those three into a church that is armed to the teeth and down the street from where a Russian cell of SVR agents is waiting. It wouldn't take much to over-power them, and none of them is ready for a potential fire-fight. No offense Kristen, but you're a fucking librarian, not Wyatt Earp," I said.

"Yeah, but it won't be just her," said Jake. "It'll be every-body."

"What?" I said. "Now I know you're crazy."

"I can show you a way to tie all of these people together with slip knots. Kristen can march them into the church. If no-body's there, great. Problem solved. But if you meet up with someone, you'll have Al, Mark, and Maureen with you. And we can give them some small weapons to hide. What do you think?" asked Jake.

"It sounds dangerous," said Al.

"Dangerous as hell," said Mark. "I'm in."

"Yeah, why not? Let's go nose-to-nose with these

fuckers," said Maureen.

"What if John Segen is there, waiting?" I asked.

"Good point. You need a back-up plan. If he's there, show him your prisoners, then tell him you'll make the switch back here on your farm, and you're doing it because you feel safer here. Demand to see Natalie alive, then bring everybody back. We'll be waiting for Segen either way," Jake said.

"That sounds dicey," I said.

"It's certainly more dicey if we run into him, but it's the risk I prefer to take," Kristen said.

"It will be dangerous, but the real danger is from the Russians, and Josh and Boo are keeping the Russians busy for now. Vinny, Tommy, and I can hunker down here and wait for John Segen. Eddie, I'm giving you a shotgun and a walkie-talkie. They get into too much trouble, you call me or bust in shooting," said Jake.

"This is insane," I said.

"Sí. Super-loco," said Estela. "I'm in too."

"Does anybody else think this is kinda fun?" asked Morgan.

"Are you nuts? You're taking on a crazed church, Russian assassins, kidnappers. All of you are on the Most Wanted list of a man who already tried to kill you once. This is fun?" I said.

"For Pete's sake, Eddie," Jake said. "It's goddamn World War III. If you can't have a little fun, the days are just empty."

"Insane. Every one of you. But I have nothing better to do, so I guess I'm riding shotgun," I said.

"That's the spirit. But you're not riding shotgun. You're driving. Now put them all in the Hummer. Kristen, do you have any long rope or extension cord?"

"Yes," she said.
"Bring it to me, and I'll set you up," said Jake.

❖ ❖ ❖

Kristen got out of the Hummer holding a shotgun. I had parked it right in front of the church, almost up on the sidewalk. Mark, Morgan, Estela, Maureen, and Al got out of the car, tied together with their hands wrapped behind their backs, each one tied in a slip knot, but connected by one large piece of rope that the Faust Farm had provided. They marched in the church in front of her. The receptionist—a different volunteer than the one that Morgan and Estela had met before—sat slack-jawed at their entrance.

"Uh, ma'am, can I help you? Ma'am you can't come in here with that gun. Oh my, ma'am, I'm gonna call someone, hold on a second," she said. Billy James and Emery Butler saw the procession from one of the sitting rooms and ran into the lobby.

"Can I help you, ma'am?" Billy said. "What's all this about? Mark, is that you?"

"Shut up," Kristen said. "I have what you wanted. Now give me my fucking daughter."

"Ma'am I have no idea what you're talking about," Billy said.

"Can the bullshit, Jesus-freak. I know my daughter's here, and I know why. You want these people? They escaped you and came to me. But they mean nothing to me, so I brought them here. Now get my daughter out here fast or so help me God I will start shooting," Kristen said.

"Look, some of this I think I understand. I do know that Father Joe wanted to talk to these folks, but that had to do with breaking and entering and assault on one of our congregation. But coming in here with ropes and a gun? And you say your daughter was taken? I don't know anything about that. Why don't I call for Father Joe now and find out?" Billy said, trying to calm everyone.

"He's at the school," said the receptionist. "I can call him."

"Stop stalling me. I'm not a fucking idiot. Where is she?" Kristen said.

She pumped the shotgun and fired it into the ceiling. Pieces of a light fixture fell to the ground with some stucco. Billy flinched and Emery looked like he soiled himself.

"Oh God, don't shoot again, don't shoot again!" Billy said.

"Alright, all three of you, get over there by that shelf," Kristen said. "Stand next to each other and grab the shelf."

Billy, Emery, and the receptionist walked over to a bookshelf with cylindrical legs and supports. Each one grabbed one of the supports with both hands. The receptionist was crying, and Emery was shaking violently.

"Alright boys, get it done," said Kristen.

With that, Al and Mark—who were on the two ends--pulled on the rope and the knots came undone. They took the rope over to the shelf and started winding it around the arms of the people there. Within a few seconds, Billy, Emery, and the receptionist were all tied tightly together to the bookshelf.

"Ladies, you're up," said Kristen.

Morgan and Estela ran to the back of the church and opened the broom closet. After a few seconds of fumbling around for the latch, the door sprung open and they slid it aside, revealing the secret staircase below. They flicked on the light switch and ran down the steps. Sure enough, at the bottom was Natalie Faust, bound and gagged. She tried to speak, but it came out a muffled grunt. Estela pulled out the knife Jake had given her and cut the ropes holding her to the chair, while Morgan gently pulled off the duct tape from her face.

"Oh, thank God," said Natalie. "How did you know to find me here?"

"You think you're the only one who gets tied up down here? Been there, done that, got the shirt and hat," said Morgan smiling. "Now let's get the fuck out of here."

They ran up the steps. Kristen was waiting anxiously, the worry telling on her expression. She turned to the church members tied to the bookshelf and pointed the gun at them.

"You fuckers better pray to that Nazi god you worship that my daughter comes out of your goddamn basement in one piece, or you will not live to see tomorrow," she said.

"Ma'am, for the last time, we don't know what you're talking about," said Billy.

On cue, Natalie came sprinting around the corner and ran to her mother. Kristen shoved the shotgun into Maureen's hands and embraced her daughter. The two clung together as one and rocked gently.

"Um, who is that, and where was she?" said Billy.

"I ought to shoot you kidnapping assholes right now," said Maureen. "But I'm gonna leave you tied there instead. You can explain what happened to whoever finds you."

"Mark, what are you doing with these people?" said Billy. "They're criminals. How could you have assaulted Oleg like that? What happened to you?"

"Billy, it's a shame. I think you are probably a decent guy married to an attractive whore and devoted to a church that serves the devil and spikes the Kool-Aid. But I don't have the time or patience to save you from it, so good-bye," said Mark.

"Let's go home," said Kristen.

And all six of them came out and hopped in the Hummer. I spun wheels and sped the fuck out of there.

CHAPTER 20—
FAMILY FEUD

The Jeep rolled up on the wrong side of the street across from Kristen's house, the middle one on the farm. The driver's side opened up, and a lone figure got out and shut the windowless door. He was dressed in a polo shirt and jeans and was wearing a baseball cap.

"Stay here," said John Segen to the others in his vehicle. "I'll call you if I need you."

John stood out in the middle of the street, about halfway between the Jeep and the house and just waited. After about two minutes of silence had passed, he finally spoke.

"Okay. You gonna make me do this, huh? Alright. You know why I'm here. And you know what I want. Give me what I want, and I will give you what you want," John said.

The screen door of Kristen's house swung open and out limped Jake Fisher. He was in a T-shirt with the sleeves cut off and a pair of athletic shorts. His wrists and hands were taped with athletic tape. His sweat-covered skin shone in the fading afternoon sunlight. The tinges of gray on his temples gleamed a little more than usual with the sun on them from this angle, and the scars on his face were showing white on his tan skin.

"I don't think I have what you want, John," said Jake.

"Well, well. Coach Fisher. Mr. Hall of Fame. The Legend himself. What are you doing here?" John Segen asked.

"I might ask you the same thing, John," Jake said. "And unlike myself, I'd imagine that trespassing is one of the answers."

"It just might be none of your fucking business," said John.

"Afraid you got that wrong, too, John. I'm here because it is expressly my business," Jake said.

"Your business, huh? I bet you think you sound tough, talking like that. Well, you know what? I'm tired of hearing how great you are. What a great coach. What a great teacher. What a great guy. You're nothing but a fucking fake. You're a liberal asshole. Brown-lovin', fag-lovin' fake asshole," said Segen.

"Now John, you know that's not true. I'm a registered independent," said Jake.

"You're a registered smart-ass," said Segen.

"Better than being a registered dumb-ass, which is about where you land, I think," said Jake.

"Well, I'd love to listen to you run your mouth all day, but like I said, I have business here, so why don't you get out of the way so I can conduct it?" said Segen.

"Okay, but you never asked me what my business was, being here," said Jake.

"I don't give a shit," said Segen.

"Now, John, that's just being impolite. No need to be rude. Just ask me. I'll tell you what my business is," said Jake.

"God damn, I don't have time for this shit," said Segen.

"Come on, John. Just ask. Ask me what I'm doing here," said Jake.

"Alright, motherfucker. I give. What are you doing here?" said Segen.

"Stalling you," said Jake.

A dumbfounded look descended upon John Segen. His face puckered a little, and he squinted at Jake for a moment with his mouth open. Jake could see him trying to work through it.

"I'm stalling you. That's my job," said Jake.

"What the fuck are you talking about?" said Segen.

"About a half an hour ago, my friends went to the church, descended the stairs to the secret room in the basement, and took back Natalie Faust from your tender care," said Jake.

"My...I don't know what you're talking...I," John stammered.

Segen's face suddenly read panic. He fumbled for a line, a word, an answer that wouldn't come.

"That's okay. Take your time and let it sink in," said Jake.

Then the realization set in that the jig was up—that his well-laid plan was busted and he was caught red-handed. Suddenly, John Segen's face turned to fury.

"You son of a bitch. I'll kill you," said Segen.

"There you go, being impolite again. You know, John, now that you've been stalled, the first half of my job is finished. All I have left is the second half," said Jake.

"Oh yeah, and just what the fuck is that?" said Segen, his face red with anger and embarrassment.

"Kicking your ass," said Jake.

John Segen was nervous for a moment, but his anger buoyed him. He sneered and reached into his right pocket and pulled out a switchblade. He pressed the button and the blade dramatically snapped into action. He smiled slightly at the dramatic effect the knife had. Then he turned and looked over his shoulder at the Jeep and whistled. It was one of those loud whistles that can quiet a crowd.

"Well it's a shame the pastor told me to leave my gun home, but lucky for you, I decided to bring my switchblade anyway. You may find kicking my ass a little harder than you expect," Segen said. "Boys, bring the hardware out."

John's two sons, Clayton and Brett, jumped out of the car with baseball bats. One was tall and beefy, the other smaller but lean and muscular from head to toe. They brandished the same smile as their father.

"The three of us are gonna thrash your ass and leave what's left of you in the street for your friends to find," said Segen.

"Ordinarily," said Jake, "I would find 3-to-1 odds a nice challenge. But today I am gonna be generous."

"What do you mean, generous? You're gonna give up and turn tail again like you did when Wes Kent ran you outta the school?" said John.

"No. I mean generous, as in spread the wealth. See, my boys like a good scrap themselves, and it just wouldn't be right for me to hog all the glory."

On cue, Tommy and Vinny walked out of the house onto the porch. Tommy was holding a *bokken*, a wooden Japanese practice sword. Vinny had his *nunchakus* draped over his shoulder. They both stood with arms folded in front of them defiantly.

"Nice entrance. We didn't even practice that," Jake said to them.

"We're good at the whole showmanship thing," said Tommy.

"So now what?" asked Vinny.

"So, pick one and have at it. How 'bout I'll take the old fucker in the middle," said Jake.

With that, Vinny ran towards Clayton, the larger and older of the two boys. Clayton wielded a large aluminum baseball bat, which he swung hard at Vinny when he got close. Vinny lithely jumped back as the bat missed him and the momentum carried Clayton through. Vinny swung the *nunchaku* in his right hand straight down and smacked Clayton on the head. The beefy boy dropped to a knee and grabbed his skull. Vinny then used the left one and swung it horizontally. It connected with Clayton's cheekbone, and he dropped onto the ground. One final kick to the head and Clayton was down for the count.

"One down," said Vinny with a smirk.

Tommy had a much smaller weapon than Brett. The *bokken* was solid ash wood, but compared to the 33-inch wooden bat Brett had, it looked puny. But Tommy knew how to use a sword, especially one shaped like a *katana*. He stood immobile with the *bokken* turned down at his waist, facing backwards towards the ground. Brett was feinting left and right, then finally went in for big swing. Tommy timed it perfectly and stepped inside the swing, rapped Brett on the head, and spun away as the bat flew past him. Brett scowled.

"Ow! That hurt," said Brett.

"Wait till you feel this one," said Tommy, who raised his *bokken* as if to swing, causing Brett to lift the bat to block him. Then Tommy dropped down in a crouch and swung low, connecting with Brett's knee.

"Ow, you fucker," Brett reached for his knee and hobbled away, then angrily raised his bat to swing it in a chopping motion, as if he were splitting wood. Tommy parried the swing with the *bokken*, spun again and this time drove the pommel of the bokken hard into Brett's ear. The smaller man dropped his bat and held his suddenly bloody ear, and Tommy

we might be followed. As we pulled up, everyone got out in a celebratory mood. Smiles, hugs, and high-fives all around. When everyone looked at the Segens tied in the back of the Jeep, the smiles deepened.

"Looks like you had some luck," Jake said.

"We sure as shit did," I answered back. "Looks like you did too. Everything go as predicted?"

"Not exactly. I didn't think he'd have a switchblade," said Jake.

"Oh shit, are you hurt?" I asked.

"No. And on the plus side I got to break his arm," said Jake.

"It's the little perks in life like those that truly make it worthwhile," I said.

"Kristen," Jake said. "Nat okay?"

"She's fine, just fine," Kristen answered. "Thank you Jake."

She gave Jake a big hug, then looked behind him at the Segens.

"What do you want us to do with these three?" Jake asked.

"Well, it looks like they were bad boys," Kristen said. "We're educators. Our job is to address and change bad behaviors. So, what do you say we go change their behavior?"

CHAPTER 21—THE MAD SCIENTIST

Wendy looked down at the mutate's dead body on the table in frustration. She was sure this approach would work. In fact, it had. The mutate's coloration had begun to revert right before everyone's eyes. The Colonel frowned. He thought her idea had merit too. But he also feared that the means by which her combined treatments were applied were not enough to mimic the way in which they had originated —that being a nuclear bomb—which was impossible and impractical to duplicate anyhow.

The younger CBRNE soldier who had done the brain scan stood with them. He had been privy to the Colonel's theory about having to duplicate the explosive speed with which the treatments had been applied. He had wanted to speak then, but held back. Now he could barely hold it in.

"You know, sir, that your idea is a good one," he said.

"Idea, son?" said the Colonel. "What idea is that?"

"The one about duplicating the explosive speed of the initial bomb in administering the treatments. I think it's spot on," the young man said.

"Well, that's nice, son, but good luck finding a nuclear bomb to help this along," the Colonel said.

"Not that we could find a way to do it any other way," said Wendy. "Damn it. I thought for sure that would work."

"Ma'am, begging your pardon, but there is another way

to do it," he said.

"What do you mean? You're actually going to bring a nuclear explosive device in here?" Wendy said.

"No, ma'am. The device doesn't have to be nuclear," he said.

"What are you talking about, son?" the Colonel said.

"I'm talking about using an NNEMP," the young man said.

"A what? Ray, is this another one of your insane government acronyms?" Wendy said.

"Yes, it is. It stands for a non-nuclear electro-magnetic pulse," said the Colonel. "But that's no more possible to get in here than a nuclear bomb."

"Begging your pardon, sir, but you're mistaken. We can make one right here," he said.

"What? What are you talking about?" the Colonel asked.

"Sir, the NNEMP's are usually short-ranged weapons that require a chemical explosive as their initial energy source, with the rest coming from inside the bomb itself. But there are other ways to create what you need. A large enough microwave generator could do it. So could a low-induction capacitor hooked to an antenna. We have both of those here on the premises, sir. The microwave emitter is the most transportable," the young man said.

"What's the catch?" said the Colonel.

"Excuse me, sir?" said the young man.

"I said, 'what's the catch?' If this was easily done, we'd be doing it all the time. We'd have thought of it and done it already. CBRNE would have brought it to me. We've had a think-tank on this project now for nearly a week. Don't tell me this is the first time something like this has been mentioned," the

Colonel said.

"Well, no sir. It's not. But the top brass said no," he said.

"Why did they say no, son?" the Colonel asked.

"Because of the side effects, sir," the young man said.

"You know, son, an old colleague of mine in the medical field once told me, 'there's no such things as side effects. Just effects.' So stop dancing around the topic and get to the damn point," the Colonel said.

"Well, sir, side effects—I mean, effects--include the destruction of electronic control systems critical to the operation of many ground vehicles and aircraft. Not to mention just about every other machine working in this tent, sir," the young man said. "We would be able to administer Ms. Yubashiri's treatments in the way you suggested, but then all the power in the area would go out," he said.

"Damn," said Wendy. "We'd need those things to keep the mutates alive, monitor their progress, and do everything else we do."

"How about a gas generator?" the Colonel said. "We could have generators at the ready when the power goes out. We have such things in place at lots of government installations. We'd just need smaller versions of them."

"Um, there's a decent chance they might explode sir. NNEMP's send out a powerful static charge that can cause explosions to fuel containers and vehicles," the young man said.

"So, you're saying we'd have one shot, and if it doesn't work completely, the whole mobile hospital and lab here are rendered useless, along with nearby vehicles?" the Colonel asked.

"Hard to say for sure, sir, but that would be a possibility," he said.

"So, what would you recommend, son? How could we

do it?" the Colonel asked.

"Well, if we had generators on standby outside the NNEMP's range, we could bring them in right after the pulse and hook them up. If we had the main power source ready for hook-up, we could theoretically zip them back in and hook them up within a few minutes, depending on the range of the pulse," he said.

"Zip, huh? And just what is the range of the pulse, soldier?" the Colonel said.

"That's just it, sir. We don't know. Depending upon the power and size of the NNEMP, the range can vary from a few hundred yards to over two hundred miles. I would essentially be making one about the size of a suitcase. There's a lot of unknowns, sir. That's why the think tank dismissed it," he said.

"So why are you telling me this now?" the Colonel said.

"Because you're the officer in charge, sir. You can override this with a word. You have the power and authority to make it happen if you want to. I just thought," he began.

"Thought what, son?" the Colonel said.

"I have been here since the beginning of the set-up. I met those people who helped you. I met that woman's husband. They seem like good people, sir. And if we can do something to help them, we ought to try. I mean, just because the particulars aren't certain doesn't mean the experiment should be scrapped, sir. We'd never have phones, cars, rockets---any of that stuff—if we were too afraid to try, sir."

"What's your name, son?" the Colonel asked.

"Mazzaros, Sir. Lieutenant Eric Mazzaros. I'm a physicist assigned to CBRNE, sir," he answered.

"Lt. Mazzaros, how long would it take you to make this thing and get it ready to implement?" the Colonel asked.

"Generator hook-ups and all?" Mazzaros asked.

"All of it. How long?" the Colonel asked again.

"Maybe three or four hours with help, sir. That's my best guess," Eric said.

"Make it happen," the Colonel said.

"Yes sir," Lt. Mazzaros said.

Lt. Mazzaros scrambled off to begin his project. Wendy smiled and looked at the Colonel.

"Are you sure about this, Ray?" she asked.

"Sure? Hell, no. But certainty is a luxury one has to learn to live without during times of crisis, and I think this qualifies as a time of crisis," he said.

"That quote. The one about effects and side effects. I told you that," she said.

"You did indeed," the Colonel answered back.

"You quoted me in front of me?" she asked.

"Just trying to look cool in front of my colleague," he said.

She went up on her tiptoes and gave him a quick kiss on the cheek.

"I guess it worked," said the Colonel.

CHAPTER 22—
SEEDS OF DOUBT

"So, who are you again?" Father Joe asked.

"Billy Joe Johnson," said Josh.

"You said Johnston before," said Lou.

"The 't' is silent most of the time. I was trying to impress you," said Josh.

"Whatever. Why are you here again?" Father Joe asked.

"He says you told him that Oleg would pay him a bounty for a black man snooping around the church," said Lou.

"I said no such thing. Why would I do that?" said Father Joe.

"No, not him," said Josh.

"You said it was Father Joe. The preacher," said Lou.

"I said 'church man,' as in the man in the church, you dumb fuck," said Josh.

"Hey, watch it punk," said Lou, puffing his chest out.

"Easy, gentlemen. Let's figure this out. So, Mr. Johnson, is it?" asked Father Joe.

"Yup. Johnston. With a 't,'" said Josh. Lou frowned.

"Very well, then, Mr. Johnston. Why don't we make our

way to Wes Kent's office and see if we can settle this now? Would you like to come, Oleg?" Father Joe asked.

"Olaf. Yup. That's the feller what's supposed to pay me," Josh said.

"I know nothing of this. I will come along to see what this idiot is talking about," Oleg said.

"Well, now, that's not very nice," said Josh.

The four of them walked up the corridor to the main hallway on their way to Wes Kent's office—formerly the principal's office—located behind the Main Office near the rotunda and the school entrance. Josh exhaled. He glanced over his shoulder and noticed the Russians starting to leave the wrestling room and follow him up the hallway. He was fairly certain they would head back to their quarters, and he was hoping it wasn't in the same direction he was going. Once they hit the main hallway, Father Joe turned right, and Josh checked over his shoulder to see where the Russians went. Thankfully, Aleksandr was looking right at him and gave him a wink as they turned left.

"Is everyone going to shower now?" asked Aleksandr.

The general consensus was everyone would grab their clean clothes, then walk back to the locker rooms where the shower facilities were. Once everyone got their clothes, Arsen and Valentin exited first and headed down the hallway, both still discussing Oleg's prowess on the mat. Buvaisar started to follow, and Aleksandr put a hand on his chest and a finger to his own lips to call for silence. Arsen and Valentin moved on down the hallway, and Aleksandr waved everyone to him.

"We have a problem," he said. "You saw man with cowboy hat speak to me?"

"*Da*, Yes, Aleksandr, what of it?" said Anatoly.

"He is SVR double agent from Pripyat," Aleksandr said.

"*Derrmo,*" said Maharbek. "Bullshit."

"*Nyet,* Maharbek Davidivich. He even spoke Russian to me," said Aleksandr.

"Speaking Russian doesn't make you Russian. Any American spy could do it," said Buvaisar.

"He knew things," said Aleksandr. "He knew about those two. Valentin and Arsen. He said they are not the real Valentin and Arsen. He said they are CIA spies trying to infiltrate our group. He says Oleg doesn't know."

"And you believed him?" Buvaisar said. "How stupid are you?"

"He had a gun to my head. He could have killed me. He could have killed all of us if he wanted. We were all tired and sitting together and he had a gun. Maybe two of them. But instead he chose to tell me about those two. He said he could not blow his cover, that even Oleg did not know he was here, as he is posing as a double agent," Aleksandr.

"*Ty che, suka, o'khuel blya,*" said Maharbek. "Are you fucking crazy, asshole?"

"He picked them out from all of us. Why would he do that? How would he know? It makes no sense if it's not true," Aleksandr said.

"He's an American spy trying to fuck with your head," said Buvaisar.

"Wait just a minute, Buvaisar," said Anatoly. "Let's think about this. We heard the shot. We saw him shoot at the black man, so we know he had a gun with bullets."

"Yes, that is another problem. Who was the black man?" asked Maharbek.

"He said even he didn't know. He said he paid the man $200, said he would shoot at him and miss and all he had to do was run away. He used him to get in here to give us the message," Aleksandr said.

"It's a trick," Maharbek said.

"Wait a minute," said Anatoly. "What did he tell us to do with Arsen and Valentin?"

"He said to kill them quickly before they find out too much. He said they are actually American spies," Aleksandr said.

"It's an American trick," Maharbek said.

"Maybe," said Anatoly. "But you must ask yourself, what Americans even know we are here, and what motive would they have for this? Why not kill all of us if they want us dead? What good would killing those two do for an American spy?"

"He has a point," Buvaisar said.

"And those two knew a great deal about Oleg. They knew more than we did," said Anatoly. "Maybe they are here to kill him."

"Another good point," said Buvaisar.

"They are always together. They don't really socialize with us," said Maharbek.

"They're alone right now, in fact. Why not just wait for the rest of us? We all shower together all the time at the gym," said Aleksandr.

"There's no way an American spy picks them out for any reason other than luck. Why not choose another of us. Why not Maharbek, or Buvaisar?" said Anatoly.

"The man called me out specifically. He did not want Arsen or Valentin. He could have chosen anyone. How would he know those two always separate themselves unless there is something to what he is saying?" said Aleksandr.

"Oleg could be in danger as we speak," said Buvaisar.

"Or those two could be spying or plotting something right now," said Aleskandr.

"Or reporting to their American superiors about our presence here," said Anatoly.

"We have to make a decision, then," said Maharbek. "This has consequences, no matter what we decide."

"What if we just tie them and torture them into telling us what they know?" said Buvaisar. "We can set up waterboard, maybe use battery from car. Then we get information from them, instead of other way around."

"What if they are waiting for us?" said Aleksandr.

"What do you mean? There are four of us," said Buvaisar.

"I mean, what if they are here to kill us all? If we try to subdue them and something goes wrong, we die. I think trying to capture and torture them is a mistake. Too many risks. People hear us. Maybe we go too far and kill one. Or one of us gets injured or killed ourselves. Too many risks. For all we know, they recognize the cowboy and are waiting for us. No, it must be all or nothing," said Maharbek.

"If we kill them, and they are not spies, they will be replaced," said Anatoly.

"And we go to the Gulag in Novosibirsk," said Buvaisar.

"Maybe not. If we explain what happened, it will look like we were being cautious, trying to protect Oleg," said Maharbek.

"But what if they're not even here to kill Oleg?" said Buvaisar. "And what if it is all a mistake? Or the cowboy is lying."

"Oleg doesn't know that. If we all agree that's what the man said, Oleg must believe us," said Maharbek. "And if cowboy is lying, Oleg takes care of him. He is with cowboy right now."

All four of the men looked at each other. They were silent for a long moment.

"I never liked either one of them," said Anatoly.

"But we must all be in complete agreement on this, if we do it. We all say the cowboy told us Oleg's life was in danger and to kill those two. We can even say we were going to try and subdue and interrogate them, and they fought back. And we must act quickly, while they're alone," said Buvaisar.

"That is actually a good plan," said Aleksandr. "If we all have same story."

"And we must not draw attention," said Anatoly.

"Does everyone have a suppressor?" asked Buvaisar.

"Of course," said Maharbek. "I even have Sergei's too."

"And I have Dmitri's," said Anatoly.

"So? Are we agreed? We kill them now, tell Oleg together later," said Aleksandr.

Another long silence prevailed. The men looked at one another.

"Agreed," said Anatoly.

"Agreed," said Aleksandr.

"*Da, harasho*," said Buvaisar. "Yes. Good."

"We go now," said Maharbek. "Get your pistols and your suppressors. We kill them in the shower, wash their blood down the drain, and pitch their bodies into the dumpster."

The four Russian assassins, each still sporting their kurtkas, packed bags of clean clothes, just as they would have done after a workout. Inside those bags, in addition to clean shirts, underwear, socks and track suits, were Yargin PYa pistols--each filled with 18 rounds and a suppressor to reduce the noise of the gunshots—and combat knives.

Anatoly led the group, his smaller frame and quicker walking pace moving him ahead of his three teammates. They rounded the corner at the gym and walked around past the custodial offices and the Athletic Director's office to the area where the locker rooms and showers were located. Anatoly turned and looked Aleksandr in the face.

"You are sure you know what you heard?" Anatoly asked.

"Certain. Completely certain," the large man said.

Anatoly leaned his shoulder into the door, which led to a small corridor connecting the back locker and shower areas with the larger hallway. Anatoly held up his hand for a moment. Everyone went silent. He turned to the other three and whispered, "no shower running." The other three began to zip open their bags. Anatoly burst in and looked around.

The locker room was empty. Arsen and Valentin were gone.

"They've gone to kill Oleg," said Anatoly.

CHAPTER 23—
TORTURE

"Kristen, easy does it now," Jake said.

John Segen and his sons were sitting up in the back of the Jeep, tied to the roll bar with bailing twine. John's elbow was dislocated. His arm was going in two different directions and it looked awful. It had to be painful. In addition, his nose and mouth were bleeding, and it looked like he was missing a tooth. His sons, Clayton and Brett, were hurting as well from the thumping given them by Vinny and Tommy Fisher, respectively. All three of them probably had concussions.

And Kristen was laying into them with stockman's cane.

The cane was all wood, curved classically at the end. It was light but strong, and she had been swinging it with two hands, crashing the handle onto John's face. She had only hit the boys in the arms, but they were already groggy from the blows rained upon them by Jake's sons. As we watched her, we all cringed a little each time she brought the cane down upon them. I wondered if she was out of control. Jake spoke to her, but it wasn't doing any good.

"No, I will not 'easy does it.' This man kidnapped my daughter. He brought harm directly to my doorstep. He did it to gain information as to the whereabouts of my friends—*your friends*—so that his comrades could kill them. Are you hearing me? *Kill them!* I don't know this man past a cursory hello after school, but I can tell you this: He has perpetrated an act of war upon my family and friends, and it will not go unpunished or unavenged. Mama bear is pissed off," Kristen said.

"But Kristen," Jake interrupted.

"Jacob Fisher, how dare you lecture me," Kristen said. "Aren't you the guy who killed two people in front of the school and maimed a third? Didn't you knife someone and concuss three others in a Wal-Mart? Have you not been shooting mutated human beings by the handful? And did any of those people—or creatures—any of them kidnap your kids? Huh?" Kristen asked.

Jake swallowed hard.

"I'm betting they didn't. I am betting, though, that you defended yourself and your people in every one of those scenarios to the best of your ability given the circumstances. Would you say that?" Kristen asked.

"Well, yes. I tried to. Yes," said Jake.

"Then please tell me how I am supposed to protect my family now that these dirtbags know where I live and are partnered up with Russian assassins and a corrupt church who has directed those assassins to kill our friends? What the fuck do you think is going to happen if I let these people go?" she asked.

"Um," Jake stammered.

"Right. Um. That's all anybody can say. Though it caught most of us by surprise, we are currently in a World War, even though none of us is currently fighting it. And these three sleazeballs are collaborators with the same enemy that bombed our country, our state, our county seat—hell, they even bombed the next town over, but we were lucky enough to avoid that. And what do you do with collaborators in a war, Jake?" Kristen asked. "Come on, Mr. Semper Fi Marine Corps man. What do you do with collaborators?"

"You don't execute them," said Jake.

"Are you sure? Because I always learned that you jail them, you torture them for information, and you execute them when they are of no more use," Kristen said. "Abu Graib? Guantamo Bay?"

Jake was silent.

"And I'm betting that your new mercenary friend would agree. I'm betting when he comes back, he'll offer to do it for me," said Kristen.

Now all of us were silent.

"Kris," said Maureen.

"Don't say it, Mo. Think about it. What happens if we turn these assholes loose? Do you think they learned their lesson? Do you think they're going to go join the Rainbow Coalition now or start a Planned Parenthood group? Or join PFLAG? I'm sorry if I sound cutthroat, but nobody else here just had to rescue their bound and gagged daughter from a secret room in an extremist church occupied by Russian spies," seethed Kristen.

"Yikes," I said. "She has a point."

"You do have a point," said Jake. "Actually, you have several points. And I'm sorry if I was judgmental. We hold them here until Josh gets back, then take his recommendation for how to deal with them. We are at war, and they are collaborators, kidnappers, and vermin. Where do you want to put them for now?"

"In the corn crib. We can padlock it. They won't get out," Kristen said.

We moved the Segen boys into the corn crib. It was a double-fenced container with a door that had a place for a lock on it, and Kristen had a combination lock. Jake felt bad enough that he gave them a container of water to share between them. John Segen's arm looked awful and would probably have to be broken once more in order to re-set it correctly for it to be useful once again. His sons were definitely concussed and clearly showing signs of it. Once they were locked away, everyone wandered back to the house to get some refreshments. Kristen and Jake lingered a bit at the corn crib as most of us moved on.

"Thank you," Kristen said to Jake. "I know you have misgivings about this."

"I do, but to be honest, I'm not sure I have any better ideas," Jake said. "You're right. These people know where you live. They can come after you anytime they want, and they have the full backing of that crazy-ass church and its hired Russian assassins behind them. There's really nothing else we could do."

"Except kill them," Kristen said.

Jake froze for a second, then looked in her eyes.

"Which neither of us seems to have the stomach for the moment," she added.

"Killing someone in battle is one thing. Killing them in cold blood—that takes something else entirely," said Jake.

"I'm not bloodthirsty, Jake. I just want to protect my family, and I wanted revenge on those creeps for what they did," Kristen said. "But if it comes down to me or them--that's an easy decision."

"I don't blame you. Really. Not one bit. In some ways, I was treating this like it was a game. Like it was some high school brawl with minimal consequences. I hate that guy and everything he stands for. I'd watched him operate for years, trying to get inside every circle of influence or petty power that he could weasel his way into. He's always been a self-aggrandizing, ass-kissing phony. But I didn't care, because with me he kept his distance and used Facebook as his weapon of choice. But since I'm anti-social, a social network wasn't a threat to me. Today, though, his chosen weapon was a switch-blade," Jake said.

"Holy shit, really? He used a switchblade on you? What did you use?" Kristen said.

"Just these," Jake said, holding his hands up.

The tape around his hands and wrists were filled with dirt and dried blood.

Kristen looked at him and smiled. "It's nice to see a real man step up and do the job for a change."

Jake nervously raised his eyebrows.

"Don't worry, Jake. I'm not hitting on you," Kristen said. They both laughed nervously.

"That's probably for the best," Jake said.

"I know. Maureen said you're all kinds of fucked up in the relationships department," Kristen said.

Jake pressed his lips together hard and grinned uncomfortably.

"Don't worry, I heard it all. Still married. Sort of. Your wife is a mutant who tried to kill you."

"Mu-*tate*," Jake corrected.

"Mutate. Whatever. Saying you two are estranged is a fucking understatement," Kristen continued. "And supposedly there's something about an Asian scientist woman?"

"Wendy. Wendy Yubashiri. And nothing's going on there," said Jake.

"Sure. That, of course, depends on your definition of nothing," said Kristen. "Or your definition of 'going on'. Neither of which is anywhere close to the definitions that Maureen and I use for those terms."

Jake laughed nervously. Then there was an awkward silence. Kristen stood there in the setting sun, her brown hair slightly unkempt and pulled back in a ponytail. She was smallish to medium-sized, her skin was bronzed from time outside. She had crows' feet at her eyes that showed depths of feeling and somehow didn't make her seem older. There was the slightest hint of a streak of grey showing in the sun on one side, and her eyes were full of soul. Jake found himself momentarily mesmerized by her.

"Word has it you've always had fantasies about librarians," she said with a smile.

"Who told you that?" Jake said.

"Who else? Ten guesses. You've got to be more careful about to whom you reveal your darkest secrets on cross-country bus rides, Jake Fisher," she said. "Maureen's my best friend."

Jake swallowed hard and felt himself having a little trouble catching his breath.

"We're having a moment, you know," she said, smiling and looking Jake directly in the eyes.

Jake started sweating profusely as Kristen just stood smiling at him. The timing of it was almost comical. He wiped his forehead with his taped hand.

"Geez. Hot for early summer, don't you think?" Jake said.

Kristen laughed out loud. She put her arm around Jake and started walking back.

"I'm sorry. I like torturing you," she said.

"Apparently the torture thing seems to be a hidden part of your personality," said Jake.

"Don't worry. I'm not dangerous. At least not as dangerous as I hear this Wendy woman is," Kristen said. "Besides, what could be more desirable than dating someone you work with who lives next door to her husband?"

They both laughed out loud at that.

"Maybe another lifetime, Jake Fisher," she said.

"Yeah. Maybe another lifetime," he said.

As they separated, she reached out gently to take his hand just before releasing it. I saw the look on Jake's face, and it was almost painful to watch. Poor Jake. I had never seen him lose a fight yet, but he sure couldn't have been more awkward around women. I could see the attraction to someone like Kristen. She was smart, tough, was a deep thinker, and yet also had a ruthless side. All of those were qualities that Jake himself possessed. She was almost his age and looked it—but was very well preserved. Some women have a way of glowing even more after they hit their forties, and she was one of them. I'd seen pictures of her in her younger days hanging up in her office in the school library. She was unquestionably attractive then, but somehow even more so now.

I found myself rooting for Jake again, like I was on the trip to Washington. Wendy and I had had a talk. It started with me giving her a lecture, and it ended with her thrashing me with a lecture of her own, which led to me later lecturing Jake. Lotsa lectures on that trip. I knew that he would never find peace until he had come to a more stable place with Laura.

Laura was his wife. She was the woman he chose to spend his life with and raise a family with. Their relationship had become strained when the boys had gone off to college, and before they had time to work on it, the Cataclysm had intervened, and turned her into a monster. No, that wasn't right. Even among those orange-skinned creatures she wasn't a monster. She was caring and nurturing to them, and still gentle with her sons. Whatever resentment Laura Fisher harbored before the weapon dropped had stayed with her in her mutate form. I wondered if Wendy and the Colonel had had any luck in treating her. One thing was for sure, Jake Fisher clearly still had unfinished business with his wife, Laura, no matter what form she took.

CHAPTER 24—
TEST PHASE

"Okay," Lt. Eric Mazzaros said. "I think I've figured out a way to make this work, sir."

"Well, I hope so, son. I gave you the green light several hours ago," the Colonel said.

"No, sir, I mean to the side effects. The mass frying of machines all around us," said the young physicist.

"Well, don't hold back now, lieutenant," said the Colonel.

"We are going to need to build a Faraday cage around everything except the patient," he said. "We're going to need metal foil, and we'll need to wrap it around some kind of skeleton. Maybe using PVC. If we could find some copper, that would be even better. But if I'm right, we can use this microwave generator to create a forceful bonding of the two chemicals you have for treatment, and they should, in theory, enter the bloodstream of the patient at enormous speed and pressure. Kind of like, all at once, which should mimic the way the bomb created her in the first place. The rest should be up to her DNA. She is an outlier. She's one of the very few whose DNA responds differently to Ebola. It's allowed her not to revert the way those lower mutates did. From what you tell me, she even kept some of her speech patterns," Eric said.

"That's right. I heard her myself," the Colonel said. "She

struggled, but managed to get two words out."

"That also helps. At least I think it does. I'm not sure that even with my machine that the devolved mutates could ever come back to normal. But she might. She's at a higher level, sir."

"I'm well aware of that, son," said the Colonel. "Now stop yapping and start building. Do you need any help on the Faraday cage?"

"I could use a few extra hands down here," Lt. Mazzaros said.

"I'll get the brigade to send some. If I can snag you a half a dozen, how long until we are at go-time?" asked the Colonel.

"Half an hour? The electronic equipment is ready, and Ms. Yubashiri already has the treatment ready, right?" Eric asked.

"Correct," said Wendy. "It's all set up for simultaneous distribution."

"Um, I think, ma'am, that we will need to bring her out of the coma first," Lt. Mazzaros said.

"That could be problematic," Wendy said. "She's likely to struggle when she wakes up. We'll need to have her re-strained, and you'll have to be ready to go within a small window or she could harm herself trying to escape."

"I understand ma'am. I'll do my best," Eric said.

"Get to it. I'll get some help down here," the Colonel said.

About a half an hour later, Col. Raymond Cannaveral had summoned nearly a dozen members of CBRNE to help Lt. Mazzaros with his project. He had fast-tracked it, putting it at a higher level of importance than the other tests and studies having to do with the lower mutates, who were scattered about the laboratory being X-rayed, tested, and studied closely.

Lt. Mazzaros had fashioned a clear plastic container all around Laura Fisher's area and examination table. Inside it was a large microwave generator that was configured with a mechanism to administer an explosively driven amount of the two combined medicines simultaneously that Wendy had been using to treat radiation sickness and Ebola in the mutates. Around that container was a makeshift Faraday cage composed of reflective metals utilized to shield the surrounding area from harm. Outside the Faraday cage were numerous X-ray machines and monitoring devices hooked to Laura Fisher. It looked like a science experiment or a scene from a low-budget Frankenstein movie.

"Um, Ray," Wendy said. "Does this kid know what he's doing? This looks like someone got carried away with an erector set."

"The kid sounds like he knows what he's doing," the Colonel said.

"He also got turned down due to the dangers associated with his idea," Wendy said.

"The Faraday cage should work, so long as it blocks all of the sensitive equipment, and there's little chance of a real explosion," the Colonel said.

"Little chance?" Wendy asked.

"Practically none. There would have to be some kind of combustible material inside the Faraday cage at the time of the pulse, and even then, it wouldn't be very powerful. And see for yourself—there is nothing combustible here. We'll be fine," the Colonel said.

"Yeah, but will she be?" Wendy asked, pointing at Laura Fisher.

Lt. Mazzaros handled the finishing touches on his set-up and then indicated to Wendy that he was ready. That was the signal Wendy needed to begin to bring Laura Fisher out of the coma.

"Okay," Wendy said. "I am cutting off her anesthetic now."

She turned a few dials and waited. It would take a little time for a human being to come out of a medically induced coma, but no one was completely sure how quickly an alpha-level mutate would do the same. A few minutes went by. Nothing happened.

"Should we inject some glucose?" the Colonel asked.

"We can. It's often used as a therapy for this," Wendy said.

She grabbed a hypodermic needle and a vial of glucose nearby. She injected Laura with a small dose of glucose. The effect was immediate. Laura Fisher opened her eyes and screamed wildly. She tried to sit up, tried to lift her arms, but her restraints were holding. She thrashed and turned side to side, arching her back and trying to kick her legs to no avail.

"Eric, are you ready? She's resisting," Wendy said.

"Ready. I am initiating. It will take a little bit to get going," he said.

While the microwave emitter was building up power, Laura Fisher was beginning to loosen her restraints. She turned to her right and saw Wendy. Their eyes locked for a moment, and Laura's face went blank and her body went still. Wendy wondered what was happening, then Laura took one more glance into Wendy's eyes, then erupted.

She let out a blood-curdling shriek, strained every muscle in her body, and the restraints snapped apart like rubber bands pulled to their limits. The only ones that held were those on her ankles. She thrashed her upper body madly, reaching for anything she could find. She ripped the pulse-ox meter off of her finger and grabbed the wires and yanked hard, and the machine—which had been placed outside the Faraday cage, came crashing inside. It took with it a small cart on wheels with X-ray materials, including some plates, some pictures, and a bottle of a contrast agent known as diatrizoate used in radiology patients as a diagnostic agent. The bottle went crashing to the ground and shattered, the diatrizoate landing very near the microwave emitter.

Laura Fisher continued to wreak havoc on anything within her reach, but no one dared try to restrain her as the electromagnetic pulse was about to occur. Thankfully she had not yet ripped out the tubes for injection of the antiradiation and Ebola treatments, as they were harder to reach. She turned for a moment and looked again at Wendy, and her face went cold. She reached out her orange finger and pointed at her.

And then the electromagnetic pulse went off.

It hit the mechanism for administering the treatment, and the fluids exploded into Laura's body. Her back arched and she cried out. Her body spasmed violently as if it were having a seizure. Then she went completely still. The microwave emitter was still pulsing, when the diatrizoate liquid reached its area of influence.

And then it exploded.

Laura, her table, the Faraday cage, the microwave emitter—everything close just flew in the air as the benzene gas from which the diatrizoate was derived reached combustion. It blew Lt. Mazzaros out of his chair and onto the ground, knocking his face shield off of him. It had enough power to knock Wendy and the Colonel back several steps, and they were a good twenty feet away already. Nothing else in the vicinity was combustible, so the explosion had nothing else to latch onto besides the small amount of vaporized diatrizoate, but that coupled with the powerful microwave emitter had provided enough of a bang to make it appear that a cyclone had touched down in the middle of the lab.

There was a nominal amount of smoke that was dissipating, and as everyone began to get their bearings back, the area that was dedicated solely to studying and treating Laura Fisher was in shambles. Monitors, vials, equipment—all lay on the floor overturned several feet away. Laura's lab table where she had been restrained was on its side five feet away from the bent Faraday cage.

And she was gone.

"God, I blew it," Eric said. "What the hell happened? Where's the patient?"

Lt. Eric Mazzaros coughed a little and strained to get back on his feet. CBRNE crewmen had come in ready to put out any flames—but there were none. Wendy and the Colonel looked at each other with astonishment.

"Are you okay?" she asked.

"Yeah, yeah, I'm okay," the Colonel said. "What happened?"

A CBRNE crewman who had walked in and started surveying the situation lifted his hood and frowned at Lt. Mazzaros.

"Somebody forgot the X-ray contrast agent," he said, eyeballing the young physicist.

"Sorry, I didn't see it. Didn't know it had anything combustible in it," Eric said.

"Benzene derivative," said the CBRNE crewman. "And unaccounted-for variables like that are why we told you not to bring that goddamn microwave emitter in here in the first place, Mazzaros. And now your one shot at being a hero is dead. Literally."

"Oh no," Wendy said. "Look at that operating table. It's demolished. Oh no, Laura."

"Gone," said the Colonel. "She's just gone. Look at that mess."

"Sorry sir," Eric coughed back. "Sorry."

"Damn right you're sorry," the CBRNE crewman shouted.

"That's alright, son," the Colonel said. "It's my fault. I overrode the protocols on my authority. I was desperate to help Jake Fisher out and saw how close Wendy's solution had been with that other mutate. This one's on me."

"Colonel," Eric began.

"Sir," the crewman interrupted.

"No, I mean it. I'm not exactly a tyro at this stuff. I could have checked the area as well. I know enough chemistry to figure out that you don't mix an NNEMP with anything with Benzene, and I knew better. This one's on me, and that's the end of it."

"Ray," Wendy said, "Look."

"No, not you too. I'm not gonna look. I'm taking responsibility for authorizing a long-shot, and in situations like that, one has to be extra thorough in the preparations, and I delegated that out and shouldn't have. If there's any music to face, I will be first in line," the Colonel said.

"No Ray, that's not what I mean," Wendy continued. "Look. Over there."

Standing over in the corner next to a ripped, smoldering hospital gown, was a tall, slender, orange figure with flowing white hair. She was dirty, unkempt, and clearly a bit shaken, but she stood there staring at the four individuals standing near the area where she had been prone for weeks. She was naked and was covering up her breasts with one arm and her pelvis with the other.

"So," Laura said, "Is there any place a girl can get a shower and some new clothes?"

CHAPTER 25—
BUSTED PLAY

Boo Andrews was frantic. He had sprinted out of the school building, taking Josh Rimone's hint to do so, certain that the bald cowboy would be following him in short order. He had run out the loading dock exit, along the same back corridor where the coaches' office and wrestling room had been. There was a clear line of sight into the corridor from behind the dumpster where Boo was crouching. He had seen Josh get stopped by the one he assumed was Oleg, and then someone in a priest's collar had walked up. Boo reckoned that this man was the infamous Father Joe.

If Josh had stuck to his story, he had the means to convince anyone that either Oleg or Father Joe had sent him to the other one for a bounty, and by playing stupid enough, could have been left alone when one or the other tried to verify, perhaps giving him a brief window for escape. But his backstory wouldn't have worked if both of those individuals showed up—which they did. That meant he'd had to improvise. And while Josh was as good as anyone alive in their profession at improvisation, neither Oleg nor Father Joe were going to be played for fools.

Boo had seen them march him towards the area that he surmised was the main office. Boo had hidden on the terrace outside the cafeteria where he could survey the entrance to the building and the rotunda. Sure enough, Father Joe, Oleg, and a beefy fellow who looked like a football player had walked Josh back to the main hallway to verify his story. The crew had moved into the large, airy cafeteria and started talking. And Josh looked nervous. Boo had an idea, but he would have to hurry and hope that Josh was thinking on the same wavelength that he was. He reached in his pockets to take out the set of school keys Maureen had lent him and took off running, saying a little prayer to himself as he ran.

Back in the cafeteria, Josh was sitting on a tall stool, and Oleg and Father Joe were in his face asking difficult questions.

"Okay, say it one more time. Who was the man at the church that told you to find Oleg for a bounty?" Father Joe said.

"I told you before, he never gave me his name. But he was at the church when I brought that black fella in," Josh said.

"Well, what did he look like?" asked Father Joe.

"Medium height, kinda brownish like hair, I guess," said Josh.

"Did he have a beard?" Father Joe asked.

"I don't remember," Josh said.

"You don't remember a man you spoke to less than a half an hour ago?" Father Joe said.

"I was paying attention to my prisoner, Padre. You woulda done the same," said Josh.

"I would have remembered every detail of the encounter, you twit," Father Joe said.

"I have an idea, Father. Leave him with me for a few minutes and I can find out anything we want to know," said Oleg.

"I don't know if we're there yet, Oleg, but I'm not saying no entirely to that idea," Father Joe said.

But Josh Rimone had done this many times before in

much scarier situations. He stayed in character, and he stuck to his story.

"Look, Mister Oleg, sir. You are all kinds of scary. I do not want to tussle with you. But nothing you could do to me could make me tell you something I just don't know. Please, there's no need to be violent here. We're all on the same side," Josh said.

"I wonder if that's true," Father Joe said. "And how could we verify it? Maybe, Oleg, I should turn him over to you now."

"No, no, Father. Please don't. I'm on your side. I mean, I was so tickled when I heard you changed the name of the town. I love it. New Plymouth. Like the Pilgrims. It's a great idea," Josh said.

"You were at the rally?" Father Joe said.

"No sir. I couldn't make it. But my friend told me about it. He made it sound great," Josh said. "That's why I was bringing that black fella to you. I figured he didn't like the whole idea of the New Plymouth stuff, bein' as how you said we was all supposed to be white Protestant and pure," Josh said.

Father Joe stared at Josh skeptically.

"And I'm all those things," Josh said.

"All what things?" Father Joe said.

"White, Protestant, and pure," said Josh grinning.

Father Joe frowned.

"Okay, maybe not so pure, but the other stuff," said Josh.

Father Joe almost allowed himself a smile.

"Lou," Father Joe said. "Go tell Wes I need every male who was at the church during the past hour over here now. Pronto."

"Yes sir," said Lou.

"And if none of them have ever seen you," said Father Joe. "Oleg here will make sure nobody sees you ever again."

Oleg smiled an evil smile at Josh, who offered his simpleton's fake nervous grin back.

Just then, Josh heard footsteps behind him in the main hallway. Arsen and Valentin were dressed in casual clothes with their small duffel bags in their hands and were walking towards Oleg. Farther back, the other four Russian agents were walking quickly in the same direction.

Shit, Josh thought to himself. *They've compared notes, and now I'm fucked. Looks like I'm not gonna make it out of this one alive. I wish I hadn't handed my gun over to them, but they seem to have had me nailed from the get-go. I'm glad Boo took off before he got nailed too. Unfortunately, this operation looks too tight to be loosened up by my shenanigans. Jake Fisher and his crew are gonna end up following me to the gates of Hell in short order,* he mused.

Arsen and Valentin started to turn towards the cafeteria. Valentin went to reach in his bag to get his contact lenses.

And then both of the young Russian agents' heads exploded.

"Holy fuck," yelled Josh.

"What are you doing?" screamed Oleg, who immediately pulled out Josh's gun, flicked off the safety, and pointed it at the closest of the other agents, which was Anatoly. Oleg shot Anatoly in the leg and he dropped to the ground in pain. The other agents held their hands up, letting their Yargin PYa pistols dangle visibly for Oleg to see.

"Don't shoot, Oleg! Don't shoot!" Aleksandr said. "They were going to kill you. We had to stop them. They were American CIA."

"What? Are you out of your mind? Who told you that?" Oleg said.

Aleksandr looked at Josh.

Josh lightly shook his head no. Oleg turned and looked at him confusedly.

"What are you looking at? Who told you that?" Oleg shouted.

"I have to blow your cover, I am sorry," said Aleksandr.

"Cover? What cover? What are you talking about? Speak quickly or I will shoot you next," Oleg hollered.

"*Ya proshu proshcheniya, tovarich,*" said Aleksandr, "I'm sorry my friend. This is greater need."

"What is this about, Aleksandr?" Oleg said.

"This man is undercover double agent from Pripyat," Aleksandr said. "He did not want to blow his cover but wanted to warn us that those two men were not Arsen and Valentin. They were CIA agents pretending to be them. They were going to kill you, so we stopped them. This man risked everything to give us this information."

"*Ty che blyad!* You fucking idiots! Those men *were* Arsen and Valentin!" Oleg shouted. "I have known them since they were boys. I picked them myself for this mission because I could trust them. This man is nothing. A charlatan, and obviously in league with the people we are searching for! And you have been duped, you idiots!"

"Oleg turned and emitted a primeval growl at Josh. He slid Josh's gun into his own belt, then grabbed Josh by the lapels and lifted him off the ground, screaming at him, then threw him backwards in the air onto his back, where he slid head first into one of the cafeteria doorstops. Then Oleg pulled the gun back out and pointed it at Josh.

"I don't know who you are, but you are going to die

now," Oleg said.

Then a shot rang out.

The bullet slammed into the glass to the cafeteria doors, shattering it into a thousand pieces inside on top of Josh. Oleg turned to cover his face, then looked back, confused. The sound of a high-pitched engine whining suddenly roared out of the hallway and into the rotunda, and another shot rang out, and Oleg dove for cover. Josh brushed glass off his face and grabbed his cowboy had, rolled over and looked out into the hallway where he saw Boo Andrews gunning the engine of a Harley-Davidson motorcycle towards him, revving the throttle with his right hand and firing a pistol at Oleg with his left. All of the Russian agents dove for the ground, wondering what was happening. Josh got to his feet like lightning and hopped on the back of the motorcycle, which had slowed but not stopped. Boo was spraying his shots in all directions, trying to pin down anyone who might fire back. Then he popped a wheelie—almost throwing Josh off—and gunned it down the hallway to the other exit.

The cycle's tire hit the push bar and the door flew open. Buvaisar, Aleksandr, and Maharbek fired their pistols, but Boo and Josh were long gone and out of reasonable range.

"Follow them!" Oleg shouted. "Get in the van, now!"

Oleg took off running to the front entrance where the van was parked. Maharbek, Buvaisar, and Aleksandr all followed Oleg with their Yargin PSa's. They looked at one another in horror at the thought of what Oleg might do to them following this colossal blunder. Father Joe pulled himself up on a cafeteria table and looked out the door in wonder and alarm. Then he looked to his left at Anatoly, who was bleeding out on the floor. Oleg's bullet had hit the major artery in his upper leg. Anatoly looked pale and barely conscious, lying in a pool of his own blood. Next to him, Arsen and Valentin lay unmoving, their heads exploded like eggs that had dropped from a high countertop.

Father Joe put his hand to his mouth for a moment, fearing that he would vomit. He heaved twice, but nothing came out. He walked quickly out of the cafeteria towards Wes Kent's office. Wes was already on his way out with a puzzled look on his face.

"Father," said Wes. "What is Lou talking about? Get everyone who was at the church the past hour? What's that all about?"

"Don't worry about it. We figured it out," Father Joe said. "But we have another problem."

"What's that?" Wes asked.

"Other people are learning about what we're doing here. We were infiltrated, and now there are casualties. Call everyone in our inner circle and get them over here now. We must dispose of these bodies and clean up the mess," Father Joe said.

Meanwhile, the four remaining Russian agents were speeding in their van after Boo and Josh, who were riding a stolen Harley-Davidson motorcycle. Josh was having some trouble holding on. Boo was gunning it up and down the hilly town, and it felt like a bad roller coaster ride.

"We've got to shake them," Boo yelled.

"Or we're dead," Josh shouted back.

"Any suggestions? I don't know my way around this town," said Boo.

"Me neither, really," said Josh. "But I have an idea. Take this left."

Boo turned left quickly, but Oleg was right on him in the van. The Russians were about a tenth of a mile behind with clear visibility. They were headed towards Chubby's— Josh's favorite restaurant—at least this week. Chubby's was next to a large corn field. Most crops in the area were either soybeans—which were low enough at this point in the year to fertilize—or feed corn, which was starting to get about as tall as an average man. Josh directed Boo into the corn field, and they rode between rows, the leaves raking their faces viciously. They rode for about five minutes, then stopped and turned off the engine right in the middle of the field, surrounded on all sides by row after row of corn. Then they ducked down and just waited and listened.

In the distance they could hear loud cursing.

In Russian.

CHAPTER 26—ALL HAIL THE QUEEN

Laura Fisher sat calmly in the Colonel's office on a leather chair. She was wearing standard Army-issue exercise clothes, including a gray Army T-shirt and black sweatpants. She was clean and fresh, having showered for the first time since the bombs fell weeks ago. Her long, straight hair had turned mostly back to her original dark brown, despite one solid white stripe that ran all the way from her crown to her bangs. It was still damp, despite having had some time to blow it dry with Wendy's hairdryer. Her skin had not reverted back for some reason, and it glistened orange, appearing smooth and almost shiny. Laura was in her early forties, with a fit, muscular figure that offered no trace of her having given birth to enormous wrestlers two decades before. She sat with her legs crossed patiently as the Colonel set up a camera on a tripod to record the interview. Wendy had already placed another recorder on the desk as a back-up.

"I know I've asked you this, Mrs. Fisher, but you're sure you're feeling alright?" said the Colonel. "Do you need anything else before we begin?"

"Call me Laura," she answered back, "And the sandwich and soda you gave me were just fine, thanks."

"We, we have so many questions for you, I'm not really sure where to begin," the Colonel said.

"Not a problem," Laura answered back. "I'm fine, I'm

prepared. Ask away."

"Okay," said the Colonel. "I've already done an introductory piece with your name and the explanation of the history of your case, so these questions are for you in particular, and will focus mostly on the results of our experimental treatments. Okay?"

"First of all," Wendy jumped in, "do you know...what you are?"

"Yes," said Laura. "My current status is a product of an exploding Russian weapon that fused a new kind of radiation and a weaponized version of the Ebola virus. I am called a mutate—an alpha, I believe, due to my appearance and my higher cognitive abilities."

"How do you know all that?" Wendy asked.

"I overheard everything you've said the past few weeks," Laura replied. "Even in my coma."

"But you couldn't really communicate weeks ago, right?" asked Wendy.

"Wrong. I could communicate. I had trouble talking the way I am now," she said.

"Why is that?" Wendy asked.

"I don't know," she said. "I can't explain it. I know that I wanted to speak but was physically unable to do so. Kind of like a stroke patient who can't verbalize, but knows she wants to. But now I can."

"Amazing," Wendy said.

"We've checked all your vital signs, and they seem normal. Do you feel different than you did before the experiment?" the Colonel asked.

"Yes. I feel—I'm not sure how this sounds—more complete now. I felt somewhat incomplete before," she said.

"And that sandwich and soda, they aren't bothering

your stomach?" the Colonel asked.

"Not at all. Why would they?" Laura asked.

"Because you all, I mean, mutates, eat only flesh, right?" the Colonel asked haltingly.

"No. That's not right. We eat whatever is available. Lately that has been human flesh," she said, grimacing. "And the idea of that nauseates me to think about now, but we aren't limited to that. It was simply the easiest option. It was right there, plentiful. It's not like we're vampires or something that can't eat real food. We ate--*we eat*--based on opportunity."

"But don't you die after not eating flesh for a day?" the Colonel asked. "We had a subject that died when he wasn't fed."

"Are you sure that's why he died? Are you sure there weren't other variables involved? I mean, you likely had him restrained, yes?" Laura asked.

"Well, yes, we did," the Colonel said.

"And I'm guessing he fought against those restraints?" Laura asked.

"Most violently," the Colonel said.

"As would you in a similar situation, right? My guess is that perhaps the stress gave him some kind of MCI," she said.

"MCI—you mean a heart attack?" Wendy asked.

"Yes, I mean a heart attack. A myocardial infarction. I have a medical background. I kind of figured you did too," Laura said. "Pardon my use of professional terms."

Wendy and the Colonel looked at each other sheepishly, blushing a tad.

"We do. I guess we just didn't expect you to. Sorry. This is new to us. You were grunting and shrieking last week, and now you're using medical jargon. It's just a bit of an adjustment," Wendy said.

"Yes, we're all making adjustments of all kinds these days, aren't we?" Laura asked.

"Okay, next question. Why is it that some of you seem to revert to a lower sort of primate, like a Neanderthal or something, and you, and a few others, resemble homo sapiens more, and seem to have more upper level brain function?" Wendy asked.

"I don't know why. I only know that some of us are slightly different than others. Some of us are...smarter, to use a simplified word. We can communicate better, more clearly. We understand the surroundings more and can convey it," Laura said.

"How do you do that?" asked the Colonel. "How do you communicate?"

"It's complicated," Laura said. "Some of it is hormonal, some of it is through primal communication means, like grunts and shrieks. But—this will sound strange—I just kind of know what they're thinking. I'm not sure how. I'd say it's telepathy, but it's more than that. It's almost hive-minded, if that makes sense. I can read what the lower mutates are thinking, or know what they are likely feeling, and I can communicate to them what they need to do. I would suppose that the other alphas are the same way."

"Fascinating," said the Colonel. "So why do you direct them to eat flesh, rather than to break into a convenience store and steal Twinkies, for example?"

"To be honest, I'm not sure the former version of me could make them understand that. I knew, I always knew that grocery stores and convenience stores had food, but it was almost like I didn't have the words for those things, so it was just easier to eat what was around," Laura said.

"Do you know how to communicate that now?" the Colonel asked.

"Yes," said Laura. "I know how to communicate anything to them now."

"Wow," the Colonel said. "Why is that?"

"I don't know. I just can. I know I can. It's like I'm in touch with all of them," she said.

"Incredible. So, you know what the others in the lab are thinking?" the Colonel said.

"And feeling. Mostly they feel. They don't use higher thought processes. Mostly they have instincts that come from the reptilian part of the brain. But I can direct them. Get them to do what I want them to. In some respects, I always could, but now even more so," Laura said.

"Like a queen bee?" Wendy asked.

"Like a queen bee," Laura answered. "They are eusocial. Dedicated to the whole."

"How many are you in touch with?" the Colonel said.

"All of them. But my range is not unlimited. I'd really have to concentrate to know exactly how far, but if any are within range, I can feel them. Sense them. Talk to them," she said.

"Test yourself for a moment. We have been tracking a pack in the northern part of the city. Near Rockville. Can you feel them?" the Colonel asked.

"It doesn't work like that. They can't interpret the images they see, only experience them. In my current state, I can interpret them, but I can't just go and look for them. Do you understand?" she asked.

"Oh, okay," the Colonel said, a little deflated.

"Wait. Let me concentrate a little. Maybe I can see something I know," Laura said.

Laura Fisher closed her eyes. She took a deep breath, straightened her posture, and exhaled in a kind of meditation. Wendy stared at her. She couldn't believe how beautiful she was. Cleaned up and with her hair partially returned to normal, Laura now had an air of the alluring. Her orange skin made her look exotic, and her hair—now with the white swoosh going through it—accentuated that look completely. She had big, deep brown eyes and full lips that were almost white themselves, much lighter in shade than her glowing orange skin. She was well-spoken and smart—which added even more to her striking features.

Wendy found her thoughts going to a weird place. In addition to her scientific fascination with a now articulate subject of what she had been studying for weeks, Wendy felt a sudden air of hopelessness. How could she possibly compete with this woman, this creature, for the affection of Jake Fisher now? Before, when they were estranged, when Laura was little more than a beast who ordered the death of her husband, Wendy found herself in solid standing for an unpredictable future with the man she had become infatuated with. But now —this exotic, brilliant beauty in front of her made her feel suddenly ugly and unworthy. It began to deflate her—then she caught her thoughts flying wildly away and brought them back into the here and now—her test subject. Her science project was about to demonstrate her new abilities.

"There is a pack near the University of Maryland. I can see the buildings there. I recognize them. There are several packs on campus, actually," she said.

"College Park? How far is that, Ray?" Wendy asked.

"About fifteen miles," the Colonel answered. "You can read them that far away?"

"Yes. Maybe farther, but I don't know that I'd recognize where all of them are. But I know College Park. And there are several groups there, roving. There's only one alpha in the area now, and he's directing them," she said.

"You are communicating with him right now?" the Colonel asked.

"Yes. He, he sees me as his superior. He's reporting to me. His thoughts are much clearer than the lower mutates. They mostly send images, feelings, fleeting thoughts. He can almost put his thoughts into a more complete form. Like sentences, sort of, if that makes sense," Laura said.

"Unbelievable," the Colonel said. "Can you ask him things? Like, with your mind?"

"Yes. I can reach out to him with my thoughts and get things back from him. He's giving me a report right now of the groups he can sense. He's in charge of three packs in that area, but he's lost touch with one of them," Laura said.

"What's that mean?" Wendy asked.

"Give me a moment," Laura said. "He is asking me to find out what happened to one of the packs near there. He's lost his connection with them and wants to know if I can feel them or know where they are."

"Fascinating. This is just plain fascinating," the Colonel said.

Her face looked confused for a moment, almost in pain. Her eyes were shut, and she shook her head slightly as if to deal with unprocessed images.

"And I sense one near the College Park packs, but down nearer the water, lonely, looking for another pack to join. He's unable to contact any of them," she said.

"Can you tell what happened by reading his thoughts?" the Colonel asked.

"A little. It's different with the lower ones. Their thoughts are jumbled. All fleeting images that I have to try and put together. Let me concentrate a little," she said.

Wendy and the Colonel looked at each other in disbelief. Wendy shook her head as if in awe, and the Colonel caught himself smiling in wonder.

"The lonely one—he lost his family to violence," she said. "He's grieving and hasn't eaten in days. He needs to find another group. His own pack, they were killed. Humans that attacked them. Humans...on horses? That can't be right. Horses? I keep getting people on horses. I, I can see the images from his memory. Yes. Horses. Three humans on horses, with weapons. One has a sword, one has a bow, and the other I can't tell. Oh god, it was Jake and the boys."

"Your husband and sons?" the Colonel asked.

"Yes," she said, opening her eyes and shaking her head as if coming out of a trance.

"It was Jake and Tommy and Vinny. I saw them," she said. "On horseback. They killed the rest of his pack."

"Jake told us about that group he fought down by the water. Said the boys saved his life. You saw all of that?" the Colonel asked.

"If I concentrate hard enough, I can actually see fleeting images of their memories. This one I just made contact with— it ran into my own family, and it cost him his own," she said.

Laura's face looked in pain, almost as if she wanted to cry.

An awkward silence hung as Wendy and the Colonel eyed one another.

"Yes," she said. "I remember my family. I remember everything they did. Everything I did. I know you're wondering that."

"Can you read our thoughts too?" Wendy asked.

"Not completely. I can read your emotions somewhat, your feelings. I know kind of what you're thinking based on that," Laura said.

"How is that possible?" the Colonel said.

"I don't know. I just can," said Laura.

"Is that new?" the Colonel asked.

"Yes. At least the clarity that I now possess is new. It came to me after the experiment. After the explosion that nearly killed me and destroyed your lab. I can, in effect, read your thoughts," she said.

"What am I thinking, then?" the Colonel said.

"You are wondering how much you can learn from me about my kind. About the mutates. You're wondering if I can give you the information you'll need to eradicate them. Now you're wondering if I will agree to do that," she said.

"Unbelievable. That's exactly right," the Colonel said.

"And this one," Laura Fisher said, pointing at Wendy. "This one wants my husband."

CHAPTER 27—SET-UP AT THE O.K. CORRAL

"Holy fuck, that was close!" yelled Josh Rimone.

He had one hand mashing his cowboy hat onto his bald head, the other gripping white-knuckled to the seat beneath him on the motorcycle stolen by Boo Andrews.

"Having fun yet?" Boo said.

"Yeah, that was fun," Josh said. "And a little too fucking close for comfort. Oleg had me dead to rights."

"I thought you had it all under control. That's what you signaled to me," Boo said.

"I thought I did too. And then my two lies ran into each other," Josh said.

"Oleg and Father Joe? Together?" Boo said, laughing.

"Fucking nightmare," Josh said. "If I had just a few minutes either way I could've squirmed out enough to slide outta there. But those fuckers caught me lying."

"You couldn't Gomer-Pyle-it-up for them?" Boo said with a smile.

"I did. The stupid southern hayseed routine bought me what little time I had," Josh said.

"Which turned out to be just enough, thanks to the white knight on his steed," Boo said.

"Um, dude. Don't know if you have mirrors in your house, but," Josh grinned.

"Okay, black knight on his steed. Whatever. I saved your ass, and I am so deeply *not* in your debt anymore that it's not even funny. In fact, I'd even go so far as to say you owe me some now," Boo yelled over the engine's roar.

"Not gonna fight you on that. But this job isn't over. Those fuckers are gonna find us. They can hear the Harley's engine, for one. Why the fuck are they allowed to have such loud engines anyway? I actually got ticketed once for my Camaro being too loud, and it cost me two hundred bucks to get a specialized muffler for it. And these things sound like goddamn tanks," Josh complained.

"The Biker Gang Lobby has always been influential in Washington," Boo said.

"Must be all the golf they play with senators," Josh replied.

"So, what now?" Boo asked.

"Get our asses back to the farm ASAP," Josh began. "Then we gotta find a way to bring this thing to a close. We gotta set up a showdown."

"Like the O.K. Corral?" Boo asked.

"Wyatt Earp and Doc Holliday," Josh said. "Somebody ain't coming home after this."

"I hope it's not me. I kinda dig this hog between my legs," Boo said.

Josh leaned over and smirked at Boo.

"Too easy, dude. Too easy," Josh joked.

The two pulled up to Kristen's farm in high fashion, with the loud engine roaring and dust flying behind them.

"Where have you two been?" I asked. "And where'd you

get the Harley?"

"Boo had sex with a Hell's Angel," said Josh. "Then snuck away on his bike after he fell asleep when they were spooning."

"Dude," said Boo. "That's gross even for a gay guy to have to hear."

"Thanks Boo. The visual of you with a fat old guy with a long gray beard, though. Priceless. Can't un-see that in my head. Ever," I said.

"Josh here just tangled with Oleg and almost got himself killed. Thankfully, the dashing and handsome black knight swooped in and saved him," Boo said.

"Why do you have to be a black night? Did Josh make you say that?" I asked.

"You're so predictable now," Boo said. "I told you to let me stay a white knight."

"Speaking of white knights, where's our Blackbird?" Josh said. "We have to make some plans."

"The Blackbird is over here," Jake said, walking up to the house with Kristen.

"Wow. You called yourself that? This whole experience has been so healthy for you," said Josh. "You must be dealing with frustrations in a positive way now."

"You could say that. I just broke a guy's arm in a knife fight," said Jake.

"Nice! That's what I'm talking about. Positive expression of your feelings. Your therapy is almost complete. Whose arm was it?" Josh asked.

"John Segen. Asshole flunky of the preacher's. He and his sons kidnapped Kristen's daughter."

"Nat? Holy shit! Did you find her? Is she okay?" Josh asked.

"All taken care of," said Kristen. "Thanks for asking. We split up. Half of us went to the church to find Nat, the Fisher boys stayed here and mopped up the kidnappers."

"Where are those fuckers?" Josh said.

"In the corn crib. John Segen's arm's broken and his sons got knocked loopy. We're trying to figure out what to do with them," said Kristen.

"Kill them. Are you kidding?" Josh said.

"Told you," said Kristen to Jake.

"Josh, that's a bit extreme," Jake said.

"So's kidnapping, dude. I mean, who are these people? Snatching a young girl up? For what? Intel? You bet your ass I'd kill them. Want me to? I won't give it a second thought," Josh said.

"Just hold off a second," Jake said. "Let's debrief a little and figure out what we're doing next."

"Good plan," said Josh. "And we have some good news. We whittled the numbers down quite effectively. They had seven healthy Russian agents, and they're down to four now. Much more do-able for us."

"What do you mean, 'down to four?' What happened?" Jake asked.

"Short version? I convinced four of them that two of them were spies. When one of them killed the other two, Oleg shot him in the leg. He looked like he was gonna bleed out," Josh said. "Seven minus three equals four."

"Tell him the rest," said Boo.

"Then Oleg tried to kill me," Josh said.

"And then I saved him. Like a damsel in distress," Boo said.

"He did save me. Hate to admit it," Josh said.

"So, they have four now, and we have three ex-military, a VMI Keydet, a college wrestler, and a few others who have mixed it up a little. Still, I'd like to keep the others less involved if we can," Jake said.

"Limit collateral damage, huh?" Josh said.

"To paraphrase, there is no collateral damage. Just damage," said Jake.

"Fair enough," Josh said.

"Josh thinks we need to set them up and have a showdown. Get this thing done all at once. Especially now while they're reeling from their losses. They'll be in-fighting by now, doubting themselves, and really, really pissed off. Now's the time," said Boo.

"A final showdown, huh?" I said. "Like the O.K. Corral?"

"This kid gets it," said Boo.

"Don't compliment him. He gets surly," said Josh.

"I am not surly," I said. Josh laughed.

"So, what are your thoughts, Josh? Where do we have this showdown?" Jake asked.

"Not sure yet. Gotta think it through some. It needs to be in a place where we can use our numbers, maybe hit them from a distance. Boo brought some sniper rifles. Can your boys shoot?" Josh asked.

"Yes," said Tommy.
"We can," said Vinny.

"We can use them. Sniping from a distance. They'll be safe," said Josh.

"With Russian special agents running around?" Jake said.

"Safe-*er*, then. Away from the main action," Josh said.

"And where is the main action gonna be?" Boo said.

"I always like the home court advantage," said Josh.

"Not sure we should do it here," said Jake. "Kristen's husband and in-laws could come back anytime. I'd hate to see them hurt. Plus, you're advertising the place that Kristen and Natalie live in. It's bad enough John Segen and his sons know. How long do you think Kristen and Nat are gonna survive here if word gets out that they've harbored enemies of the church and live here in the sticks with no means of defending themselves?" Jake asked.

"Not for nothin', Jake, but that ship has sailed," said Josh.

"What do you mean?" said Jake.

"They're already in danger, and always will be so long as this church operates, so long as any of these people are alive and breathing. Either we go scorched earth and kill all of them, or Kristen and Nat are gonna have to find a new place to live," said Josh.

"Scorched earth?" Jake asked. "The whole goddamn town is in on this now at some level."

"So, you understand what I'm saying, then. Right?" Josh said.

A pained look overcame Jake's face as he turned to look at Kristen and Natalie. The home they had always known would have to become a stranger to them.

"Oh god, Kris, this is all my fault," said Maureen.

"No it's not," said Kristen.

"Yes, yes, it is," said Maureen. "I came here to you and they found us. I put you in danger. Now you have to leave your home."

"No different than you, right?" said Kristen. "Looks like we get to stay together a little longer."

Maureen and Kristen hugged. They both reached out for

Natalie, who joined in. Each of them dropped a few tears on each other. It was a poignant moment, and the rest of us felt like voyeurs on the outside looking in. Al DeFillipo walked over and hugged them all with his long, wiry arms and lay his head on top of Maureen's.

"Okay. Not here, then," said Josh. "Hmm."

"Hmm—what?" said Boo. "What does 'hmm' mean?"

"What if we took the fight right to them. Right in their backyard?" asked Josh.

"Their backyard, dude. You said it yourself," said Boo.

"But it's Jake's backyard too. And his sons. And every other fucking person here except you and me. They know the school as well as anybody, and way more than the Russians do. What if we met them on the fucking fifty-yard-line in the football field?" asked Josh.

"Are you serious?" I said. "That's too obvious."

"That's my point," Josh said. "Make it obvious. Force them to do battle there on the turf."

"That's insane," said Mark Longaberger.

"Actually, it sounds way cool," said Vinny.

"Gotta say, it does sound cool," said Tommy.

"They'll slaughter us. It's a killing ground," said Jake.

"It's a killing ground for both sides, Jake," said Josh. "And we're gonna get there first. They have no reason to guard that place now, right? I mean, there's no town meeting there this week is there?"

"No. They have no reason to use it now, to my knowledge," said Longaberger.

"What if we set up in the press box with snipers— Tommy and Vinny. Boo can stand guard there to protect them. He can snipe and also have a sidearm if somebody somehow makes it up the bleachers to the press box, however unlikely that is. There's a hill on the far side with some trees. I can set up there with another sniper rifle. All four of us can see anybody approaching. It's backed up to the hill. Nobody is coming from behind. They'll all be walking over from the school. We stand you guys in the center of the field, maybe bring the douchey Segen trio as even more bait, and taunt them into meeting you in the center of the field. Then we pick them all off as they make their way into the stadium. It's practically flawless," said Josh.

"They won't fall for it. They'll suspect something," said Jake.

"What are their options? You know of their existence; you know of their plans and their alliances. They have to come and kill you. What else would they do?" Josh said.

"They could try to circle around," said Jake.

"There's no circle. There's only one way to approach that field. And we will be all over it," said Josh.

"What if they don't send everyone?" asked Jake.

"Then we shoot whoever's there and whittle the numbers down more. Shit, we could even threaten the preacher guy that if he doesn't give them all up, we'll kill him too. He's a collaborator. Any of us would be within our rights. That slimy fucker is all about self-preservation," said Josh.

"Dad, it's a tight plan," said Tommy.

"It does sound like it could work," said Mark Longaberger.

"I admit, it doesn't sound bad," said Boo. "But Jake, you and your buddies are gonna be prime targets with bullseyes on your backs. Are you gonna be okay with being bait for the trap?"

"Did you bring any Kevlar?" Jake said.

"Tons," said Boo. "I got a dozen vests. I brought the kitchen sink, dude."

"I want every one of them wearing Kevlar," said Jake.

"Done," said Boo.

"Alright," said Josh. "Showdown at the O.K. Corral."

"I haven't been on that field since the 11th grade," said Tommy. "And I sat the bench most of the time anyway. This will be way more exciting."

"It should indeed," said Josh.

"So how do we set the trap?" I asked.

"First, we get all of you vested up in Kevlar, like Jake said. Then we arm you if at all possible. Then we sneak into the stadium and set up. Then we send the good Padre a little message he can't ignore. They're gonna be on edge anyway. They've had three agents die right in front of them in the cafeteria. It will be a big blow to confidence and momentum for the Russians, and it'll fuck with the locals big-time. Especially the squeamish ones. We'll need to capitalize on that. The Padre will want some closure on this shit," said Josh.

"So will Oleg," said Jake.

"Yes, he will. Jake, be careful with Oleg. That fucker's good. He doesn't miss anything, and he's smarter and tougher than the rest of them put together," said Josh.

"Well you two pick him off before he gets to the fifty-yard-line and I won't have to worry," said Jake.

"Why didn't I think of that?" said Josh.

CHAPTER 28—
CRUMBLING EMPIRE

Billy James was starting to sweat profusely but had just begun to loosen his wrists a bit on the shelving that he and his fellow church members had been tied to. There had been some grumbling, some accusations, and a good bit of confusion when the horde of people had descended on the church lobby and accused them of kidnapping. Billy hadn't known what to think about any of this, to be honest. He had conflicts about the Russian collaboration, he had misgivings now about his own pastor's intentions, and now he was somehow an accessory to kidnapping, though he hadn't known anything about it.

Pablo was sweating as well and was cursing at their now-departed captors in Spanish. Somehow, to Billy, Pablo seemed completely resolute. The idea of collaborating with Russians didn't bother a man who came from Spain and had lived in Mexico a portion of his life. But to a small-town country boy like Billy, everything seemed very un-American. For Pablo, the Almighty had a vision of what his church should look like, and that vision included straight Caucasian men in charge of everything. As soon as Father Joe had renamed the town New Plymouth, Pablo's devotion to the cause became unwavering.

There was also a portion of Billy that felt a little guilty about the racism the church seemed to be founded on. His wife, Roz, never seemed bothered by it, but they hadn't had much chance to discuss things since Father Joe's big town meeting and the arrival of the Russians. Billy definitely had questions he wanted to discuss, whether it was with a wife who didn't seem to respect him or a friend who had the same concerns he did. But Billy had always been a member of the church since he was a boy and had always taken direction from Father Joe without hesitation. There was no question that Father Joe was brilliant and understood long-term plans better than Billy ever would. Oddly, it was Billy's faith in Father Joe and in Christianity that kept him afloat as he struggled to free his wrists.

Emery was failing. His knees shook, his breathing was shallow, sweat poured down his shirt, and he struggled to stand. He was groaning, but it almost seemed to be from a panic attack. Billy hoped that someone would come cut their bonds and save them soon. It would not be long before he got his wish. His wife, Roz, and her friend Addie Segen walked in the front door inconspicuously gossiping about the town's new name and finding a way to capitalize on it by making merchandise with "New Plymouth" all over it.

"Oh, we can absolutely sell T-shirts," said Roz. "We need to get lots of colors, though. People like certain colors, and we really should have options."

"I always liked those T-shirt and baseball cap combos you see at some places, you know? Like a two for one deal? I think those would go over great," said Addie.

Then they looked to the left and saw everyone tied to the shelf.

And screamed.

It was hard to imagine to whom they were screaming, but panic was definitely the first reaction for both women.

"Roz, honey. Can you get me a knife or a pair of scissors please?" Billy said.

"Oh my god. Oh my god. Who did this to you? Who did

this? What happened?" Addie babbled.

"Roz, a knife, or some scissors?" Billy said.

Finally, Roz went to the receptionist's desk and grabbed a pair of scissors. After a few seconds hacking away at Billy's bonds, they broke, and he was free. Within a few moments, everyone else was as well. Emery dropped to his knees and grabbed his chest.

"Em, what's wrong?" Billy said.

Emery's face looked pale, almost to the point of having a blue tint to it. He struggled to breathe, then dropped over to his side. Roz began chest compressions, but he was completely unresponsive. No breath. No pulse. No movement. Emery Butler was dead.

"*Madre de Diós*," said Pablo.

"Oh my God, he just died," said Billy.

Pablo took a deep breath, closed his eyes, crossed himself, and turned to Emery's immobile body, then leaned in and began to make a crossing gesture over him.

"*Requiem aeternum donat eis domine, et lux perpetua luce at eis*," Pablo said.

"What was that?" Billy asked.

"I gave him his last rites in Latin. I am still Catholic, first and foremost," said Pablo

"I can't believe this," said Roz. "What the hell happened here?"

"A bunch of people came in and tied us to the shelves and started ranting about some kind of kidnapping," Billy said.

"What? A kidnapping? Who got kidnapped?" Roz asked.

"Apparently it was this one woman's daughter. She was

crazed, and she had a bunch of teachers—those friends of Jake Fisher's—come and tie us up while they ransacked the church. One of them was Pablo's daughter," Billy said. "And Mark Longaberger was with them."

"Is that true?" Roz asked Pablo.

"Sadly, yes. It appears my daughter is so far gone that she has no care for the well-being of others. She is an accomplice to murder now, in addition to her other sins," said Pablo.

"Those sons of bitches," said Roz. "And what was the bullshit about kidnapping? They just wanted to destroy the church and needed an excuse."

"Well, dear, they actually did come out of the back of the church with a young girl who had been tied up. A teenager," Billy said.

"What? Well, that doesn't condone murder," said Roz.

"I don't think they meant to murder Emery," said Billy.

"Well ask Emery if he cares what they meant. It all turned out the same, didn't it?" Roz said.

"Honey, there's something really wrong here," said Billy. "All of this. It's so, so weird. The new town name, the Russians, this kidnapping. All of it. It's wrong. We're fighting a World War with many enemies. We shouldn't be fighting amongst ourselves."

"Well, you go solve the world's problems, Billy, and I'll find a casket for poor Emery here," Roz said.

"Addie, they said it was your husband that did it," Billy said.

Adeline Segen's face went numb. Her eyes went flat, her expression turned to nothingness. She didn't answer, didn't confirm or deny. She just kind of vanished.

"Addie?" said Billy.

"Billy, leave her alone," said Roz. "These people killed one of your best friends. A man who helped frame this very church. And you're defending them? What the hell's the matter with you?"

"I'm not defending anyone. I'm asking questions. And Emery, God rest his soul, was not my best friend, and he was very, very old. It's sad what happened to him, and maybe it didn't have to happen, but look around you, Roz. Something here is very, very and I don't think I could see it until right now," said Billy.

She slapped her husband across the face.

"Be a man, for once in your life, William James, or I will leave you right here, right now," Roz said.

Billy held his hand up to his cheek, which was turning red while he glared at his wife.

"Billy! Do something!" Roz shouted.

"What would you have me do, dear?" Billy said. "I don't know where these people are, and I don't know what I'd do if I found them. They outnumber us, and they have weapons. And somewhere around here Jake Fisher and his sons are walking around. I'm not sure there's anything we can do. And I'm not sure what the whole story is. But maybe Addie can help shed some light on this."

"I said leave her out of it," said Roz.

"But she's in it, dear. Look at her. Look at her face. She knows. She knows her husband kidnapped that girl. She knows why that girl's mother came here to look for her. And she was right. The girl was here. I didn't like being tied up any more than you would, and I'm crushed that Emery had to die, but I can't shake this feeling that we are in the middle of something really bad here. I understand now why they did it. Look around you. What the hell has happened? The world is coming to an end. Cities are dead. We are a small spark of life in a dead country, and we're responding to that by renaming a town, dedicating ourselves to racist, homophobic propaganda, and kidnapping? Is this the church you want to serve? Ask yourself," said Billy.

"These people have been our friends for years. I'm not going to abandon them now. Can't you see that, Billy? We *are* somebody now. We matter. We're important. We run this church, we run this town, and there are only a few towns left in the whole state of Maryland. We are close to being the most important people in the state, and who knows how many states are even left out there? Do you even know that? No, you don't. Because you are a fucking spineless jellyfish, Billy! I could stand being married to a sheep, but not a jellyfish. I'm not going back to being a nobody. Never again. Get out. Get out of here now. We are through. Take your wishy-washy ass out of this church this instant. Do you hear me? Get out!"

Rozlyn James' last statements were screamed at a pitch Billy had never heard from her before. She was bordering on hysteria. Billy slunk out the door with his head down and his feet shuffling. He looked back over his shoulder. Addie was hugging his wife. Pablo was looking down at Emery. Everything Billy knew was crumbling before him, and even when he questioned it, those people he loved dug in. They doubled down on indefensible arguments. And in the middle of everything seemingly spinning out of control, they told him to leave. As he eased out the front door for what he thought would be the last time, he heard the PA system squawk.

"This is the Emergency Broadcast System with a message from the President of the United States," the message squawked.

A few seconds of static were followed by the familiar voice of the President of the United States, whose presence was absent for most of the past several weeks since the first bombs dropped. Besides one message spinning defiant rhetoric, the White House had been silent. Part of that was due to the mass communication destruction brought on by the Russians. But the man who had taken to social media daily to convey his thoughts before the war began had gone largely silent once bombs had been dropped on his country. That silence was broken.

My fellow Americans. It has been verified by numerous sources that China and North Korea have brazenly attacked our Pacific West Coast, bringing destruction and death at untold levels in Hawaii, California, Oregon, Washington, Nevada, Arizona, and Colorado. To avenge those American deaths, I have authorized a massive retaliation against both of those countries. Our Pacific fleet is launching intercontinental ballistic missiles at strategic locations even as I speak at Beijing and Pyongyang, as well as other strategic targets. Make no mistake. We are at war. And we are going to win that war on all fronts. We have been hit on the front porch by some countries, and we have been hit in the back door by others. We are the most powerful country in the history of the world, and our wrath will be felt by those countries foolish enough to engage us. May God bless us all, and God bless America.

Then the squawk returned. "This has been a public address by the President of the United States as part of the Emergency Broadcast System. Stay tuned in for further announcements as they come."

Billy's mouth hung open. Nobody had heard much news about the West Coast, and with New Plymouth and the former residents of Emmitsburg so caught up in all things Russian, it had been easy to forget that we indeed had many other enemies involved in the global conflict. The message had been vague and without much detail, much like the last one the President gave. Billy wondered how a President who had been so vociferous in the past could become a disciple of brevity now. Again, the thought went through his head: *Something isn't right here. Like really, really wrong. And it's time to do what my wife says and be a man. I'm out. I'm done with this place,* he thought.

The West Coast. That meant Los Angeles, San Francisco, Portland, Seattle, Phoenix, the NORAD defense system in Colorado. All of it gone, just like that? Billy shook his head in disbelief. Just then he heard footsteps running towards the church. Oleg and three other Russians—all of the bigger ones, Billy thought—ran by him and into the lobby. Billy hesitated a moment to watch what would unfold.

"Did you hear that message?" Oleg said. "All of it?"

"Yes," said Pablo. "We heard every word of it."

"And what did it say?" Oleg demanded.

"It spoke of attacks on our West Coast by China and North Korea, and the president mentioned retaliating against both of them," Pablo said.

"There was no mention of my country? No mention of Russia?" Oleg pressed him.

"No," said Pablo.

"You're certain. No mention whatsoever?" Oleg said. "Was the phrase, 'back door' uttered."

"I think so. I can't be certain, but I think so. Why?" Pablo said.

"*Shto eta?*" Buvaisar said to Oleg. "What is it, Oleg?"

"It may be nothing. Or it may be everything," Oleg said. "For now, however--for us, it is meaningless. Now we regroup, collect our weapons, and formulate a plan to find those men who taunted us, who caused the deaths of our comrades, who threaten everything we are doing...and we kill them. Slowly. We torture them for what they have done. Go. In the back and downstairs," Oleg said. "To the planning room. I will join you in a minute."

"Pablo, what is Emery doing on the floor?" Oleg said.

"He is dead, Oleg," said Pablo.

"What? How is he dead? How did this happen?" Oleg asked.

"There was a kidnapping. A young girl. Her mother, accompanied by all of the people you have been looking for, came in here with guns. They tied us to the shelving and took back the girl. Emery's heart failed. He died almost immediately. I don't know what to say. It all happened so quickly," Pablo said.

"What kidnapping?" Oleg said.

Silence. Pablo looked at Roz and Addie.

"What kidnapping?" Oleg demanded.

Addie looked at the floor. Roz had a pained look on her face.

"My husband," said Addie Segen. "He wanted to help with your investigation. He wanted to find out where those people, those criminals were who attacked you, the ones who were snooping around. He kidnapped a girl whose mother was a friend of theirs. He wanted to press her for information. He was going to trade her for the information. He wasn't going to harm her."

Oleg closed his eyes and pressed his lips together tightly. His nostrils flared.

"And they found the girl?" Oleg said.

"Yes," said Pablo. "She was in that room downstairs that you use, apparently."

"Did you know of this?" Oleg said to Pablo.
"No," Pablo said. "I am only learning of it now."

Oleg nodded slowly.

"And where is your husband?" Oleg asked Addie.

"I don't know. He hasn't come back yet," she said.

Oleg nodded silently again.

244

"And why did he not speak to me of this?" Oleg asked.

"He wanted to surprise you," Addie said.

"To surprise me?" Oleg asked. "Well, he has done that, hasn't he? Mrs. Segen, your husband may not be coming back at all. If he came into contact with either of the two men I encountered an hour ago or with this infamous Jake Fisher, it is possible that he is already dead."

"What? Why would you say that? What men did you encounter?" Addie screeched.

"Two men infiltrated the school and manipulated my team into harming itself irreparably. Then they escaped on a motorcycle. I believe it is likely that they are allied in some way with Jake Fisher," Oleg said.

"Jake Fisher? Who the hell cares about him? He's a crippled old man who can't get out of the way of his own ego," Addie said.

"This is the same man who singlehandedly killed three marauders with his bare hands and fought off four more at the local Wal-Mart, yes?" Oleg asked.

"Well, yes, but so what?" Addie said.

"Perhaps you should not take him as lightly as you do," said Oleg. "I know that I do not."

"But he's no match for my John," Addie said.

"No? And how many men has your John killed?" Oleg asked.

"None. But he's been in lots of bar fights. He can handle himself," Addie said.

"I have been told that Jake Fisher single-handedly killed seven Iraqi terrorists in Baghdad when he was a U.S. Marine. Was your husband in the military?" Oleg asked.

"Well, no, but," Addie stammered.

"I say again, it is possible you will not see him again if he decided to try to harm Jake Fisher or his friends. Your husband is a bungler who sought favor from people in power and influence, and he is now likely paying the price," Oleg said.

"Who the hell do you think you are?" Addie demanded. "If you're so tough, why don't you go do something about Jake Fisher?"

Oleg grabbed Addie Segen by the neck and shoved her hard up against the East wall of the church. He leaned in so close that he could smell the spearmint gum on her breath covering up the smell of stale cigarettes.

"I *am* 'so tough'. And I am going to skin Jake Fisher's sons alive in front of him before I kill him with my own hands. And once that is done, I am leaving this idiotic town and church to consume itself in its own twisted dreams of power and mediocrity. And if you are lucky, I will kill you as well and spare you the fate of the rest of your comrades. But right now, I think not. Right now I think it is much worse to let you live to see the failure of your husband, the failure of your church and town, the fall of your pathetic pastor, and the fall of your pathetic country. The thought of you living through all of that entertains me greatly," Oleg said.

He released her neck and turned to Pablo.

"Emery was a pedophile and a pervert," said Oleg. "I'm not sure why you tolerated him as long as you did. He is better off dead as well."

Then he spat and walked away to the back of the church.

"*Madre de Diós, no puede ser*," said Pablo. "*Es el diablo.* He is the devil."

Roz was crying, and now so was Addie.

"I'm done with this place," Billy whispered to himself at the door, as he turned to walk out. "Heaven help us all."

CHAPTER 29— SETTING THE TRAP

Tommy and Vinny Fisher were setting up their sniper rifles in the press box of the Hunter's Run High School Football Stadium. Boo Andrews had spared no expense. Each boy got a Barrett .50 caliber sniper rifle, a weapon deadly from up to two miles away in the right hands, with a bullet so large that it could blow a concrete block away on its path to a target.

"Jesus, Boo," Josh said. "You gave the kids Barrett fifty-cals? That's like giving hand grenades to kittens to kill smaller kittens."

"That analogy is so far off I'm not even gonna dignify it with an answer," Boo said. "But do you really want to be under-armed for this showdown?"

"Point taken. But how come I didn't get one of those?" Josh said, pushing his bottom lip out in a pout.

"Because you have to be able to move more quickly," Boo said. "You not only have to be able to hit a faraway target, you might have to run and shoot as well. You can't do that with a Barrett fifty-cal."

"Another point taken. Stop making so many good points. It sets a bad precedent," Josh said.

"You are getting the Wilson Combat Tactical Recon .308," said Boo. "It's super light, and still deadly up to 800 yards. Hopefully we won't need more than about a hundred yards, but in case we do, here you go."

"Nice. Really nice," said Josh. "Good choice. I'm glad I called you."

"Just call me the Candyman," said Boo. "Cause I mix it with love, and make the world taste good."

"And each one of Jake's buddies is wearing a Kevlar vest strong enough to stop anything that isn't armor piercing, apart from a direct shot at close range," said Josh. "Another good move. Did you give any of them handguns?"

"Not all of them. Some of them didn't know how to use one, and Jake thought that bullets flying everywhere might be a bad idea," said Boo.

"Good point. You Marines are such good point guys," said Josh. "What's Jake packing?"

"He's got a semi-automatic pistol, a Barretta 92 series," said Boo. "And a really wicked looking trench knife."

"And you?" said Josh.

"Same as you on the lightweight Wilson sniper rifle," said Boo, "and my preferred Walther P22 Rimfire pistol."

"Good taste. The man has good taste," said Josh.

"I gave Tommy and Vinny a couple of Glock .9 mm pistols too, in case things get dicey," said Boo. "Let's hope they don't need them."

"Let's hope," said Josh.

"So how are you going to get these guys to come to us?" Boo asked.

"That's already started. Kristen left the outside door cracked to the church's secret room. I left a little note scrawled on their white board there for the good Padre, complete with some Russian shit-talking," said Josh. "Then I called that fat-ass Wes Kent and taunted him. And finally, my coup de grace," said Josh.

"What's that?" said Boo.

"A really nice surprise. As it turns out, Hunter's Run's Wi-Fi is functioning. The net doesn't have much new stuff, but the Wi-Fi is essentially up and working. And I happened to have with me a super-secret spy device from a friend. It's like Bluetooth on steroids. It takes over everything within a mile radius if I want it to—if I ask it nicely. I currently have the PA systems in the church, the school's Main Office, and the gymnasium all tied in together and ready to go. We should be able to hear it on these big-ass speakers out here, too," said Josh.

"Now you're just showing off. You're trying to one-up me," said Boo.

"And I have," said Josh.

"How's your Russian?" Boo asked.

"Impeccable," said Josh. "Wanna hear?"

Josh looked down at the fifty-yard line. The small stage that Father Joe had used for his town meeting was still there, set up. Standing next to it were Jake, Maureen, Al, Kristen, Mark, Estela, Morgan, and me, of course. I wasn't crazy about being bait, but I wasn't gonna let these schmoes have all the fun, so I put on the heavy smelly vest that everyone else had on and stood next to the stage.

Then I heard Josh speak in Russian. I don't understand a word of Russian, but I asked Josh what his message was, and he gave me a small cheat sheet in English that he had written up. I'll sum up what he said here, translated for you.

Oleg—it's me. The guy who got your friends to shoot each other? Well, actually, you did some shooting too, didn't you? I have a message for you. Russians are pussies. I say that, and I immediately want to apologize to pussies for making the comparison. I am smarter than you, better than you, and I have been beating you at every turn. And now I have a present for you. Lots of presents, actually. Every person that knows your dirty plan and every person who has been a royal pain in your soft Russian ass is with me at the football stadium right now. All together on the field. It should be easy for someone like you. For anyone, actually, but I know that you are a broken old man commanding a group of soft, stupid Russian cowards, so this isn't anything more than a cruel taunt to you. If you have any testicles left, I invite you to come finish your business here. My friend Jake Fisher and I have a bet. Jake says you'll come because you're military, but I told him that only applies to American soldiers, not chicken shit post-Soviet Russians. I hope to see you soon!

"Well, I don't speak Russian...but I can say your tone and inflection sound every bit the smart ass you are in English," I said.

"Your affection is much appreciated," said Josh.

"What did you say?" I asked.

Josh gave a summary of the taunting language he gave— the one I gave just now.

"Wow. I'd be pissed enough to come here and try to kill you myself," I said.

"He's already pissed, believe me. Him losing three guys? Two of them he hand-picked because he knew them. That was all my doing. He wants to cut my dick off and shove it in my ear," said Josh.

"We're not gonna let him do that," said Boo. "At least not the ear part. That's just gross. Besides, it could get stuck in there and we'd never get it out."

"Are you suggesting that I'm so poorly endowed that my Johnson would actually fit in my ear canal?" Josh asked.

Boo laughed out loud at that.

"What is wrong with you two?" I asked. "We're about to have a giant shoot-out here and you're joking about each other's junk."

"It's how we cope, Princess," Josh said. "Marcus Aurelius said 'death smiles at all of us. All we can do is smile back'. You'd be surprised how many of us act like this right before a firefight."

"Actually, I wouldn't," I said. "Jake's like that too. Smart-ass to the end."

"Better than," Josh began.

"I know—better than being a dumb-ass. Jake says that too," I said.

"Well why don't you go and join your boyfriend down on the fifty-yard line so we can get this party started, huh?" Josh said.

"He's not my boyfriend. You macho types are all the same," I said.

"Wait, you're gay?" Boo said.

"You couldn't tell?" Josh replied.

"There's not a mark or a brand on people, you doofus," said Boo.

"No, but, you know," Josh said.

"No, I don't. What?" Boo said.

"He's a little light in his loafers," Josh said.

"Light in his loafers?" Boo asked.

"He behaves with a slightly effeminate mannerism," said Josh.

"See? You *can* use your words when you try," said Boo. "But effeminate doesn't equal gay. Gay is a preference for partners, sexually or romantically. Effeminate is a behavior trait that refers to being womanlike, and that may or may not reflect homosexual tendencies or preferences. Don't necessarily equate the two."

"Wow," I said. "You're articulate for an arms dealer."

"I went to William & Mary. So did Jake. We're smart people. Josh is smart too, don't let him fool you with his coarseness," said Boo. "We're deep thinkers. And that means you are as guilty of buying into stereotypes as our bald buddy here."

"Now wait a minute," I said.

"Stereotypes exist for a reason," said Josh. "They come from reality."

"Maybe, but reality and pre-disposition are two different things," said Boo. "I'm black. I like fried chicken. But I don't like fried chicken because I'm black. The two are not pre-disposed to mutual inclusion, even if eating fried chicken turns out to be a cultural norm for African-Americans. Eddie here is slightly effeminate. He's also gay. While that stereotype may exist in the world, it isn't a rule like one of Newton's laws of physics. Sure, stereotypes exist. They may even be representative of a culture—but they're not a default."

"God damn, we are covering some pretty heavy sociological shit today, aren't we?" Josh said.

Just then the walkie-talkie squawked, and I heard Jake's voice.

"Are you all done philosophizing yet, or can we get this murder-fest going? I see movement coming out of the school," Jake said.

"What? You heard all that? Did we have the PA on or something?" I asked Jake.

"I didn't hear anything. I just know Boo. He loves to hear himself talk and wax philosophic. Even more than I do. I just figured he was being himself and you two got caught up in it," said Jake.

I looked at Boo, who was deadpan.

"Dude, he just nailed you," said Josh.

I snickered.

"He's no better than I am," said Boo. "He's the same way. And besides, I've been holding the button in on the walkie-talkie the whole time anyway."

Josh and I both snickered and nodded skeptically. Boo frowned.

"Just go get in your spots," Boo said.

Josh grabbed his rifle and started walking toward the hill behind the bleachers and the tree cover there. I went down the steps of the bleachers to the field. Boo set up behind a trash can near the ramp entrance to the press box. The boys lifted the windows in front of their chairs, and I saw two large gun barrels poke out. Josh, Boo, and the boys all used the scopes of their rifles as a way to survey things from a distance. Jake and the rest of us were at a distinct advantage being at field-level. It got me a little worried.

"Are we gonna be alright down here?" I asked him.

Every single person on the field turned and looked at Jake after I spoke that question. Jake turned and looked at them for a moment before answering, feeling the gravity of everyone's anxiety all at once.

"No promises this time, Eddie. These people are gunning for us. They've always hated you and me. We knew that when they ran us out of our own school. They have been gunning for others of us ever since the girls discovered the secret room and the chemicals in the town water," Jake began.

Estela and Morgan smiled at us.

"They got deadly serious about it when another one of us played hero and prevented the girls from getting murdered," Jake said.

Mark Longaberger straightened and smiled.

"Then they added names to the list when others of us

aided, abetted, and harbored their targets," Jake said.

Al, Maureen, Kristen and Natalie smiled.

"We're all in this together. We can't keep running. We do this now, and then it's over, for better or worse," Jake said.

"You all know what to do when the shooting starts, right?" Jake asked.

"Yeah," Maureen said. "We all get underneath this stage, grab the stash of guns you have waiting there, and shoot at any legs we don't recognize."

"Guns?" I said. "I thought you didn't want us having guns for this."

I looked under the stage. There were easily a dozen pistols and one AR-15 lying beneath the stage near the middle.

"Holy shit, Jake! There's a goddamn arsenal under there," I said.

"I didn't want Oleg or his cronies to see us with weapons. They're sure to know it's a trap coming in, and they'll have something ready for us, no doubt. But I'd rather this crew look helpless now and have access to means to defend themselves if things go wrong," Jake said.

"There's a shit-ton of firearms in this stadium," I said.

"That's why Josh called Boo. It's what he does now. He sells arms to people who need them. He doesn't usually get mixed up in stuff personally anymore. That's just old debts," Jake said.

"I'm glad you two buried the hatchet. It's clear that you were very good friends before. It took something pretty serious for you to let all that go," I said.

"Yeah," Jake said. "I'm glad too. Really. I should've let all that stuff go long ago. And I'm indebted to all of you for helping me do that. Boo and I were very tight, and if we get out of this shitstorm maybe we can be again. Let's hope we all live long enough to see it come to fruition."

CHAPTER 30—
COUNTER MEASURES

Oleg waited. The four Russian agents were sitting on a bench outside the school, listening. His three teammates stared at him with wide eyes as they all listened together to Josh Rimone's insulting message in Russian. Josh's Russian was far from impeccable, as he may have claimed, but it was definitely adequate enough to achieve his goal. Buvaisar, Maharbek, and Aleksander were furious. They were animated. They were shaking with anger. Maharbek's left leg was firing up and down like a piston of nervous, angry energy. Buvaisar was pacing back and forth angrily. Aleksander was sneering and fondling his pistol.

And Oleg sat perfectly still.

"How can you just sit there?" Buvaisar said. "You heard what the American bastard said about us? And you just sit there? What is wrong with you?"

"I want to kill him myself with my bare hands," said Aleksander.

"We are going, *nyet*? We go to kill him now," said Maharbek.

Oleg just sat motionless with no expression.

"Oleg, tell me you are not going to kill him," said Buvaisar.

Oleg looked at Buvaisar.

"Of course we are going to kill him, *suka blyad*," said Oleg. "We are going to kill them all."

"Then let's go!" shouted Buvaisar.

"Slow down Buvaisar," said Maharbek. "It may be a trap, you know?"

"Of course it's a trap," said Oleg. "Why do you think they are openly inviting us?"

"Because they are arrogant Americans who like to talk," said Aleksandr. "Because now that we are only four, they think they can defeat us. That is why they call us pussies."

"They call you that to make you rush into a trap they have set for us. Don't be a fool," said Oleg.

"Don't tell me you're not going in," said Buvaisar. "Our comrades need to be avenged. If you won't do it," he paused.

"Calm yourself Buvaisar. They will be avenged. But we need to be intelligent about this. Yes, it is almost assuredly a trap. But many times, the hunter loses himself when he looks to trap the bear. We will need to put them on the defensive. Who among you is the best shot from long distance?" Oleg said.

"That would be me," said Maharbek. "I had highest scores in sharpshooter school."

"We will put you on the school roof with my sniper rifle," said Oleg. "And you will pepper them with shots. Make them run. Make them scatter. Pick off as many as you can from that distance. The three of us will enter together, hands raised. Then the fastest of you..."

"That would be me," said Buvaisar.

"You will run to the concession stand and hide in the entrance there, taking as many as you can. They will run and panic in the confusion, and Aleksandr and I will get hostages.

Preferably women. Americans are soft. They will surrender if we threaten a woman. A few cuts with a knife to the wrist and they will watch her begin to bleed out, and then they will surrender," said Oleg.

"Then what?" asked Aleksandr.

"Then we slaughter them all and leave this hell-hole," said Oleg. "Maharbek, get all of the ammunition you can for our best sniper rifle. There should be enough for perhaps fifteen shots. You will need to conserve them, as you will act both as our distraction and also as our backup. Save five shots for the finish at the end. Take your ten shots at the beginning where you see them set up. We will coordinate with transmitter and receiver, and I can tell you where to look."

"What do you want me to do?" asked Buvaisar.

"The entrance to the stadium has a covered area protected on two sides by brick walls. You will be safe there. Your job will be to harass them even more, once Maharbek begins. When you see them react and move, you react and move. You will use the Kalashnikov and your Yargin. Kill as many as you can. Move quickly. Shoot and then take cover, and then move and shoot again. Your job will be the most fun. You will be like American cowboy," Oleg said.

"I like this job," said Buvaisar. "Run back and forth. Kill as many as I can. Yes. I can do that."

"Alek, you and I will be the biggest targets. We will offer ourselves up as if we are surrendering. We will need to carry two pistols. One clearly visible, one hidden. We will offer ourselves up with Buvaisar, convincing them that there are only three of us left. Then when Buvaisar runs, it will look like he has broken ranks. They think they have made us break ranks already, so we will use it to our advantage. You and I will pretend to plead for mercy, walking up to the stage in the middle of the field where many of them are waiting. Then once the shooting begins, we will run to the middle, grab two hostages, and force them to surrender. You are the strongest. If any of the men come to stop us, you must stop them first," Oleg explained.

"I will stop them. Don't worry," said Aleksander.

"Buvaisar and Maharbek, be sure to listen to your communication devices. Once Aleksandr and I have hostages, we will need to talk to them. Lull them into thinking they know what we are going to do. Get them to lower their guard. Then, when I give the signal, we finish them. Does everyone understand his role?" Oleg asked.

"*Tak tochno*," they said in unison. "Yes, sir."

Oleg smiled.

"Yes. We know our jobs. Now let's go partake in our favorite sport," said Oleg.

"Killing Americans."

CHAPTER 31— NEGOTIATIONS

Wendy's eyes bulged and her mouth slid agape. Laura Fisher was looking at her, finger directly pointing at her face. And she was smirking.

"What? No, I, uh, I just. Jake is my friend, that's all. My friend," said Wendy.

"And you want him," said Laura. "I can smell it on you when you say his name."

"Look, Jake saved my life. I'm very thankful for that. That's all," said Wendy.

"I can also tell when you're lying. And you're lying," Laura said.

"How can you know that?" asked the Colonel.

"I don't know," said Laura. "I just do. I'm certain of it. Just like I'm certain now that you are nervously wondering if I can find high level classified information by reading your mind."

"Oh," the Colonel said.

"Don't worry. I can't. It doesn't work like that. It's instinct. Pheromones. Smell, some logic. All of that bundled into some kind of truth that buzzes in my brain. I know that you, also, hold my husband in high esteem," said Laura.

"I also owe Jake my life," said the Colonel.

"You poor fools," said Laura. "If you only knew him like I did."

"Well, we don't," said Wendy. "So let's just move on."

"Wow, you're really uncomfortable right now," said Laura. "I think there's much, much more to this. You don't just find him attractive. You're in love with him, arent' you?"

Wendy scowled and looked at the ground.

"It's easier to reduce it to saying that he saved your life, and you're thankful, though, isn't it?" she asked.

An awkward silent moment hung in the air as Wendy scowled at Laura.

"Maybe you should be thankful too," said Wendy sharply.

"What do you mean?" said Laura.

"He saved your life too," Wendy said.

"Ha! How did he save my life?" said Laura. "By hunting me down and killing my packmates?"

"By going after you, that's how," said Wendy. "Even though you tried to kill him."

"He saved me? By going after me? How do you figure that?" Laura sneered.

"Because that man over there was going to have every one of you killed by his brigade," Wendy said, pointing at Colonel Cannaveral.

That caught Laura off guard. She looked nervously at the Colonel, who looked tense as well. Wendy rose to her feet and pointed at Laura's face.

"That's what they were all going to do. There's a task force created just to end all of you. And that's what would have happened if Jake hadn't come down here to get you, and then everything changed. We no longer studied your kind to slaughter you, we studied to save you. And we did. You are now not only much closer to human; you've acquired special abilities. None of that happens if Jake doesn't risk life and limb to get to you. And it surely doesn't happen if you succeed in killing him. If that had happened, they'd have cut you all down in the subway and moved on. So maybe you ought to be thankful to your husband as well," Wendy said.

Laura's face went cold, and her eyes thinned a bit.

"Whatever," Laura said. "When you hear what I have to say, none of that will matter anyway."

"What do you have to say?" the Colonel asked.

"I'm going to make you an offer, Colonel. One you can't refuse. Though I doubt that you have the authority to give me the answer yourself."

"Okay, you have my attention. What is your offer?" the Colonel asked.

"You want to study my kind. That was harder before I gained the ability to communicate. Now, thanks to you all, I have a lot more than that. I know things about my kind. My race. My—dare we call it species? I can give you that information that you seek. I know it intrinsically," said Laura.

"How do we know you won't lie to us?" Wendy said.

"Because I have no reason to. We don't have some grandiose war strategy. We are a new species trying to understand itself, and only a handful of us can even do that in part. I can't stop you from killing us by withholding information. But I might be able to stop you by *providing* information," Laura said.

"Okay, now you really have my attention," said the Colonel. "How can you convince me that you all aren't a threat that needs to be eradicated? Especially when you've killed people I know in front of me and tried to kill my friends."

"I can control them. All of them. They will do what I say. I'm the highest form, which makes me the queen bee. As I said before, they are eusocial. Hive-minded. I can make them do anything, because their new DNA configuration tells them to do what the alphas tell them, because the alphas know what's best for the hive. And I am *the* alpha and the omega," said Laura.

"Okay, that was creepy," said Wendy. "Now you sound like you're power-crazed."

"I have power. It's not a boast, just a fact. For whatever reason, the weapons didn't kill me, and they didn't turn me into one of the lower primate versions of my kind. And now, thanks to you, my status is as high as it can get. It's just the way things are," said Laura.

"So, what is it that you want, then, in exchange for your cooperation?" Colonel Cannaveral said.

"I want to live. I want *us* to live. I want a place where we can be alone and thrive, and the world won't bother us because we look or sound different than they do. I can help my kind cooperate and build a society, but I can't do it if we have to live off of corpses in the subway tunnels and have to run from being hunted all the time," Laura said.

Wendy and the Colonel just looked at each other.

"That's an intriguing offer," said the Colonel. "But we hunt you because you hunted us first. You might be evolved, but my first dealings with your 'species' was locking myself in a lab and nearly starving to death while your people ate my friends. If I turn you loose, what's to say you don't use that space to kill and eat my species?"

"I understand your skepticism. This is all new for you. But it's new for me too. I can't explain some of the things I know now. I just know them. And I know that I can help us make a society. But we need space, and time, and resources, and we need to be left alone," Laura said.

"You're looking for an Indian Reservation deal," said Wendy. "Land and autonomy in exchange for peace."

"That may be an oversimplification, but essentially, yes. That would be fine," said Laura.

"The Native Americans got an enormously raw deal on that," said Wendy. "Ask them now if they think they were treated fairly."

"Not my problem," said Laura. "I would agree that what we did to the Native American population in this country is about as horrific as anything anyone in the world has done in history. But that's not my concern. We can raise our own food, subsist on what we have, and not bother any humans. In exchange, I'll give you everything I know and cooperate with you, and I'll order my people to cooperate with you. You won't get a better deal than that."

The Colonel sat up straight in his chair and inhaled. Wendy looked nervously back and forth at him and Laura.

"Besides, if you change your mind, and we're all in one place, we're easier to exterminate," said Laura.

Wendy shivered at the brutal accuracy of the comment.

"You're right," the Colonel said. "And we won't get a better deal than that. But it's going to take some time, some politics, and this decision is so far above my head it's not even worth mentioning. And let's not forget this is low on the priority list. We're in World War III, our president barely shows himself, and our communications systems need major repair before we can coordinate cross country."

"All of that is true. I don't expect miracles. What can you give me in the meantime?" asked Laura.

The Colonel thought about it for a minute. Wendy

tapped her foot nervously.

"I am basically in charge of Washington D.C. right now. That could change, but I'm in charge of the CBRNE battalion in this area and we have jurisdiction over the city. They have cleaned many of the streets of the dead, but we haven't gone into any residences, apartment complexes, or anything like that. To my knowledge, a small percentage of people in the city survived. There are some that made it into bomb shelters—especially the military and the politicians—but regular people just died where they stood. Give me a few days to locate a housing facility for you. Once it's been established, you and the local members of your group—are you okay with us calling you 'mutates'? The members of your group can live there and clean up the dead bodies to use as you see fit. There's no way we can give all of the casualties in the area the burials they deserve. It's a prudent, expedient, and even somewhat harsh answer, and if I'm ever pressed on it—which I doubt will ever happen--I can simply say that the mutates cleaned the bodies out. Once you're established, you can reach out to other mutates in the area, begin gathering them here. Then we can transport them to a location of your choosing if it's approved by the Department of the Interior, assuming I can even find that guy. It's not much, but it's a start," the Colonel said.

"It is a good start. I can live with that, and I will work in conjunction with you two daily to help you gather information. You can inoculate my people to make them non-contagious for Ebola so that your people are safe, and the information exchange can begin. Once we get started, we can start negotiating on a place of my choosing for my people to go and live," Laura said.

"Are you going to try and build a civilization? Like, raise babies or something?" asked Wendy.

"I don't think we can reproduce. I'm not sure why I know this, but I have no sexual urges whatsoever and neither do the lower primates, and we should have seen something like that by now. I think the radiation ended all of that. But sadly, child-age mutates do exist. And no, Colonel, I don't mind that term, I suppose. All it takes is one Russian bomb anywhere near children are living. Those children will need to be raised, grow, and become adults that contribute to the society as well. But it is not a self-sustaining civilization by your definition," Laura said.

"But then won't you just die out?" asked Wendy.

"Not as long as the Russians keep using that weapon we won't," Laura said. "We already will have several generations to tend to as it is. That will be enough for us."

Wendy's eyes widened a bit and she turned to look at the Colonel, who nodded solemnly.

"And what happens if something happens to you, Laura Fisher? What if you die, and there's no one to lead the mutates? Will it just be chaos, then?" asked Wendy.

"That's actually a good question. Pretty much all of this hinges on a single person: you," said the Colonel.

"I would like to see if I can train the alphas to use more of their brains, to get closer to where I am. I think it can be done, at least to an extent," said Laura. "Maybe your Lieutenant Mazzaros can bring his chemistry set to a less combustible place and try to repeat the process."

Laura smiled at her own joke. Wendy raised her eyebrows and almost caught herself laughing.

"We'll have to see about that. That machinery isn't cheap to utilize," said the Colonel.

"Neither are thousands of guns, assassins, and clean-up crews you'll need to eradicate us. Nor are the excavators you'll need to bury the tens of thousands of mutate bodies you'll have from wholesale slaughter," said Laura.

"Alright, alright, you make a good point. No need to guilt me into trying something. I'm going to cooperate with you. I think it's in everyone's best interests to do so. The President has delegated lots of daily operations to the military and isn't worried about policy so much. Hell, we're not even sure we can assemble Congress just yet. We haven't gotten accurate counts for anything. So let's move ahead with this part of the plan. I will get on the horn with the Secretary of the Army. He's a member of the Joint Chiefs and can get me answers quicker than anyone, and I know that he's alive. You, in the meantime, can stay here in the residential apartments that exist in the Pentagon. Wendy and I are already staying here, so you'll be under our charge," the Colonel said.

"*She* is in charge of me?" said Laura. "She's a chemist. Why would she have any say over what I do?"

"She's been on the front lines of the mutate issue since day one and knows as much or more about your biochemistry than any other person in the country. Maybe the world. She is still leading all studies in this arena," said the Colonel.

"But I am going to provide you with everything you need. She's unnecessary," said Laura.

"She's even more crucial now. Someone has to do something with all of that information that you're going to provide. Sorry, it's non-negotiable," said the Colonel.

"Hmmph," said Laura. "Well that's going to be pretty awkward, then, isn't it? As soon as Jake gets wind of all of this, he'll be here in no time. And then we all get to stand in a room together. Won't that be fun?" Laura laughed mockingly.

Wendy frowned at her.

"Don't worry, dear," said Laura. "I won't torture you for too long. I have much bigger plans out West."

"Out West?" asked Wendy.

"Yes. You see, for reasons outside my control—thanks

to both the Russians and you, your Colonel and that cute Lt. Mazzaros—I am a new creation in charge of a new species. They are my family now. It's not that I don't love my sons. I do. And I want them to be okay. But there is a higher calling now that I can't explain. I need to take my fellow mutates to a place that is hard to get to, deters visitors due to its isolation in a harsh environment, yet has enough resources to sustain us indefinitely," said Laura.

"Pretty specific description," said Wendy.

"So, what are you asking for?" asked the Colonel.

"Zion, Utah. I want Zion National Park. And that, too, is non-negotiable," said Laura.

CHAPTER 32—
CAMP DAVID

The chopper landed at Camp David on the helipad. The wind from the blades blew into the surrounding trees in the beautiful landscape of the Catoctin Mountains. Men dressed in black suits surrounded the area, and one in particular ran up to open the chopper door and help the passengers out. He reached up and offered an arm, and an older man dressed in a blue blazer, a rumpled white buttoned-down shirt, and khaki pants took it. He stepped down from the chopper with his free hand holding onto his hair, which was blowing in every direction due to the chopper blades. He released the other man's arm and started walking towards an array of golf carts all parked in rows at the end of the helipad. All of the men surrounding the chopper got into one of three of the nearly dozen golf carts waiting nearby. The one who had run to the chopper first got in the driver's seat with the older man and turned to him.

"Welcome to Camp David, Mr. President."

The President nodded in acknowledgement and pointed at the winding golf cart path and simply said, "Aspen."

"Yes sir," said the driver, and he set off on the cart path to the Aspen Lodge, one of the main cabin areas used for hosting the President, his family, and any guests.

"Are my people here already?" the President asked.

"Yes sir. The Joint Chiefs, the Defense Secretary, and your personal staff all arrived about fifteen minutes ago. They had to go through the checkpoints at the intersection of Route 15," the driver said.

"They took the main roads?" the President asked.

"Yes sir. They wanted to see Frederick, gauge its status. The Joint Chiefs actually drove past Fort Detrick briefly," he said.

"Good. I want to hear about that," the President said. "And radio up to Aspen and tell them to get lunch going. I'm fucking starving."

"Right away, sir," the driver said.

The driver picked up his walkie-talkie and radioed the President's demands to the kitchen staff, who were already on call. They began preparing frantically. The President's personal staffers relayed the number of people being fed and their preferences, and the kitchen staff, always prepared for such quick and demanding turnaround, rose to the occasion.

Standing outside in the shade of tall, ancient hardwood trees surrounding the compound were the Joint Chiefs of Staff. Included in that group were the secretaries of the Navy, the Army, and the Air Force, as well as the highest-ranking officers from the Marines and the newly created Space Force. Each was in full dress uniform, which meant that each suffered from the sweltering summer heat. It was considerably better than the humid Washington D.C. weather. The cool Catoctin Mountains provided an easier atmosphere by comparison, but anyone who has ever worn a military uniform in the summer understands the challenges of trying not to perspire so profusely as to draw attention. Large outdoor fans aimed at the walkways were a big help.

"Is he here yet?" General Peery of the Navy asked. "It's hot as hell out here."

"He's here," answered General Steers of the Army. "Didn't you see the chopper?"

"All I saw was sweat in my eyes," said Peery.

"It shouldn't be long now," said General Baughman of the Air Force. "That old bastard won't go ten minutes without a sandwich."

The other generals laughed. All of them were colorful, old school soldiers with years of experience and knowledge earned from careers spent all around the world. They talked tough, straight, and plain—like soldiers—but each held advanced degrees and blistering intellects. And each had strong and relatively thorny personalities.

"You all right Greg?" Baughman asked Marine Corps General Greg Gibson, a powerfully muscled African-American Marine whose arms were too big for his sleeves.

"Yeah, I'm fine. Thanks Wayne. I'm just hot, like Ed is. Wouldn't mind getting inside. I mean, the shade here is better than the sun in D.C., but I still wouldn't mind some AC instead," said Gibson.

"So is the new guy here?" Gen. Baughman asked.

"The Space Force guy?" answered Gibson. "I think he's already inside, with the Homeland Security people."

"That makes him smarter than us," General Peery said. "Let's just meet him inside."

"I'm with you," said Gibson.

The four generals entered the building and walked into the living room area of the Aspen Lodge, where lunch was being served on this day. The President himself stayed in Aspen, and he preferred to host gatherings in his own quarters, strongly favoring a "home court advantage" when bandying words with the Joint Chiefs. Each Joint Chief would be staying in his own cabin on the grounds of Camp David, whose facilities were simultaneously rustic, technologically advanced, and marvelously complete.

A man in a black suit entered from the Western entrance and announced, "the President of the United States." The members of Homeland Security and Space Force rose from their seats on the couches. The Secretary of Defense and the Joint Chiefs were already standing. The President breezed in with a half-hearted wave and sat down at the head of the table.

"Gentlemen, let's eat first. I could devour a goddamn bear by myself right now, and I'm sure as hell not going to discuss business on an empty stomach," the President said.

The catering staff then brought out the feast, which included numerous artisan sandwiches, salads, drinks, and desserts. The group ate voraciously and quickly, knowing the President to be one who tended to wolf down his meals with blinding speed and then sit impatiently for everyone to finish, usually interrupting everyone's dessert to get started. The Defense Secretary and the Joint Chiefs knew this drill, and each of them began eating his dessert early. The newly appointed Secretary of the Space Force, however, was in his first such meeting, and was trying to make a good impression by eating slowly and methodically.

It didn't work.

The President started speaking, and the catering staff immediately took the hint and began quietly clearing the table. The Joint Chiefs had quickly finished their meals and the Space Force General, Michael Moyer, had only gotten through half of his sandwich and hadn't touched his dessert before he found to his dismay that the caterers had removed all of it from his presence. The President's staffers had replaced those meals with briefs printed and bound for each member to refer to and peruse.

"Alright gentlemen, I'm going to need a verbal status report on each front, if you please," said the President.

An awkward pause ensued as General Moyer looked confusingly at his bound report, then looked around at the other Generals, whose lips were pressed tightly together.

"It's all in here, correct?" Gen. Moyer said.

"Yes," Gen. Gibson replied. "It's in there."

"Then, why are we...?" he began.

"I don't read those," the President said. "I'm a people guy. I prefer to hear it from people. You all are people. So, let's hear it. Ted, you want to go first?"

Theodore E. Steers, the Secretary of the Army was a smallish, dark-haired man with glasses and sharp features. Thin, wiry, and with a look about him that suggested he didn't miss a detail, Steers had been at his post for over a decade like most of his colleagues.

"Well, Mr. President, we have mobilized troops in Europe and Asia, and they are moving towards points in Moscow and Beijing. They have slowed due to air resistance from the North Koreans, and before we advance any further, I wanted to request some support from General Baughman and the Air Force," Gen. Steers reported.

"Wayne?" said the President.

"Logistically speaking, Mr. President, we have a cluster-fuck. I need carriers to get my largest, newest, fixed-wing aircraft into Asia, but currently the Navy is tied up getting fighter jets there," said Baughman.

"Ed?" said the President.

"He's right, Mr. President. Due to the emergency response we've had to muster for the first round of bombs, all aircraft carriers are currently in use. My suggestion is either land-based or short-range aerial refueling options for the Air Force until such time as we get a carrier free, and even then, it's gonna be months getting them back to the states."

"I hear you, Ed," said Gen. Baughman. "Our only other viable option is getting them to Alaskan bases for refueling, but the Russians hit us hard there, sir. I'm not sure what weapon they're using—I'm guessing it's chemical—but every single person on all nine of our military bases in Alaska is dead. And I have some really weird-ass reports coming in from fly-byes that said there's some kinda orange things roaming around the bases that are attacking anyone who comes near."

"Orange? Are they bears or something?" asked the Defense Secretary.

"Bears?" echoed Space Force Secretary Moyer.

"That was my thought too, but we have pictures. They are humanoid, but most of them hop around like monkeys or apes. There are a few that walk upright. They all have white hair and are wearing some semblance of clothing. I don't know what the fuck they are," said Baughman.

"Are you kidding me? Orange things? Apes?" said General Gibson.

General Baughman tossed color printouts from the Air Force surveillance planes he sent. Clear shots of mutates roaming around the Alaskan military bases slid across the table to the President.

"Actually, gentlemen, I've seen these. And so has Secretary Steers," said the President.

"The Army is currently working on a project in Washington regarding these creatures under Army Colonel Raymond Cannaveral, who is commanding the CBRNE brigades out of Maryland and Virginia," said Steers. "Preliminary reports indicate that these are mutated human beings that did not die as a result of the new Russian weapons, which seem to be a combination of a new kind of radioactive bomb that creates an exploding airborne version of the Ebola virus," said Steers.

"Jesus, Mary, and Joseph," said Gibson. "Exploding airborne Ebola. That'll kill millions."

"It already has, Greg," said Steers. "Except for the naturally occurring small percentage of people immune to Ebola. Those poor devils mutate into those creatures, which Col. Cannaveral has dubbed 'mutates.' Apparently, they are carnivorous and aggressive, as well as carriers of the virus to anyone who gets close."

"Dear God," said Peery. "What are we doing in response to that?"

"Well, Ed, CBRNE has cleaned up most of Washington, which is why you likely didn't see any while we were there. They're studying them intensely at the Pentagon and have made some very considerable advances in short time. Ray— Col. Cannaveral, that is—is due to contact me very soon with some updates. He narrowly escaped them in what we believe was the first contact anywhere at Fort Detrick. Ray believes that the lead lining in the walls of his lab spared him from death or mutation, which could be a key to surviving future Russian attacks from this kind of radiation, called Brenerium."

"That's a lot of information, Ted," said Gibson. "How is it we're all just hearing this now?"

"A lot has happened in just a span of a few weeks, Greg. Col Cannaveral has some of the best minds from NIH working with CBRNE. The problem is that apart from the massive amount of death caused in small areas by these Russian weapons, we also then have to contend with the mutates that remain in those cities where the bombings took place. There are theories circulating," Steers began.

"Theories?" asked the President.

"It, it might not be prudent to put forth any theories just yet, Sir," said Steers.

"Come on. Out with it. We don't hold back in here," said

the President.

"Well, sir, Colonel Cannaveral has postulated that the Russians may have gone with this type of weapon in the cities in order to minimize the damage to infrastructure," said Steers.

"But why would they want to do that?" asked the President.

"Well sir, Col. Cannaveral's conjecture is that the Russians want to take over the U.S. and move in themselves," Steers said.

"What?!" said Peery. "You mean physically take over the United States, as in occupy us?"

"That's the guess, Ed," said Steers.

"That's crazy," said Gibson.

"Maybe crazy like a fox, General," said Moyer.

"What do you mean, Mike?" asked Gen. Gibson.

"I'm just spit balling here, but the Russians only have one legitimate warm-water port in the Black Sea, and that's problematic. They're surrounded by enemies—Ukraine especially right next door—and getting ships through the Dardanelles is extremely difficult. The Bering Sea is frozen for a portion of the year, and so is the North Sea and the northern Atlantic. Taking over the United States provides them with arguably the greatest natural resources in the world by far and another country to colonize for Mother Russia," said Moyer.

"Countries don't just take over entire other countries anymore," said Gibson. "That hasn't happened since World War II."

"That's because of the balance of power and alliances like NATO," said Moyer. "But if you have the ability to do it, and the whole world is at war, to the victor go the spoils. While we're dicking around with North Korea and China on the West Coast and Cuba and Venezuela in the Gulf of Mexico, Russia is sliding right in by killing our urban population," said Moyer.

"That's nonsense," said the President. "I don't believe that theory for one second."

"It actually sounds pretty goddamn brilliant to me," said Baughman. "Underhanded and conniving just like those Rusky bastards."

"It could make sense," said Peery. "It would also explain why the Chinese and North Korean attacks are so limited."

"How's that?" asked the Defense Secretary.

"Well, if Russia is trying to move in, they're running this show. They give Central Pacific targets to the Chinese and the Koreans to appease them. They let China take out NORAD in Colorado. But the real prizes are the cities of the Central Plains and East Coast. There are ports in the Gulf of Mexico, in the Great Lakes, and all across the Atlantic. And that would also explain why the Mexicans are neutral in all of this. Depending on the result, they could theoretically have new neighbors," said Peery.

"We're the strongest country in the world. We have the best technology and the best people in history. No one is going to take us over just because of a few bombs," said the President.

"And a few—what were they called Ted, mutates?" said Gibson.

"Mutates or bombs be damned," said the President. "We just launched a shit ton of missiles at China and North Korea, which should get them off our ass in the Pacific."

"Except in Hawaii," said Peery. "They're occupied already."

"And Alaska," said Baughman. "Nobody's left there, and

the Russians want it for the oil and natural resources."

"Fuck Hawaii and Alaska," said the President. "They're not even real states, and they didn't vote for me anyway. We're protecting the continental forty-eight states just fine. I want to see plans for improvement on taking Asia and South America quickly. You guys solve your goddamn logistical problems or you can find yourselves new jobs."

"But Mr. President," said Baughman.

"But nothing, Wayne. That's it. Now I want to talk to Space Force," said the President.

"Yes, sir?" answered Moyer.

"Do we have any laser defensive weapons up and running up there?" the President asked.

"Well, sir, it's hard to tell due to the massive satellite damage in the first bombings. They took out all our communications. In fact, it's the number one problem in the country right now. People don't really know anything," Moyer said.

"Can't they just use the Internet?" the President said.

"It's not up everywhere, Sir. The transmitters are down all over the place. It's not reliable, and people in the country who don't have access to cable have virtually nothing but the Emergency Broadcast System, and that's assuming they're listening to the radio. It's like the left hand doesn't know what the right hand is doing, sir. We're the only ones who really know what's going on, and we're way behind," said Moyer.

"I didn't hire you to give me all of that defeatist pessimistic bullshit," said the President. "Get somebody to fix the transmitters and the communication, and bomb the fuck out of Asia and South America, will you please? I'm getting a little tired of the Venezuelan President's bullshit, too."

"But sir," said Moyer.

"Any other issues will be handled by the Defense Secretary, my cabinet, and my staff. I'm taking the tunnel back to Washington," the President said.

"The tunnel, sir?" asked Gibson. "Back to Washington?"

"Washington's safe, now, right Ted? You said it yourself. Now that we can reestablish ourselves there, it makes for a strong message. We've been away from Washington and the Capitol for too long. Some of you guys may have seen the city, but I've been hopping around from bunker to bunker and I need to get back. I've already called for Congress to reconvene. That should be happening soon. The American people need to see us strong and in command and doing something about all these goddamn bombs dropping on us. They want to hear about progress. So, give them some progress, gentlemen. That is all," said the President. "Oh, and Ted, hang back for a moment, I have something for you."

"Certainly, sir," said Steers.

The Army secretary offered a quizzical look in response to the President's request to his friend in the Navy, Ed Peery. Peery noticed the awkwardness of the situation and offered some banter to ease Steers' nerves.

"Um, when are you leaving, sir?" asked Peery.

"As soon as possible, Ed," said the President. "I can't stand it here. Too out of the way. Nice golf course, though. Probably going to get in a few holes before I go. To release the tension. It's tense being President during a World War."

"I don't doubt that for a second, sir," said Peery, glancing at Steers cautiously. "Not one second."

CHAPTER 33—THE TRAP IS SPRUNG

"Okay, everybody ready?" Jake said over the microphone.

"Sniper one, ready," said Tommy from the left side of the press box.

"Sniper two, ready," said Vinny from the right.

"Sniper three, ready," said Josh.

"Guard dog, ready," said Boo.

"Okay, how about you guys? Eddie—is everyone vested up? Does everyone know where their weapon is located?" Jake said to the crowd at midfield.

"Ready to go, boss," I said.

At Jake's request, Boo had given everyone names and had given some combination of headsets, ear pieces and mics to each of the shooters, himself, and to me. My job was to coordinate all of the bait. We were the bait. Al, Mark, Maureen, Kristen, Estela, Morgan, and me. Of all of us, I was probably the least high up on the Russians' shit list, because all I had done was defy them and leave. Everyone else had either spied on, harbored fugitives against, or assaulted one of the Russian assassins headed our way.

"Do you think they know it's a trap?" I asked.

"Of course they do. They'd know it was a trap if it was

set beautifully. This is obvious," said Jake.

"Then why bother going through with it?" I asked.

"Because the confrontation is coming. Because we can control the preferred place of engagement. We have the high ground, we have control of the technology in this location, we have a tactically superior situation, and we have a back-up plan. Confrontation was unavoidable, Eddie. At least now we can control some of it at least," Jake said.

"We could die here," I said, frightened for the first time since the Wal-Mart incident.

"We could've died in the school from the thugs. We could have died again in the Wal-Mart. We could have died at Fort Detrick from the mutates. We could have died in Front Royal with the convicts. We could have died a dozen different times on the trip to Washington and back. Every day is a party, Eddie. Death smiles at us," said Jake.

"All we can do is smile back," I answered.

Jake smiled at that and patted me on the shoulder.

"We'll make a Stoic of you yet, *amigo*," he said.

"I'm getting there," I said.

"Here they come," said Josh. "I see three of them coming out of the nearest exit from the high school."

"Three? I thought you said there were four?" Jake said.

"There were four," Josh said. "I'm sure of it."

"Unless another one got shot in the crossfire in the cafeteria and didn't make it," Boo said.

"There were four chasing us. I'm sure of that," said Josh. "Either one got the sniffles, or they're up to something."

"They're up to something," said Jake. "Boo—check the roof."

"Already there, homeboy. Nothing yet. But if I were

Oleg, I'd have somebody on that roof too," said Boo.

"There really isn't another tactical position. There's nowhere from behind us to sneak up on. The only other structure near here is the concession stand, and they have to march right through those gates to get to it. Keep your eyes peeled on that roof, Boo," said Jake.

"Like you gotta tell me," Boo said.

"Like anybody could ever tell you anything," Jake said.

"Jesus, Jake, don't get him started talking again. He gave me ear cancer the last time, just from sheer volume," said Josh.

"That's not even a thing," said Boo.

Oleg, Aleksandr, and Buvaisar walked up to the gate entrance and opened it. They started walking in along the fences that ran along the outside of the track and walked down towards the concession stand. There was a larger gate entrance there, and Oleg very slowly opened it and left it open. Then the three of them stopped, and Oleg put his hands up.

It was deathly quiet.

"That's far enough for now," said Jake, who moved out from behind the stage into the open. I got nervous for him. The rest of us were standing behind the raised stage that Father Joe had spoken from weeks ago during his rally. It came up nearly to our chests, so it gave us the feeling of a little more safety in that we could duck down out of sight. Truthfully, though, if anyone decided to start shooting at ankle level, we would all have lost our feet to bullet wounds. Jake, however, was in the open, arms up and spread like Oleg.

"Let the negotiations begin," said Oleg.

"What's there to negotiate about?" asked Jake. "You're trying to kill us. Do you want to stop trying to kill us? If so, then I accept."

Oleg smiled at that.

"Your cowboy friend has had more success than I have," Oleg said. "He effectively killed...four of my men. And your history teacher friend tried to kill me by pounding my head with a rock. It seems I have more to complain about than you, Jake Fisher."

"So, we have a Mexican standoff," said Jake.

"You have a Russian standoff," said Oleg. "Very different."

"Oh yeah? How so? *Shto eta?*" said Jake.

"*Harasho*," said Oleg. "In a Russian standoff, there is no truce. We both know that neither of our sides can permit the other to leave alive. If you leave, you could provide information of our whereabouts and our alliance with the church, school and town. If we leave, you know you can never live without looking over your shoulder."

Morgan and Estela hugged each other tightly.

"Maybe we don't mind looking over our shoulders. At least that way we get to live," Jake said.

"You are a wrestler, no? And a U.S. Marine? We both know you cannot live that way," Oleg said.

"Maybe not. But they're not Marines. Let them go, and you and I can settle up," said Jake.

"That settles nothing. It changes nothing, regardless of who wins. We still have to kill each other. This is what you Americans call 'zero sum.' There will be winners, and there will be losers. Winners get to live. Losers do not. There is nothing in between," Oleg said.

"Okay, then let's get down to business," Jake said. "I know you're not stupid. We have the high ground. We have snipers in place. And we outnumber you. Surrender and we let you live."

Oleg laughed out loud.

"And then what? What do you do with us? Tie us up somewhere? Drive to Washington and hand us over to someone in a tank? Our countries are at war. If I surrender, our death is inevitable, one way or another. No, we both know how this is going to go," said Oleg.

Just then, Buvaisar pulled out his gun, screamed and fired at Jake. The shot missed, but all of us ducked when we heard it, which allowed Buvaisar to take off running to the concession stand. Shots rang out from above. Boo was trying to hit Buvaisar, but the Russian was too fast. Confusion set in. The boys each fired a round from their huge Barrett sniper rifles. Each one hit right where Oleg and Aleksandr had been standing, but neither had waited long to start sprinting towards the stage. Each boy reloaded the large cartridge to his rifle, meanwhile Josh took shots at Oleg and Aleksander. Blood and flesh flew from the edge of Aleksandr's shoulder, and the huge Russian howled and reached for his wound with the other hand. Flesh was missing, but otherwise the Russian bear was unhurt.

Now enraged, he ran towards us at the stage. Mark Longaberger jumped at him, but Aleksander swung with his good arm and knocked Mark to the ground as if he were a nuisance. Oleg was firing his pistol at Jake, but Jake was rolling and firing himself. Each man dodged and shot with no bullets hitting their target, but Oleg managed to get behind the stage along with his huge partner. Boo had Buvaisar pinned down behind the concession stand wall. The boys had just reloaded and were preparing to shoot, when the glass in the press box exploded into shards. Maharbek had fired from the school rooftop two hundred yards away. Both boys ducked down from the window. Buvaisar, still hiding away from Boo's aim, had a direct line of sight to the stage, but was about eighty yards away. He lifted his Kalashnikov and began firing. We all ducked beneath the stage. All except Al. I looked back to tell him to get down, and noticed him looking confusedly at his shoulder, where a pool of blood was growing quickly gushing down from his neck. His face twisted in realization and he dropped to the ground dead. Maureen screamed and started to run to him, but Kristen tackled her to the ground and told her not to move. I felt helpless.

Josh had a slightly better angle at Buvaisar but was over a hundred yards away. He began shooting at him to keep him at bay. Buvaisar ducked back again. Mark shook his head, trying to revive himself from Aleksandr's blow, but was slow to get up. Oleg grabbed him by the collar and put a gun to his head.

"Nobody move," shouted Oleg.

Aleksandr then walked behind the stage and grabbed Morgan and lifted her up as if she were a kitten and wrapped his good hand around her throat.

Jake ran towards the big man to stop him, but he lifted the index finger of his wounded arm and wagged it.

"Any closer and I squeeze," he said to Jake.

Jake stood still, unsure what to do. Oleg had Mark. Aleksandr had Morgan. Oleg smiled.

"It seems we know who the winners are today after all," Oleg said.

Just then Morgan twisted sideways and swung hard at Aleksandr's open shoulder wound. He howled and loosed the grip on her, allowing her to turn fully to face him, and then she kicked him in the groin. He doubled over for a second, then reached in his belt for a knife and with a swift and powerful swing, slit Morgan's throat. She gasped for air as the blood poured from her neck and she dropped.

"No! No!" yelled Jake.

Then a shot rang out from Tommy's side of the press box and Aleksandr's chest exploded, and he fell to the ground.

Another shot from Maharbek hit Tommy's rifle, demolishing it, and he dove to the floor of the press box cursing. Then Vinny fired at Oleg and missed, and Buvaisar ran out from the concession stand and peppered Vinny's side of the press box. The younger boy dove to the floor and crawled as low as he could to his big brother as Buvaisar continued his barrage.

And then, just in the nick of time, Boo shot Buvaisar, and the blonde Russian lay in a heap in front of the concession stand. I wondered where Josh was during all of this, and then Oleg backed up, holding Mark and his gun.

"Everyone stop. There are two of us left, me and my sniper. Let us go, and I will not kill anyone else, but I will take this man hostage as my security package. Come at me, and I will shoot two more people dead before any of you can lay a hand on me," Oleg said.

Jake was crouched, ready to spring, and was shaking with anticipation. Maureen was on the ground crying, Kristen hugging her and whispering to her. Estela was on her knees crying in front of Morgan's body. I was standing next to Jake, and Oleg had an angry smirk on his face.

"The game has changed, Jake Fisher. Now all I wish is to get out of here alive. Let me do that, and no one else need die today."

"I'm not a fool, Oleg. Take that man with you and he's as good as dead anyway," said Jake.

"True. I owe this man for the damage he caused me. But no one else in your group needs to die. Maharbek and I leave, and you will never see us again," Oleg said, backing up slowly but constantly toward the side exit of the field.

"You know that's not true," said Jake.

"Actually, it is. We have dishonored our names. When seven ex-Spetsnaz cannot finish off a bunch of teachers and little girls? You don't want to know what they'll do to us in Moscow. We will disappear. No one will hear from us again," Oleg said, getting ever closer to the exit with Mark's shirt collar in one hand and his Yargin pistol in the other. "We will go find another town and ride out this war."

"How am I supposed to trust you when your answer changes every few minutes?" asked Jake.

"Do you have a choice?" Oleg replied. "You want your people to live? You must trust my word."

"My people are already dying," said Jake. "And you are running out of time."

"With one word I can have Maharbek kill your sons. You can prevent that," said Oleg.

"Again, how do I know that's true?" said Jake, slowly inching forward towards Oleg and Mark, who were still slowly backing towards the gate.

Oleg released Mark's collar but kept his pistol at Mark's head.

"Don't move," Oleg said to Mark.

He lifted his large wristwatch, which also had a communication component inside.

"Maharbek, aim at the boy," said Oleg. "Show me your laser."

A deep voice, just audible to me from Oleg's watch, replied affirming the order, "*Da, harasho.*"

A red beam of light appeared on Tommy's chest. His eyes bugged and he looked at his father.

"Tell him not to move, Jake Fisher, or Maharbek will fire," said Oleg.

"Stay still, boy. Any harm comes to him, Oleg, and I will kill you as slowly as I can," said Jake.

"I'm sure. Maharbek, keep your laser sight on the boy

and come down the ladder. We are almost finished here," said Oleg.

The light bobbed and weaved a little, but stayed on Tommy, who's face showed pure terror. He didn't move. Jake scowled and looked at Boo. I kept wondering what could be done. Boo couldn't see Maharbek, and Jake was motionless. Oleg had Mark, and Al and Morgan were dying or dead already. Things couldn't get much worse, and I didn't see any way in which we could come out of this without any more casualties —or maybe not at all. Where was Josh? Had he been killed too? He had been involved early on, keeping Buvaisar back, but nothing but silence was coming from his hiding spot, and he could make all the difference now. Boo sensed that too and started to initiate.

"Oleg! Up here! I'm the guy who was on the motorcycle. Remember me? I have a rifle aimed right at you right now. Give me one reason why I shouldn't pull the trigger," said Boo.

"Because two of yours will die immediately and Maharbek will pick the rest of you off and get away. Jake Fisher's son and this man who hit me with a rock die first. And that's assuming you hit me in the right place," Oleg said. Then he yanked Mark's collar close to him and placed his head right behind Mark's, turning slightly to face Boo.

"Your threat is less credible than it was a moment ago, black man. You cannot hit me now without killing your man. Now let me leave, and the bloodshed is over for you," Oleg said.

"You're not getting out of here alive, Oleg," said Jake. "Follow this through to its conclusion. You might get out of this stadium, but we'll hunt you down. It's over. Let him go."

It was a bluff, of course. Jake was doing his best. But a quick look in Jake's eyes and it was clear even he didn't believe what he was saying. Oleg was still too far away for Jake to lunge at him, was using Mark as a human shield, and his partner, Maharbek, had his sniper rifle trained on Jake's son. Oleg held all the cards, and everyone in the stadium knew it.

Oleg smiled.

"So, I will be leaving now," Oleg said. "Maharbek, keep your target in sight and meet me at the gate," he said into his watch.

Oleg's comment caused Jake and me to look up at Tommy, whose face had changed to confusion. The red beam of light that was bouncing around on his body had disappeared. Jake's brow furrowed. He turned to Oleg, who was again speaking into his watch.

"Maharbek, keep the target in sight. *Ty ponimayesh?*" Oleg said, looking at the press box for his comrade's laser sight beam.

No answer came. But in a few seconds, the red laser sight returned. First it was on Tommy. Then it traveled down the press box, down the bleachers, across the field, and then onto Jake's chest. Oleg, at first with a look of concern, then smiled broadly.

"So, you see, Jake Fisher, you were right. It is over. But not the way you expected. Maharbek and I will be leaving now, and we will never see you again. But I will take this man with me and exact my revenge on him once we are gone. Good-bye, Jake Fisher. It was a pleasure working with you," Oleg said.

He backed a little farther toward the gate, which creaked as it was being opened.

By Josh.

"I'm guessing this belonged to Maharbek?" Josh said, holding up Marharbek's Kalashnikov. "Cause I know this did," he said, tossing a bloody human ear onto the turf near Oleg's foot.

At the same moment that I wanted to cheer; I could also feel myself wanting to vomit.

Oleg sneered at Josh, holding Mark's collar tight with his gun to Mark's head.

Josh pointed the Kalashnikov at Oleg.

"It's over dude. Let him go," said Josh.

Suddenly, Oleg aimed the pistol at Josh and fired. Josh hollered and went down. Then Oleg shoved Mark away and shot him in the chest. It was point blank and punctured Mark's vest, which exploded into shreds at the entrance point, and Mark fell to the ground limp. Next, Oleg turned to Jake, who was awestruck with the sudden turn of events, and pulled the trigger. Jake froze, then closed his eyes and listened.

And the gun just clicked.

He pulled again, and only a clicking sound came from the gun. He was out of bullets. In a desperate fury, Oleg pulled a giant knife from a leg holster and ran towards Jake.

"I will send you to Hell myself," Oleg screeched as he swung the knife at Jake's throat.

CHAPTER 33—THE ART OF THE DEAL

The President walked over to General Ted Steers, Secretary of the Army, and put his arm around the small, wiry soldier.

"We still need to iron out a few things," the President said. "Without consulting everyone else."

Just then a buzzing noise came from the General's pocket. He reached inside for his phone and pulled it out and saw the name on the identifier: CANNAVERAL.

"I'm very sorry sir, I need to take this. It may have to do with what we're about to discuss," Steers said.

The President sneered. "I'll get another piece of cake. Make it quick," he said.

Steers held the phone tightly to his head and walked a little distance away from the table and the President.

"My God," said Steers. "That, that's amazing."

He listened a good while longer, nodding his head as if Col. Cannaveral could actually see him nodding. Several minutes went by, and the President continued to work on his cake, staring impatiently at Steers.

"Yes, I agree. I agree. I think that's the way to go. But obviously I can't make that call. Can you hold?" Steers asked.

"Sir?" Steers said to the President.

"What is it?" the President answered.

Small dabs of chocolate stained the outside if his lips, and Steers had to focus on something else and not look at the President's face, as the sight distracted him.

"I have Ray Cannaveral on the phone, sir. And the news is frankly unbelievable. In their experimental treatments, they have essentially brought back one of the alpha mutates, Laura Fisher. She says that she will share any information on the mutates that we want, allowing us to study them further. And she also seems to be in command of them sir, kind of like a queen bee to a hive. She says she will direct them not to attack humans, sir, and will cooperate with us fully," said Steers.

"What's the catch? There's always a catch," said the President.

"She wants a place for them to live, away from society. Kind of like a reservation, sir. She says she can help them learn to farm and ranch and subsist on what's there, and as long as we don't bother them, she'll cooperate with us and no further attacks will take place. She'll even help coordinate a nation-wide trek for them to go to a designated place," said Steers.

"What's the designated place?" the President asked.

"Zion Canyon, Sir. She wants the national park."

"Forget it," the President said.

"Before you answer, sir, you should consider that in every single city where those Russian bombs drop, mutates appear. There's no telling how many more they have. They hit our communications with the first barrage, then our major Eastern cities with the Brenerium-Ebola bombs. They hit Great Plains last week with the same bombs. We already have tens of thousands if not more. Soon we'll be seeing them in droves in cities like Chicago, St. Louis, Cleveland, Kansas City. She's promised that anywhere mutates are created, she'll call them to Utah, Sir. The town of Springdale that surrounds Zion has tons of hotels, but only six hundred residents. Giving her the park and the town takes care of an enormous problem that we haven't effectively solved yet," said Steers. "And the next town over, Rockville, has fewer than three hundred. That's fewer than a thousand people displaced in exchange for this problem going away."

"Well, isn't it going away anyhow? They brought her back to normal, didn't they?" the President said.

"She's not exactly normal, sir. She's extraordinary. And Colonel Cannaveral says that experiment can't be duplicated. It involved an accidental explosion, and that she may be our only hope right now," Steers said.

"How long until she wants to get there?" the President asked.

"She hadn't put a timeline on it. She's cooperating fully with CBRNE and the Pentagon. The Colonel said she knows it will take a while. She wants a ceasefire from us in exchange for directing the mutates not to attack humans," Steers said.

"How will they live until we move them?" asked the President.

"They live on corpses, sir. At least for now. Which, I know it's gruesome sir, but that also solves another unpleasant problem heading our way, which is what to do with the millions of bodies of those killed in the bombings," Steers said.

"We bury them," the President said. "They deserve a burial."

"Sir, the Germans began cremating the Jews because they had no more room to bury them. Our estimates have our dead already approaching seven million and counting, and we don't have all of the numbers from the Midwest yet. Sir, this problem could solve itself right here."

"I see," said the President. "Six hundred people in

Springdale, huh? And only another three hundred. And you say all of the hotels can fit them?"

"There are cabins in the park already, sir, along with lots of buildings, hotels, and even an elementary school that can be easily converted into residential facilities. It solves the problem, sir," Steers said.

"Elementary school? How big?" the President said.

"Forty-nine students, sir. Easily moved to the next town over, La Verkin, which is thirty miles away. It's ideal, sir. She's thought it through. There are trains that come within only a few hours of Zion, and we can bus them from there using Army and National Guard transports," Steers said.

"This Colonel Cannaveral. Is he okay? I mean, is he competent? Does he know what he's doing?" asked the President.

"He's the best, sir," said Steers. "He's a decorated war hero and a dedicated soldier. He's one of the best leaders we have in the Army, sir."

"Can he be in charge of that whole operation, then?" asked the President.

"Absolutely. But I need your go-ahead, Sir, to make it happen," said Steers.

"Do it," said the President.

Steers picked up the phone.

"Ray, did you hear all that? Yes. Yes, it is excellent news, and congratulations on your promotion. I need to confer with the President about other matters right now, but catch up with me at 1700 hours and we can work through some of the details. Well done," said Steers.

"Now Sir, what did you want to speak to me about?" Steers asked.

"I have been in secret negotiations with the Russians for a ceasefire," he said.

"Good God, Sir! Why didn't you bring that up with the other Joint Chiefs at the meeting?" asked Steers.

"I don't want them interfering. I don't want them doing anything differently. These negotiations are delicate and not assured in any way, and I don't want knowledge of their existence to affect what we do in the meantime. It might compromise our bargaining position, if you understand my meaning. Negotiations go a lot better when you have guns trained on the other side of the bargaining table," the President said.

"Okay, but why tell just me?" Steers asked.

"Because I need the Army's cooperation in the furthering of these secret negotiations. You are the largest branch of the military and have the men to spare. You also happen to be in charge of Camp David, where I'd like the talks to take place, again, in secret. I will be arranging for a delegation of some of Russia's highest officials to come here to work through a cease-fire just between our two nations. They're willing to abandon the Chinese and the North Koreans and all of the other countries if I can provide them with some basic demands, and if things work out, they will even pressure the other countries to end the war," the President said.

"That's unbelieveable! That could be great news. But what are those demands, sir?" Gen. Steers asked.

"That's what the negotiations are for, Steers," said the President. "I'm one of the greatest negotiators in history, so you can be sure we'll get the best of the bargaining table."

"So, what do you need from me, sir?" Steers asked.

"I need you and your men to set things up for the negotiations. The Russian delegation will want to ensure their own safety, naturally, so I am allowing them to bring one hundred armed soldiers here to Camp David to protect them," the President said.

"A hundred? Sir, we can't accommodate that many. And armed? I think that's ill-advised, Sir," said Steers.

"It's already decided, Steers. Make it happen. Take whatever actions you deem necessary to maintain safety and order within your ranks. We have a truce, and these can be delicate matters, do you understand?" the President said. "I don't have a timetable, but I would like the negotiations to take place sometime in the coming months. That's an order, not a request. As details and dates get clearer, I will inform you. Make it happen, and do not, under any circumstances, disclose these proceedings with anyone else other than the personnel you plan on using here at Camp David, do you understand?"

"Yes sir, I understand," said Steers.

"Good. I'll catch up with you in Washington," the President said. "Now I'm going to play a round or two of golf before I head back. Dismissed."

Steers saluted and walked out of the Aspen lodge, shaking his head in bewilderment.

I hope he knows what the Hell he's doing, Steers thought to himself.

CHAPTER 34—FINAL SHOWDOWN

Oleg charged Jake, knife in hand. Jake met him full force, as if a spring had released. He caught Oleg's knife hand by the wrist and stopped the thrust, but the edge of the knife blade sliced Jake's forearm. Jake winced as the blood began to trickle down his arm. Oleg then swung a violent left cross with his free hand and caught Jake squarely on the jaw. He blinked hard, shook his head, and recovered. He then side-stepped and spun beside Oleg and grabbed the knife hand with both of his hands, bent it back towards Oleg and backstepped, sending the knife flying and Oleg spinning and dropping to the ground with his wrist bent unnaturally toward him. Jake then jumped on top to straddle him. Oleg lifted a knee and caught Jake in the ribs, then kicked his leg into Jake's groin, did a backwards roll and flipped Jake over his head and onto the ground behind.

Oleg got up, gritting his teeth and shaking out his wrist. Jake landed on his head but scrambled to his feet and into a crouch. The two men stared at one another about six feet apart.

"*Kotogaeshi*, the wrist throw. Impressive," said Oleg.

"*Tomoe nage*, the monkey flip. Also impressive," said Jake.

Boo Andrews came down from the bleachers with his

gun, and I had snagged the knife that Oleg had earlier.

"And now it seems your friends will save you, Marine. Too bad we couldn't see which one of us was better. But I think we already know, don't we? Your sore neck is telling you from my throwing you on your head," Oleg said.

"Do we know? How's your wrist, comrade?" Jake said back.

"Soft Americans. I'm surrounded by them," said Oleg.

"Not now, you're not. Boo, Eddie, go see to Josh. I got this," Jake said.

"But Jake, you're being stupid now. There's no need," I said.

"Do not interfere, do you hear me?" Jake said.

"I don't want to hear this macho..." I began.

"Do. Not. Interfere," Jake repeated.

"At least you are no coward, Jake Fisher. We will see if you are a warrior," Oleg said.

He ran again towards Jake, spearing him with a double leg tackle. Oleg's head was in Jake's diaphragm, his hands behind Jake's thighs, and he was driving forward like a linebacker trying to tackle a running back. It was the same move he toppled Maharbek with in their sparring session. Jake's legs sprawled back into the turf and his arms yanked up on Oleg's elbows, releasing some of the pressure. The move stopped Oleg's drive, and for a moment, the two were locked together, unmoving. Then Oleg popped his head to one side, under Jake's armpit and adjusted his arms and locked Jake around the waist, set to throw him over his head in a suplay as he had done with Buvaisar. But Jake twisted, reached over Oleg's head and grabbed his chin with the near arm, then with the far arm snagged Oleg's far elbow.

"We call this one the pimp chicken where I'm from,"

Jake said.

He twisted and popped his hips and reaped his rear leg into Oleg's while simultaneously pulling on Oleg's arm and chin to throw him, and the Russian went flying violently in the air and crashed down onto his neck and back to the turf below with a bounce. The move knocked the wind out of Oleg, and Jake ran over to pounce on him.

Oleg shook his head, then sat up and kicked Jake in the face as he approached. Jake's head snapped back, and his legs wobbled. Oleg then kicked behind one of Jake's faltering knees and he dropped to the turf. Then it was Oleg's turn to attack. He charged Jake and kneed him hard in the head, knocking him over. Jake lay on the ground trying to regain himself.

"Not bad for an American. But that is not really a compliment," Oleg said.

As Jake knelt on both knees, Oleg cocked back his right arm to hit Jake in the face. But Jake stepped up with his right leg, and with both arms blended with the blow and back-stepped. The force of Oleg's own swing coupled with Jake's move sent him sprawling hard to the turf again. As he landed his head hit the ground, and for a split second he was completely immobile, his brain reeling from another concussion —his second in only a few weeks. He stood nevertheless and turned to face Jake. Jake's arm was now covered in blood from the initial cut given him by Oleg's knife. Oleg's lip was bleeding and his face marred from the turf burn on his landing, and his vision was blurring from his head hitting the ground. Both men were panting.

"Had enough yet?" Jake said.

Oleg feinted a punch with his right hand, which Jake moved to block, opening up a shot to Jake's face. Then Oleg's left leg shot out and clipped Jake in the head. Jake's legs faltered a second and he dropped to one knee. Oleg then kicked at Jake with his other leg, which produced a loud thud to

Jake's chest, but Jake anticipated the kick and caught Oleg's outstretched leg. He locked the leg out and dropped his elbow hard on the outside of Oleg's knee. The knee buckled and an audible pop sounded as the Russian howled in pain and dropped to his hands. Jake dove onto him and the two began to wrestle on the turf, each looking for some kind of life-ending choke or submission hold.

Now the battle took an odd turn. Instead of wid swings and violent throws, the two men struggled with each other on the ground. Very little motion was detectable, but their grunts revealed their extreme effort. Sweat poured from both men as they struggled with one another, their breath coming in loud heaves now. Every few seconds during the grapple, each would try to get in one more punch, one more elbow to the face. Each landed shots to the head, and both were bleeding in several spots on their faces. Oleg's nose and mouth were bleeding; Jake's eye and mouth were bleeding. Neither man was giving in.

Then Oleg found an opening and slipped around behind Jake in what ju-jitsu practitioners call the rear mount position. Oleg was essentially on Jake's back with each leg wrapped around Jake's torso and each heel in Jake's crotch. Oleg's right arm was wrapped around Jake's throat and intertwined with his left, which was pressuring Jake's head, trying to cause him to pass out.

Pro Wrestlers call it the "sleeper." Ju-jitsu practitioners call it the "rear naked choke," but calling this move any kind of 'choke hold' is a misnomer. The recipient of such a hold is not gasping for air. The hold places blood-stopping pressure on the carotid artery that brings blood to the brain. Starved of the oxygen-rich blood, the brain shuts down and the victim passes out. Thus, many such practitioners who are "choked out" are actually starved of oxygen to the brain, not of air to the lungs. And Jake's brain was getting starved quickly.

Jake's face was purple, and veins popped on his neck as he tore at Oleg's wrists. Jake punched, clawed, and scratched, trying to make Oleg release, but the wily Russian would not leg go, knowing his enemy was in his death throes. If left long enough, such a hold could indeed result in death. In UFC and similar mixed martial art competitions, a referee or a ring doctor usually enters to prevent the hold from causing damage. Left on, though, and Jake was a goner. Both men knew that.

Tommy and Vinny had rushed down from the press box to watch their dad. Maureen and Estela, both mourning the loss of their lovers, were transfixed. Kristen and Natalie looked horrified. And I was wondering why the fuck Boo Andrews didn't do something before his former best friend got killed by a murderous Russian.

"He said 'do not interfere' to us, Eddie. That means do not interfere. This is his fight," said Boo, reading my thoughts and anticipating my comments.

"This is bullshit macho pride and nothing else," I yelled. "Get in there and stop it right now!"

But nobody moved.

Including Jake.

He was on all fours, arms shaking, with Oleg clinging to him like Velcro. His face now a dark purple, and my own heart in my throat. I feared that Jake's whacko Viking dream of dying in battle was about to come true. I never understood that kind of talk. He would say idiotic things like to get to Valhalla he had to die in battle, and to hand him a sword if I ever saw him dying. I used to laugh uncomfortably at that, but now I admit that all I could think of was where the fuck I could find a sword and wondered if Boo Andrews had one in his weapons cache. Horror showed on the faces of the girls near the stage, and the boys' deep concern for their father's life showed on theirs. I clung desperately to the hope that Boo wouldn't let it get that far, that he would intervene in the nick of time. But Boo wasn't moving, and my hope was fading.

And just when I thought I was about to have to say good-bye to my best friend, the unthinkable happened.

Jake started crawling off the field. They were already close to the edge from Oleg's attempt to escape, but their scrum had taken them even closer. Gurgling and gasping sounds were coming from Jake's mouth, and Oleg sneered and squeezed harder. But Jake kept crawling on hands and feet like a bear. His face was bloated, his eyes bulged, and the veins thrummed in his neck. And Oleg hung on.

And Jake started to climb the bleachers.

He went bench by bench, row by row with hand and foot, and Oleg dug in his heels and started shaking Jake's head like a pit bull with a chew toy.

But Jake kept crawling.

"What the fuck is he doing?" I asked Boo, but I could already see from Boo's expression that he had no idea. The rest of the group was also dumbfounded, their expressions in complete wonder. Then Josh Rimone sat up, holding the bloody bullet wound in his thigh as the sweat drained like a waterfall over his hairless body.

"I know what he's doing," said Josh, wincing at the pain in his leg and forcing a grin.

Jake climbed slowly but made it to the top of the bleachers with Oleg clinging tenaciously, waiting for his victim's brain to finally be starved of enough oxygen for him to drop dead. Then Jake reached over for the railing on the top row of bleachers. And for the first time since Oleg had begun choking Jake, he looked worried. Oleg squeezed as hard as he could, and Jake's tongue lolled out of his mouth, and his eyes rolled back in his head. Then he stepped over the railing with each leg, his bloody arms rippling as he gripped the railing with exhausted hands. And then, with both men outside the railing on the top row of bleachers of the stadium, I understood why Jake had done what he did. Oleg realized it to, and in a last-ditch effort to finish Jake off, drove his forehead into Jake's to bend it forward and further into the choke.

And then Jake let go of the railing.

He pushed off with both legs and spread both arms like an eagle doing a back dive. He laid out flat with Oleg clinging to him, and the two of them fell from a height of what had to be nearly fifty feet in the air.

As they fell, I noticed nothing but complete, serene quiet everywhere. No one spoke, no bird chirped, the wind was silent. Nothing.

And then came the thud. They hit hard. Oleg hit the cement with his back and his head. Jake's fall was broken somewhat by the Russian, but his neck had snapped backward into Oleg's face, his arms had hit the pavement, and his back had been wrenched by landing on top of Oleg. Coupled with the amount of oxygen his brain had been deprived of, Jake's injuries sent him rolling off of Oleg, unconscious.

And Oleg lay dead on the concrete.

CHAPTER 35—ZION

"I can't believe it," Colonel Cannaveral said. "They went for it."

"What part?" asked Wendy.

"The whole thing. The whole damn thing, lock, stock and barrel. Laura Fisher gets Zion and the two towns next to it, all of their buildings, and autonomy to run it like a reservation," the Colonel said.

"Who did you talk to?" asked Wendy.

"The Secretary of the Army. General Ted Steers. But he was conferring with the President. I heard the entire conversation," Col. Cannaveral said.

"Ray, that's so cool," said Wendy. "I mean, I was never a big fan of this president, but you actually got permission from the highest possible source. So, who is going to coordinate and oversee all of this?"

"Apparently I am. They essentially created a position and put me in charge of it. It sounded like the President didn't want to worry about the headache. They'll only have to displace about 800 people and then the mutates' nearest neighbors are thirty miles away," the Colonel said.

"Amazing," said Wendy. "Congratulations."

"I'd better go tell Laura," said the Colonel, easing out from behind his desk and walking toward the door.

"Laura already knows," said a voice in the hallway.

"God damn she's creepy," said Wendy.

"No need to be cruel, dear. I was on my way and your cerebral emanations were very strong and easy to read. But I would love to hear the details, Colonel," said Laura Fisher.

"There are none. You got everything you asked for and more," he said.

"More? How's that?" Laura asked.

"I suggested that the President cede the towns of Springdale and Rockville just outside of Zion as well. There aren't many people who live there anyway, and that would give you a thirty-mile buffer from the town of La Verkin and a twenty-five mile buffer from the town of Hurricane," the Colonel said.

"That was very thoughtful of you, Colonel. That will truly be helpful and assure that my people have places to live and resources as well. Was there a timeline?" Laura asked.

"No. You and I determine that. I'm the new authority on this, so you'll be working directly with me," the Colonel said.

"Will she be involved?" Laura said, pointing to Wendy.

"Well, she works here with my CBRNE brigade. Anything scientific regarding the gathering of knowledge or information in regards to your kind will be under her purview. But in terms of the logistics of relocation, no. That's just me," said the Colonel.

"Good. She practically breathes hostility whenever I enter the room," said Laura. "That gets old pretty fast."

Wendy scowled at Laura.

"See what I mean?" Laura said.

"Alright, no need to get into all that," the Colonel said.

"So, what's next, then?" said Laura.

"We set you up a semi-permanent apartment here while the National Guard gives word to the people of Springdale and Rockville that they have to leave. They'll have two months, and they'll be paid a base assessment value for their property from out of my budget, which is apparently considerable. You will spend that time communicating with Wendy on all health-related and biological information while trying to reach out to your people from a distance. I have an idea that Lt. Mazzaros can help with that. He was working transmitters before he got transferred to CBRNE. I'm wondering if he can boost whatever signal it is that you produce to reach out to your people far away," the Colonel said.

"Good idea," said Laura. "See? This is already a fruitful collaboration."

"Your apartment should be ready within the hour. Is there anything else I can do for you right now? I have a meeting to get to in twenty minutes and I really should prepare," the Colonel said.

"Well, there was one thing," Laura said.

"What?" said the Colonel.

"I would love to see my boys before I go. Do you think you could have Jake bring them down here within the next few weeks?"

The Colonel glanced at Wendy.

"Sure. I'll see if I can contact him. Hopefully he's not too tied up right now."

CHAPTER 36—
THE BACK DOOR

The President swung his putter and lightly tapped the brilliant white ball into the cup.

"I wish this place had more holes," said the President. "It has multiple tee boxes, of course, but the same hole. It gets boring after a few trips up the same real estate."

"Yes sir," said his personal assistant, who today was serving as his caddy. "I know what you mean, sir. Been there, done that."

The assistant, a tall slender man in his fifties, was doing his best to look dignified. Greg Knoll had been involved in the administration since it arrived. He had curried favor, done a myriad odd jobs, and basically handled every unpleasant task the President had set for him. It was demoralizing most of the time. This President was famous for being disrespectful, demeaning and arrogant. Greg found that to be completely true. But he also was generous with power and influence to those who were loyal. If the country knew how many national decisions had been made by Greg himself without consultation of the President, it would have resulted in massive scandal. On more occasions than Greg could count, the President had gone with his advice while eschewing that of Congressmen, cabinet members, heads of state, and even on one occasion, the Joint Chiefs. Greg admitted he enjoyed having that kind of power, and he didn't need notoriety for it either. Congressmen had to do interviews, be hounded by the press, and be answerable to the country. But not him. He liked it that way.

But he knew his time was fleeting. The President had somehow come out unscathed despite controversies, scandals, critics, and the censure of everyone from public servants to journalists. He'd found a way to keep anything negative from sticking to him. Greg called him Old Teflon. But this time, he knew, would be different. The writing was on the wall with this war. The Russians had crippled us by hitting our communication arrays first. Then this new weapon of theirs that combined Brenerium with Ebola killed people by the millions. The Russians had let the Chinese and the North Koreans handle the Pacific, but the truth was that World War III was already a rout only after a few weeks. The United States' response was to send missiles, troops, nuclear warheads and a massive naval armada to Asia. But the Russians had planned ahead for that and had supplied the Cubans and the Venezuelans with weapons of their own to hold us at bay in the south. We were surrounded, cut off from sustainable allies, and the ship was sinking.

Greg had foreseen this after only a few days. He'd smiled at his own ability to see the future during this administration, and sadly this time was no different. He had lived long enough to see the United States humbled in defeat. But what was truly frightening was the Russians' desire to take over and make the U.S. into a puppet regime of theirs where they could send colonists. All they needed was enough people dead and the infrastructure to remain intact, and this President would cave. He would cave because the one thing he feared more than anything was not being a man of influence. Above all things, he needed to ensure that. So, Greg had talked, and talked, and talked with him night after night. Unconditional surrender meant having to do whatever your conquerors wanted. Conditional surrender, however, was another matter. By halting the fight, the President could ensure his own safety and influence for the remainder of his days. And Greg would ride that coattail to the same luxuries.

At first, he had been too proud. This was a man who never backed down from a deal or a battle. In fact, he'd created more battles than he needed to have. But the devastation of the last few months had proven the nail in the coffin. If the President wanted to have anything left to bargain with, he would have to be proactive. So thanks to Greg's counsel, the President would be given a residence with servants, an annual salary on his large estate--along with housing for his most important assistants of course—for all of them to live unmolested as the Russians bothered with the business of setting up a new government in a new land.

Greg had even come up with the plan---the very plan the he'd heard the President put into play today with General Steers. He would host negotiations with a Russian delegation that demanded to have a platoon of their own soldiers to protect them—not an extraordinary request. Then, once here, they would essentially be given the keys to the back door: a hidden tunnel that stretched from Camp David to the White House. Rumors of its existence were in the air, but none were ever confirmed, and thus were usually written off as urban legends. The government had even admitted to some secrets in order to throw everyone off of its true existence. But the tunnel existed. And one hundred armed Russian soldiers would take it to the White House and "force" the President to surrender the country. General Steers and his army would be blamed for their incompetence, and the President would disappear to Florida.

And Greg would disappear with him.

EPILOGUE

Boo, the boys, and I had buried the bodies of Morgan, Mark Longaberger, and Al DeFillipo in the fields near Kristen's house. Kristen had Boo release the Segens along with a very credible threat that if they ever set foot near the house again Boo would kill them in their sleep. Then we had all driven the entire crew to Jake's house. Josh's wound wasn't pretty, but it would heal in time. Neither the femur nor the femoral artery had been pierced. He walked with crutches in the meantime. Estela, Maureen, Kristen and Natalie hung out in the kitchen and had promised to whip up a meal from Jake's meager stocks. You could smell pancakes cooking, and it was a great smell.

The boys looked after their father, who was taken to his own bed to sleep in. He had taken an abundance of over-the-counter pain pills, been given ice packs for his back and neck, and was sleeping off a battle the likes of which even some-one like him wasn't accustomed to. Boo and I were watching a bastardized version of cable television, which had old Bugs Bunny reruns on, occasionally interrupted by the same news that had been reported for the last three days.

There was room for everyone in Jake's spacious coun-try house. Those of us without injuries tended to things like cutting grass, trimming branches, and caring for Oklahoma, Jake's cat, who stayed at his side most of the time. It was a good retreat for the better part of a week.

The Colonel had called and caught us up on the amazing

story of Laura Fisher's transformation. He told us about the deal they had struck and how in a few months she would be moving with the mutates to Zion National Park in Utah. He had said that Laura wanted to say good-bye to her sons and to Jake before going and explain to them her reasons for the decision. The Colonel had expressed his condolences for the losses of Al, Morgan and Mark and congratulated us on our success at defeating the Russian cell. Finally, he invited us all to come to Washington at our convenience once everyone had healed up. A few weeks went by quickly, with the welcome boredom of a humdrum country communal life. The church left us alone. Everyone left us alone. Our insulated world was quiet and peaceful.

Then, one afternoon, I heard Boo Andrews yell excitedly.

"I got it! I got it! I'm in! I got the password," he said. Josh hobbled over on his crutches, careful not to brush his wounded leg up against the table. Jake walked slowly and painfully in from the bedroom to see what the excitement was about. I was there as well.

"What? What are you talking about? What do you got?" I said.

"I managed to hack into Oleg's watch. It's synced with his computer, his phone, his email, the works. And I just checked the last email he got, unopened. It's marked 'Kremlin.' Holy shit," Boo said. "I hit the motherfucking jackpot!"

"Holy shit indeed," said Jake. "Can you read it?"

"No. I don't read Russian. I got lucky on the pass code," said Boo.

"I can," said Josh. "Let me see."

Josh read the words in Russian Cyrillic and his lips moved as he whispered the words to himself aloud.

"That can't be right. Let me read it again," said Josh.

"What did it say?" I asked.

"It said for Oleg to prepare to bring his team to Camp David within the month and await orders. The American President is going to let the peace delegation bring a platoon of soldiers to Camp David for negotiations, at which time he will show them the secret tunnel that leads to the White House. After the negotiations, the Russians will slip down the tunnel to the White House and the President will then surrender the United States," Josh said.

"Jesus," said Boo.

"That's unbelievable. He's just going to let them come, like in the back door?" said Maureen.

"And the negotiations are just for show?" asked Kristen.

"This sounds a little crazy, even to me," said Boo

"This is bullshit, is what it is," I said.

"I'm afraid I'm with Eddie," said Jake. "I think this must be some kind of decoy. First of all, why would this President ever surrender at anything? This guy never knows when to stop fighting, even when he's lost. But the real catch is the mention of the tunnel. That's just a myth. I've been to Camp David. There is no such tunnel. Sorry to deflate your drama, guys."

"Um, Jake?" said Josh.

"Yeah?" said Jake.

"There's a tunnel."

BOOK FOUR IN THE CATACLYSM SERIES: *FIRST YEARS AFTER*

Nearly a year has passed since our heroes did battle with a cell of Russian assassins on the football field at Hunter's Run High School. As Jake Fisher and friends heal their wounds and regroup, lingering questions remain: What will become of Laura Fisher and the mutates? Will the President's plan to surrender to the Russians to save himself come to fruition? What direction with the sinister Church of Many Blessings go now? Can Jake, Josh, Boo and friends do anything with the intel in their possession to bring their country back together and stop the Russians from taking over?

New problems arise for America as North Korea lands troops and weapons on both coasts. Distrustful of their allies and impatient to make their mark, the North Koreans decide to take action in the form of occupation. How will Jake and his allies face this new threat while trying to foil a Russian takeover?

The answers lie in a journey into Jake Fisher's hometow--to the Eastern Shore of Maryland and Virginia; as well as a trip to Zion Canyon in Utah, and a much needed reconstruction of communication systems for the United States. Be on the lookout for *Book Four in the Cataclysm Series: First Years After*.

ABOUT THE AUTHOR

Jay Vielle

Jay Vielle (pen name) is a career educator and coach, but has been writing in some form or other since childhood. A career educator and coach, he has taught English and Spanish and coached wrestling at the college and secondary levels for three decades. He is a current NCAA and NHFS wrestling official, and an inductee to  both the National Wrestling Hall of Fame as well as the McDaniel College Hall of Fame. He has contributed articles to Wrestling USA Magazine and the NCAA News, as well as Op Ed articles for The Carroll County Times and W.I.N. Magazine. He is a 1987 graduate of Washington & Lee University in Lexington, Virginia, and currently lives with his family in rural northern Maryland. For more information about Jay Vielle, check out his blog page https://jayvielle.com or look for him on Facebook.

PRAISE FOR AUTHOR

Well written with outstanding characters. Stayed up half the night to finish the book. Excited to dive into book 3 and continue the story.

- RICHARD R.

This is very well paced, and has a Bourne series feeling to the books... with the multiple story lines going on.

- JON P.

BOOKS BY THIS AUTHOR

First Days After

When the first bombs drop in a global conflict, teacher Jake Fisher and thirty of his colleagues decide to hunker down in the school where they work. Jake must face infighting and an attack by local thugs in an effort to survive. When he discovers that his sons are trapped at college, he decides to go on a quest to find them. Along the way he rescues two researchers who warn him of mutated creatures who are an after-effect of a deadly new Russian weapon. Jake and his friends must face the challenges of an uncertain world gone mad in the first days after the beginning of World War III. Book One in the Cataclysm Series.

First Months After

Having realized that his wife, once presumed dead, is now a mutate, Jake Fisher and his sons have to find a way to skirt past military blockades and get into Washington D.C. to rescue her. With them are fellow teacher Eddie Reyes, who is looking for his parents, and Wendy Yubashiri, the researcher trying to reunite with her colleague, Colonel Ray Cannaveral at the Pentagon. Unbeknownst to them, however, the local pastor of an extremist church has delusions of grandeur and is making his move to take over the town and mold it in his image. To do so, he'll have to collaborate up with some very dangerous partners, who have violent ways of dealing with investigators and malcontents--including three of Jake's friends. Meanwhile, the rest of the country is just starting to recover from the first weeks after the bombs began dropping in World War III and formulating a plan to retaliate. Book 2 in the Cataclysm Series

Made in the USA
Middletown, DE
08 July 2022

68576913R00179